FOR A SECRET NEVER TO BE TOLD

BRIT ANDREK

First self-published in 2024

Copyright © 2024 Brit Andrek

The moral right of the author has been asserted.

All rights reserved.

No portion of this book may be reproduced or transmitted in any form or by any means, without prior permission from the author, nor be circulated in any form of binding and cover other than which it is published.

Cover design by Brit Andrek

First Edition, 2024

Disclaimer: I do not claim that provided content is completely accurate, though all efforts have been made to ensure the best accuracy possible. The contents of this book have been written solely for entertainment purposes. This is a work of fiction. Characters and events in this publication are fictional, and any resemblance to real persons, living or dead, is purely coincidental.

For people who breathe a little easier when lost between the pages of a good book.

PLAYLIST

STONED ON YOU / Jaymes Young
WAY DOWN WE GO / KALEO
THE BOLTER / Taylor Swift
BURN IT DOWN / Daughter
PEOPLE YOU KNOW / Selena Gomez
NO BODY, NO CRIME / Taylor Swift, HAIM
BANG BANG BANG BANG / Sohodolls
THE NIGHT WE MET / Lord Huron
REFLECTIONS / The Neighbourhood
HAUNTED / Taylor Swift
MAMA'S GUN / Glass Animals
NIGHTMARES & FLARE GUNS / Seb Adams
WHO ARE YOU, REALLY? / Mikky Ekko
THE BEACH / The Neighbourhood
WOLVES WITHOUT TEETH / Of Monsters and Men
REMEMBER THAT NIGHT? / Sara Kays
COLOURS OF YOU / Baby Queen
WHEN IT'S ALL OVER / RAIGN
THINGS WE LOST IN THE FIRE / Bastille
STUBBORN LOVE / The Lumineers
MEET ME IN THE WOODS / Lord Huron
DON'T FORGET ABOUT ME / CLOVES
STARS AND MOONS / Dizzy
YOUNG FOLKS / Peter Bjorn and John
INVISIBLE STRING / Taylor Swift
MURDER / Coldplay
NO LIGHT, NO LIGHT / Florence + The Machine
BARE / WILDES
FLAWLESS / The Neighbourhood
THE FALL / half•alive

Prologue / Lucas

The vanishing

THREE YEARS AGO

Ophelia Graham wasn't the first to vanish. She wasn't even the second, but instead the third. I always wondered if maybe I could've done something differently had I known waking up that day that she would be gone the next. Being at this strange age, when we had yet to dip our toes into the cold waters of adulthood, a lot of things went unnoticed. Including the first two disappearances. But she had mattered.

My shirt clung to my back, filthy with sweat. The store AC was turned all the way up, sending shivers down the length of my body. Trying to rub the goosebumps off my skin only sprung more of them. It was a recipe for getting sick, but you don't think of that when you are a fifteen-year-old boy.

Adam snapped his fingers in front of my face. "Hello? Earth to Lucas?"

I blinked twice at him.

One of the sodas in his hands clattered to the floor. He kneeled to pick it up. "Oh, I'm sorry, was I interrupting you?" He smiled playfully. "You got some important thoughts in there?" Adam tapped my head with his finger, careful not to drop anything else. "Wait. Don't tell me. I don't think I want to know."

"Let him dream, blondie! You're just jealous because a girl likes him and you can't even get one to talk to you," yelled Zack from the next aisle. Rafael and him snickered.

Adam rolled his eyes and bumped my shoulder. "That is so not true," he muttered.

"Yeah, and she doesn't like me. We haven't even talked outside of class." Despite Ophelia's dad working for my dad, she was like an eclipse. I never saw much of her outside of school, but that didn't stop me from looking for her in every room I entered. Hearing her name everywhere. Dreaming of her. Having a crush was like having a full-time job.

"You know, one of these days you're going to have tell her. You said you've been meaning to, right? Tonight's the perfect chance! You drool so much over her you'd think you'll drown in saliva soon."

I looked to the side, hiding a blush. The reason I hadn't said anything yet was because I was scared. But Adam was right. It was the party of the summer. Whitewood had never seen a heatwave like the one of recent days, but that only added fuel to the fire. A perfect time to meet up, drink cheap beer, and swim in the cooling water. I evaluated Adam's suggestion to not be a completely horrid one. And like he said, I'd been meaning to say something anyway.

"Maybe."

Outside, the air burned my lungs ruthlessly. I narrowed my eyes against the light as we made our way to the docks. Water sloshed against the pier, calm and lulling. Near the edges, it was clear enough to see little fish swimming in the seaweed. In the deep, the water turned into dark greenish blue.

I fished my keys out of my back pocket before climbing onto my family's little boat *Betty*. Dad didn't know the guys and I were borrowing it, but what he didn't know wouldn't kill him. He'd named the boat after my mother. He didn't usually let me anywhere near it. Not unless he was the one driving.

The boat jumped against ruffles of glistening water, and the motor purred as I steered. Near the docks, there were always plenty of seagulls, screaming for food or what else. With the wind whipping in my face and the smell of the ocean in my nose, I wanted nothing more than to scream along with them. Zack, Adam, and Rafe were talking behind me. The wind snatched away most of what they were saying, but I heard words like *girls, drink,* and *fire.* My hand moved to let the speed drop because I wasn't stupid enough to drive so far, I wouldn't be able to see land.

I heard a splash.

My neck twisted towards the sound. I cut the engine no sooner than I could run towards the boat's ledge. There was a road of stirred-up sea foam where I'd driven moments ago, but no sign of Zack. Did he seriously jump off a moving boat? I called out his name, scanning the sea.

"If he lives," said Rafael, "I'll kill him myself." He shook his head in disapproval, pushing up his glasses. Tiny specks of salt water reflected off them.

I pulled my shirt over my head, ready to jump. Idiot, I damned Zack. What if he got hurt? Had I known, I wouldn't have taken him on a boat ride at all.

Zack gasped for air and relief exploded in my chest. I was supposed to be careful and watch out for everyone. "You could've died or something." My heart was still racing.

Z's near-black hair was dripping wet. His eyes twinkled, a wild grin on his face. Cheeks and nose flushed pink. He lived as if he had nothing to lose, and sometimes it made me worry for him.

I picked up an empty soda can and threw it at him. "Not funny!" I yelled, struggling to hold back a smile.

Zack caught the can with one hand and waved it in the air. "That's littering! Now I have to call the ocean police." He threw it back on the boat.

"Yeah, I think I hear the sirens," stated Adam. He peeled off his white T-shirt and cannonballed into the water with a howl.

Rafael and I didn't leave the two of them waiting for long, jumping in next.

"Do you hear the sirens, Lucas? They're coming for you now!" Zack tackled me, and we both went underwater into the quiet cold.

I felt silly looking in the mirror. My brown hair still tousled and damp from washing it. Trying to tame it only made it spike up in odd places even more. I changed into a hoodie and beach shorts, all the while contemplating not going to this silly party at all. I didn't feel brave enough to tell a girl I liked her, knowing I'd have to see her every day at school if she didn't feel the same. And yet, I opened the door and took my first step, because what if she did feel the same?

Stars glistened like small diamonds in the sky. They illuminated my way to the beach, but the closer I got, the brighter the light seemed to grow. A bonfire. The flames reached for the stars, crackling every time they came back empty-handed. Part of the beach was enveloped with the forest. The trees ended abruptly to give way to sand. The boys waved at me from a spot by the tree line.

Zack took a long sip from his cup. I smiled and shifted my eyes to Rafael, who was sitting on a boulder next to us. Zack saw me looking. "It took him forever to climb that thing. He fell twice." His tone suggested that he thought the story absurd.

"Don't listen to him, it's all lies. I am a perfectly good climber, and he is very greatly overestimating his skills," replied Rafe, eyes narrowed.

I laughed. Rafe was the brains of the group, and that's what we loved him for. In a way, he'd always been the glue holding us together. After all, he was the reason we'd become such great friends as children.

Rafe slid down the rock, aiming to be careful, but somehow managing to trip a little anyway. He sighed, smoothing over his short dark brown hair. Zack, amused, patted Rafe's shoulder. A tinge of red worked its way onto his dark skin, shiny in the firelight.

Z bit his lip. "What a sad party. My sources told me it would be fun. Party of the summer they said." He rolled his eyes. Zack was enchanting, even when he was irritated. Pronounced jawline, brooding and handsome. Girls went crazy for that.

"What did you expect? Not every party has to end with you stealing Mrs. Thyme's garden gnomes," said Rafael. "Do you even remember that? You threw up three times the next day. Once on my shoes. Adam still owes me ten bucks."

Now that had been Zack overestimating his skills—drinking skills. Thankfully it did seem like he'd learned a thing or two since then.

"It was an improvement to her yard, if anything. I don't appreciate you guys making bets over the stupid shit I do."

Rafe crossed his hands. "It's easy money. What about the pecan pie she made you sell at the charity sale later? I thought the straw hat and overalls were a nice touch."

Zack coughed. "Right. Very nice. You'll never let me forget that, will you?"

Adam and I looked at one another. He nodded at the party, reminding me why I'd come in the first place. I pushed my way through chattering people, towards the music and laughter. I passed a girl I went to kindergarten with. We used to play pirates. I stopped, searching the crowd, and thinking how odd it was to make a bonfire during a heatwave.

As I was rolling up my hoodie sleeves, I noticed two girls coming my way. My stomach flipped. "Lucy. Arabella," I greeted. It was safe to say I wasn't exactly happy about the school's biggest it-girls approaching me.

"Love the look." Lucy brushed long, blonde hair from her face. She reminded me of a cat because of her sharp pale-brown eyes.

"Thanks. How can I help?" I asked while eyeing the other blonde. Arabella's hair was a bit muddier than Lucy's. Her long waves ran down her spine to where her lilac top ended and belly started. She was generally quiet, and I didn't mind her at all—just the company she kept. Her beauty was shadowed by the loss she carried. It was no wonder since her uncle vanished. Died, people said.

"Have you seen Zack?" She played with her hair, looking up at me with those big eyes, painted with heavy makeup.

"Why? Did your other boyfriends get bored of you?"

Lucy tilted her head, jaw tense. "Fuck you, Warren. Jealous much?"

I snorted. As if I'd ever associate myself with bullies like her. "Go on, knock yourself out." I pointed her in the right direction.

Lucy smiled sweetly and turned to leave, Arabella staggering behind. I hoped she knew what she was doing.

I didn't want to go back just yet, not with the girls there. And I hadn't found Ophelia. Perhaps she wasn't at the party at all. I wished for that not to be the case.

There was a shape by the bonfire. Her skin was bronze, and her long hair fell loosely around her head. My friend Katie.

"Hey," I said, standing beside her.

"Hello there. I didn't think you were coming." Katie's lips curled, her dimples more prominent. The fire made her eyes seem as if they were pools of lava. She was glowing in the light.

I craned my neck, flashing my teeth. "I wasn't planning to. It's good to see you, been a while. Oh, and Adam sends his regards."

"I seriously doubt that."

"What about you? All alone here? I'd ask you to join us, but I guess we've already established how little you like my friends." If it weren't for her and Adam's rivalry, Katie would probably be part of the friend group. She'd fit right in, except Katie didn't want to be where she wasn't wanted.

"You know that's not true. And I'm not alone." As Katie said that, another girl rounded the fire. The girl. It was as if she might melt into the flames herself. She was wearing a yellow dress, and her red hair was pulled softly over her shoulders. As she got closer, I could make out her firm cheeks and rosy lips.

I shuddered. All my confidence was stripped away. I felt bare and embarrassed and so in awe. Happy that I'd found her, but scared shitless at the same time.

"Hey." Ophelia handed Katie a drink and then narrowed her eyes at me. "Hey," she said again, dragging out the word, "I know you."

"Yeah, uh, our dads—" I stammered. "And school." I took a deep breath, trying to unclench my fist and relax before I'd cramp up completely and make a total fool of myself. If I already didn't look like one.

Ophelia Graham knew who I was.

It was dawning, and although the party had long ended, none of us wanted to go home just yet. The tall grass tickled my bare legs. The misty air made my nose itch. Birdsong echoed from the treetops, and the world seemed overall vulnerable as it bubbled with life. I was lost in the haze of it all.

Somewhere near me, Lucy and Zack giggled. Elsewhere, Rafael was tailing Adam and Katie, as the two bickered over something insignificant like they always did. And Ophelia, she was beside me. We made no sound as we moved, hand in hand.

It had been Zack's idea to show the girls our favorite spot. A secret place only we knew of. Well, plenty of people knew it existed, but I'd never seen a single soul besides us go there. It was an alluring lake, its surface like a liquid mirror embedded in earth's soil. Since the beach was empty now, the last of the fire's embers gone with the morning wind, Zack had proposed to move the party over to the lake. Our lake, only a short walk away from the beach.

Adam and Rafe ran, jumping into the water which hadn't yet warmed. Katie followed them, squealing as her thighs touched the water, fully clothed. Ophelia and I sat by the water's edge, watching them. Zack and Lucy stayed behind, but close enough to hear their mumbled talking. Arabella had separated from the rest, picking flowers in the meadow. She looked peaceful, humming to herself, but I'd noticed her get lost in thought more than once during the night. Dad didn't want to talk about the news, but I heard the whispers going around. There were many.

Ophelia started tracing circles in my balm with the tip of her finger. Something unsaid lingered in her eyes. Something almost sad.

"What?" I asked.

"Nothing," she said with a shake of her head. Her eyes trailed up my arm, down my chest.

By all logic, we should have been freezing. The mornings were cold, though it warmed up fast as the day went by. My skin buzzed, not from the chill. It was like a fever. This static under my skin.

My voice turned hoarse. "Tell me."

"I wish I'd said something to you sooner."

It almost made me laugh. "You have no idea. I've been trying to talk to you for months."

She looked up at me, surprised.

"You're beautiful," I whispered. She was so beautiful that I got nervous just by looking at her. I hadn't meant to say it out loud, but I wasn't sorry I had.

She readjusted her pose. "Favorite ice cream flavor?"

I smiled, her closeness tugging at my chest. How could she talk about ice cream when my heart was about to burst? All this time we'd wasted being scared. Scared of what? It all seemed senseless now. I should have asked her out the second I laid eyes on her. I was fifteen, and I didn't know many things, but I knew how I felt. People love to say you are too young to understand things about the world and yourself, but I always thought that young people feel so much brighter, clearer, and so much *more*. Somehow these things get lost as we grow up.

She smiled, shaking my arm. "Come on! What's your favorite flavor? It's important! We have lost time to make up for."

"Chocolate."

"Oh no, you're one of the basic ones."

Basic? It's ice cream. "Fine, if I'm so boring then what's your favorite?"

"Caramel vanilla in a cone," she said proudly.

"So, I'm boring for liking chocolate, but yours is vanilla?" It was hard to focus. I was tired and a little drunk. I watched her lips move, but the meaning of her words came to me with a delay.

"Caramel vanilla. In a cone." She leaned closer. Her eyes were green. Not bright green or dark. Light, like sea glass and moss. And she had freckles. Perfect tiny dots all over the bridge of her nose and cheeks, shaped like little stars.

"Oh yeah, my bad, that makes it much more special." We laughed, and my cheeks burned, but even then, I couldn't wipe the stupid grin off my face. "Any more questions?"

"Cats or dogs?"

"Dogs," I replied.

"Cats. We even each other out. Favorite sport?"

"Basketball or hockey, probably." I'd never played hockey, but I watched it occasionally with dad. I played basketball for two years but stopped when I started working at the shop.

"I don't have an answer. I know nothing about sports. What's your favorite planet?"

I raised my eyebrows. "Really? No one has ever asked me that before."

Her head turned to the side. "I'm asking now. No exoplanets, just our solar system."

I looked deep into her jade eyes as I thought about it. "I don't know. Mars or Jupiter. Maybe one of the blue ones. How different are they really?"

She scowled. "You can only pick one." Her cold fingers played with my hands, moving along my purple veins, and massaging my palms. She had no idea what her touch did to me.

"All right. Jupiter, then. What's yours?"

"Saturn."

Somehow that didn't surprise me. "Because of the rings?"

"Obviously because of the rings."

Our eyes were locked on one another. She leaned closer, so close that if she moved any more, our noses would've touched. My heart was beating fast. I'd never felt anything like it.

"I really want to kiss you right now," I mumbled. "That okay?"

Our lips touched softly at first, before either of us had much confidence. When she kissed me, I forgot how to breathe, and when she finally pulled back, it was as if there wasn't any air to breathe at all.

And then I never saw her again.

1/ Rafael

There are worse things to do than chase ghosts

Ivy purred impatiently. Her tail swayed from side to side, sending white fur flying all over my pants. I scratched her behind the ear before placing a food bowl in front of her. She didn't even notice me slipping into the living room.

"Hey, I'm off now. I'll be home for dinner."

Pops' feet were propped up on the coffee table, his wrinkled eyes glued to the TV screen. All I got was a lazy harrumph.

I rode my bike down the streets snaking before me, a few lonely cars following the puzzle like me. Zack and Adam were already waiting for me at the arcade when I arrived. This summer was different. It was the last one before university. Anticipation imbued the air, but also worry. Who knew if we'd ever live life as we knew it again? We wouldn't see each other as much anymore.

The crammed arcade was dimly lit. Always crowded by middle schoolers stinking up the place with sweat and hormones. We used to go there a lot. Now we were just visiting old memories. That's what this summer was supposed to be about. Having a good time, and—in a way—saying goodbye.

Zack put his arm around me. "Ah, I missed this. Look at blondie, he's like a glowing stick. He might burst."

Adam flipped him off, but he couldn't hide his excitement. He'd coaxed Zack and I into this. At least someone was enjoying this. Sadly, at our expense.

"But me?" continued Z, "I'll probably die of shame if anyone finds out I'm spending my Friday night with pimply kids, drinking *Pepsi*." He scrunched his nose.

Zack had shared some of his own ideas, which Adam and I had shot down. Most of them could've landed us in a jail cell. I kindly reminded him that my father was the chief of the police department, and he'd probably skip jailtime and send me straight to my funeral.

"Maybe it won't be that bad." I shrugged. "We liked it once."

"Yeah, when we were as stupid and brainwashed as those little monsters in there!" Zack gestured at the building.

His ideas had been too extreme, mine labeled as boring, so naturally Adam had won. If Lucas was there, none of us would be walking through those arcade doors.

An hour had barely passed when we decided we valued our dignity more than we'd anticipated. No kid was intimidated by us. If anything, they seemed to be judging us. It wasn't a trip down the memory lane, it was a trip to torture land. So much push and shove. I was out first, saying I had a headache. I just needed some air. Something breathable. Zack followed shortly, and even Adam couldn't go much longer.

One thing checked off the list. The evening was still young.

Zack popped a piece of gum in his mouth. "What's next? Are we building pillow forts? Tag? No, don't tell me, hide and seek? Spin the bottle? Good old times."

"Yeah, you'd like that, wouldn't you?" shot Adam back. "If you guys weren't running off after summer, we wouldn't have to do this at all."

"It was your idea."

He pushed blond hair away from his face. It was getting longer in the back. "Because you're both leaving! What am I supposed to do in autumn? I'll have to become one of those sad, sulking men with sandpaper mustaches, who spend their days loitering and scowling at little kids."

"You could go to a school in the city too," I said. "You don't have to stay here. You're smart, I know you are." I said it, but it was hopeless. Adam couldn't picture himself anywhere else. Yeah, he had the wits, but there was nothing he dreamt off. No goals. He hadn't decided what he wanted from life, and what he was willing to give in exchange.

We passed the bay, and my mind wandered to Lucas again. It had been days since he left, and I already missed him. What would it be like in the fall, then? The four of us were like brothers. We'd been friends all our lives.

It wasn't right to think of that yet. Summer had barely begun.

We passed the docks. There were people out there. I recognized two of them. Lucy and Arabella.

"Should we go say something?" I asked, even though that was the last thing I wanted to do.

"Well, yeah. We should, right?" said Zack. Zack and Lucy were complicated, and to describe them would be impossible. They never spoke in public, never did anything in public. They weren't exclusive. They didn't go on dates. But they were *something*. And they definitely meant something to each other. Lately they were spending more and more time together.

As the girls got closer, I could make out their shapes better. A baby blue dress hugged Lucy's figure, a handful of rings on her fingers, and white slide-on flats covered her toes. Arabella's wavy hair was tied back into a braid, long enough to reach her waist. Her light green one-piece matched her eyes.

"What are you doing here?" asked Lucy.

"Nothing much. You?" answered Zack. His whole demeanor changed to cool and casual.

She gestured at a yacht at the end of the dock. "Went for a ride." She pumped Arabella's shoulder. "Thank God Bells came; I would have died of boredom. Parents can be so dull."

There were few people I couldn't stand and Lucy Payne was one of them. She was a basic, entitled rich girl, whose whole personality revolved around her being pretty and popular. Making fun of people was practically her hobby. I couldn't think of anyone more annoying and unlikeable.

"So, Arabella, haven't seen you around much." I cursed myself for keeping the conversation going, but they weren't leaving, and silence would've been worse. Lucy's parents were still by the yacht.

Arabella snapped her eyes to mine. "I've been home a lot, helping mom out." She cleared her throat. "We're trying to sell the boat, but…" She played with the bracelet on her wrist.

"But?"

"Well, obviously no one wants to buy it."

"Right," I mumbled. How could I forget? Her uncle died on that thing. An accident, but still. People remember stuff like that. It had been a big thing when it had happened. My dad had been pulling gray hair figuring it out.

Adam cleared his throat and nudged Zack and I forward. "We better get going. Nice seeing y'all. Good luck with everything."

Lucy and Arabella said goodbye, and we went our separate ways.

I got home before dinner. Pops was making salmon, and I heard the clattering of dishes downstairs. Ivy was on my bed, curled up between the folds of my navy bedsheets. I turned back to my computer. I didn't know what had prompted me to search up old news articles, but there I was. Following my instinct.

All of them had the same story. Sheldon Rogers had gone fishing and drowned. They all mentioned the limp he had from a work accident months ago. They talked about his sister Iris and his niece Arabella. His body had never been found. And all of them mentioned Link Martinez and Ophelia Graham, two people who also died shortly after Sheldon. Two people whose bodies also were never found.

I scrolled down the search page, and clicked on another post. The forum below it was filled with comments, and I read some of them.

────────────*Threadeet*────────────

AlbyIsTrippin49: Can't believe the police aren't doing anything about this. Three people and not a single answer.

Cavin_Hugo: Waiting for the documentary they'll probably make about this next year lol

RoxKissez6: Easy. Murdered. Happens all the time, but people are acting like this is some new revelation.

Sienna21987 replied to RoxKissez6: No way. I thought they said one of the men drowned and the other burned to death. Nothing about murder.

RoxKissez6 replied to Sienna21987: First of all, you forget there was a third victim; a girl. Some of her stuff was missing when she disappeared, and they haven't said much about her on the news. We know nothing about her. Secondly, I heard the police arrested someone as a suspect, but then let him go. And that's when the girl disappeared. Isn't that weird? You can't just hide three bodies without any evidence. Sooner or later, they'll find something, but right now, most likely, they just don't want to cause panic.

Sienna 21987 replied to RoxKissez6: Oh, wow that's insane. The parents must be worried sick. Poor girl. I can't imagine how hard this must be for everyone.

I scrolled down until I found an older post.

AluminiumOllie: All these conspiracy theories are just bullshit. Y'all are not thinking. It's just some boring small-town shit, and no one is ever murdered in small towns. It's all a big scam for attention and money, tourism, and such. The man who vanished first was in huge depts. Everyone is just too stupid to realize that once he gets his pay, he'll miraculously turn up. What a joke. And you people are the punch line.

HiArabella.R: Hello. My family's life is not some gossip to entertain you. This is not funny, people are missing! Instead, why are none of you helping us find him?? You're all talk, but you won't lift a finger to do something about it! You should all be ashamed.

I slammed the laptop shut. Pop was calling for me. Dinner was ready.

But hopping down the stairs, my mind was on what I'd just read. I could practically hear the wheels start to spin.

2/ Lucas

The odds of meeting a corpse

New York is a city that never sleeps. It had been a while since I'd last escaped the simple and quiet small-town life. The city could easily overwhelm me, yet it also kept reminding me that there was a whole world out there to be discovered. A hive of bees. So much to explore and do and see. It was absolutely liberating to breathe different air for a change.

But that didn't mean New York was all sunshine and rainbows. At first, it was the bigger things that I noticed; how noisy the city was or how easy it was to get lost. Everything moved so fast. Always in a hurry. Suddenly, I found myself disliking the tall buildings, which hid the sky above me. It was all of it, and then somehow none of it, that I hated. So vastly different from the life back home it made me dizzy. It could've been that, with time, I could grow to accept each part of it.

No. The idea of leaving dad alone made me physically ill. He would be so hurt and disappointed in me. He wasn't getting any younger. Who else would take care of him and keep him company? We all want something we can't have. I'd always been careful never to step out of line. Ever since mom, responsibility was something I'd had to learn earlier than most my age.

I clutched the folder under my arm tightly, pressing through the crowd. I should've felt greater excitement about going home, but all I wished for was more time in the city. These past few days I'd been drowning in work. I'd barely had any time to see the sights. No surprise I felt like a stranger there. On the other hand, I missed my friends. Home was effortless. I knew exactly who I was meant to be. Being away from home gave me the possibility of who I *could be*.

A sigh quickly grew into a yawn. My eyelids were heavy, but blinking helped to keep some of the exhaustion away for the time being. A darkening veil of azure blue was cast over the sky. I rushed my steps. I passed shops and cafes. Same ones I passed every day. I would have loved to slow down and sit somewhere, but I felt like a walking zombie. My body begged to just sleep it off. Flower shops were slowly closing, last blooms selling for half their prices. Tables in bakeries were being scrubbed clean of all the crumbs. Windows of apartment buildings were lighting up one by one.

I thought of Zack. He'd lived in NYC as a kid, before his family moved to Whitewood. Did he ever miss it? He'd been so young, maybe he didn't even remember it. How do you miss something you never knew?

I passed a bookstore. It was an old red-brick building with multiple businesses cramped together side by side. The bookstore was in the middle, with a huge sign above the door. One look through the window revealed a mesmerizing chaos inside. Some of the shelves were tilted, bare wood peeking from underneath the paint. Plenty of books were stacked on top of each other on random tables or against walls. The shelves were overflowing—there clearly wasn't an inch left for more. The store had its own character, however disorganized. A personality. There were various plants, splashes of color, along with hanging lights. Paintings. I liked it, because it was interesting, bold, and daring. Like a labyrinth.

I felt another yawn coming, but before I could let it escape, I froze.

Colorful spots blossomed in front of my eyes, and I felt like passing out. My mouth hung open, and I snapped it shut. My eyes were locked on the window, mind racing to catch up. Were I to blink, the dream would end and shatter into a million pieces. The name I'd stored away long ago lingered on my lips like a spell waiting to be cast. I swallowed the letters one by one. Once they were out, there would've been no turning back.

I rushed inside, nearly knocking the door from its shaky hinges. My tiredness was gone. Vanished. I made my way through the maze of books to the back of the store. The blood drained from my fingertips, and my lips felt dry and cracked. Everything was upside down. Because surely, *surely,* this could not be real.

No. I had to be right. *Please let me be right, please let this be true.* I'd spent way too many sleepless nights pondering over this. If I wasn't right now, I didn't know what I would do with myself. It had taken me a lot of time and effort to get past what happened.

Her hair was longer than I remembered. She didn't see me standing behind her. I sent another prayer in the wind. A part of me had always felt it in my gut. I whispered her name. Low enough for only her ears to catch it, but loud enough to silence my rapid heart. Or stop it altogether.

Ophelia's back tensed. I felt a small rush of pride. "You're alive," I said, more to myself than her. "You're here."

I should've been furious. I should've yelled and caused a scene, demanded to know how and why she was alive. Why she'd never come home. I should've waved my arms and stomped my foot but it was like I'd hit a wall. I couldn't.

Slowly, she turned. My mind went blank as I stared into her round green eyes. We stayed there for a precious moment, just taking each other in. I couldn't read the expression on her face, whether it was joy or surprise or fear.

"Yes," she said back in hushed tones. "Hi."

I took a step forward. I had to make sure she was truly there. That this wasn't some cruel joke. She was alive. I shook my head in disbelief. Gosh, I felt like I was fifteen again. No time had passed.

She straightened her back, eyes still skipping over me. "You've grown," she said with a smile. "And your hair is longer."

"You've changed quite a bit too. Actually, that's not true. You are just as beautiful as you always were." My smile vanished, the first wave of shock washing away. "Where did you go? Ophelia, everyone searched for you. You just disappeared. We had a funeral. Your parents—"

She bit her lip and looked down at her feet. "Listen, Lucas, it's been great seeing you again, but I have to go. This isn't really the time. I'm sorry, I am," she said before storming off.

She didn't get far, because I was trailing right behind her. I kept bumping into people, mumbling apologies left and right while trying not to lose sight of Ophelia.

Her face darkened when I made it beside her.

"Wait. Let's talk about this. Wait!" I grabbed her arm. A tremble went through me. It felt oddly like electricity.

She gasped, turning abruptly. "Do not touch me unless you plan to lose an arm today." Her eyes were set, hands curled into small fists on either side.

I stepped back, releasing her. But when Ophelia continued her stride down a dark alley, I followed her. If she thought she'd get away so easily, she was wrong. Answers were the least she owed me. I felt a mix of joy, awe, and concern. On one hand, it was a surprise to find her alive, and on the other it was an even bigger surprise to find her alive.

"Lucas, stop!" Her voice was forceful. When I didn't listen, she stopped short before me. Shadows were beginning to crawl closer and closer, as night drew nearer. "What do you want from me? Please just go, please."

"Not until you give me some answers."

"Answers?" she said like the meaning was foreign to her.

I raised my arms only to let them drop again. "Yes! Or have you forgot that you are supposed to be dead? I mourned you! Answers are the very least you owe me." She'd managed to convince a whole town. Now she was acting as if she had no idea what I was talking about.

Ophelia sighed heavily. "Of course. How could I forget?"

"Honestly, I don't know. Please, tell me the truth. Ophelia, it's been three years and I haven't stopped thinking about you. Do you know how guilty I felt? I kept thinking I could've done something, saved you somehow. An idiot." We'd been almost the same height once. She barely reached my shoulder now. "I need to know."

We stood still for a moment. Blaring cars was the only sound.

"Give me your number," she said.

"What?"

"I said give me your number. I'll call you, and we can meet up. That's what you want, right? To talk. I'll show you New York. It'll be great."

"How do I know you won't disappear?" I asked, towering over her.

"I will call. Promise." Again, she had that determined look in her eye.

Trusting her was my only option. We exchanged our numbers, and hugged goodbye before Ophelia jumped into her car and drove off.

As I walked to my hotel, I felt nothing but wonderstruck. It was a miracle I'd happened to see her. Out of all the people, I'd somehow stumbled upon her. It didn't matter that I'd been tired from work. When the night came, I could not sleep at all. I remembered the stolen glances and smiles. Seeing her around town and at school. The bonfire party. The kiss.

She wasn't gone. Our story hadn't ended with her death.

The next day, we arranged to meet at a park. The sun warmed my face as I waited for her. Ophelia was wearing an emerald summer dress. Her hair was down, the way I loved it the best.

"How long have you been in New York?" she asked as we were strolling through the park.

"A few days. Work. You?"

"A year. I'm not constantly here though. I have friends who have a house in the most amazing spot. When I miss nature and quiet, I go there."

"How did you finish school? No one found you?" The last question sounded funny when I said it out loud, but I had been curious. How had no one recognized or discovered her?

She hesitated. "These friends of mine ... they helped me with school. They've been helping me. I know how lucky I am."

"Do they know?" I didn't have to spell it out, she understood what I meant.

Her eyes drifted up to mine. "No. They don't."

"What about you?" she asked. "College?"

I shrugged. "I've applied to some schools. I don't think dad really wants me to go anywhere far. The closer to home the better. Someone has to help out with the business, and I'm all he has. I'll have to work aside from school. It'd be a bit tough were I hours away, wouldn't it?"

Ophelia's eyebrows drew together. She chewed on her cheek. "Hey, do you want ice cream?" She squeezed my hand.

I nodded; a bit surprised. The sudden change of subject threw me, and before I could even offer to pay, Ophelia was already half-way to the ice cream stand. I scratched my neck, a bit embarrassed. Maybe we'd lost what we'd once had. What if I was annoying her, and that's why she'd been so eager to shut me up with food? Oh my God, she wanted to escape, didn't she? I'd messed it all up.

Ophelia fetched us two cones. She kept smiling cheekily. What the hell did that mean?

I stared at the ice cream cone in my hand. "How did you know I like chocolate?"

"You told me, remember?"

I felt a bit sheepish. "Right. I can't believe you remember that."

"Of course I do. We kissed that night."

"Oh, hold up." I stopped, reaching down, brushing gently against her cheek as I wiped melted ice cream from the corner of her mouth. Her lips parted at my touch. I snapped my hand back, and she looked away.

There was still much to talk about.

Ophelia offered to drop me off at the hotel, and by the time we reached it, it was already chilly outside. During the drive, she filled me in on her life so far. Her travels, her friends, dreams. I didn't want to go. I tried to stall. I took my time memorizing her face, her smell, the freckles I'd missed three years ago. The way she smiled, or how she pushed hair out of her face.

"Listen," she said, "I have to get out of the city for some time—visit the friends I told you about. We might not see for a while." Hesitance crossed her face. "Unless…"

"Oh. Unless what?"

"Look, I'd appreciate it if you didn't tell anyone you saw me."

"Oh?"

"And these friends—they expect me to bring someone." She sighed and grabbed my hand with a grunt. I looked down on our tangled fingers. And there it was again, the electricity. "Lucas." Another sigh. "This is going to be sort of weird, but do you want to go to a wedding with me?"

3/ Rafael

This is why I don't socialize

"Take a shot with me, Rafie. Live your life. Enjoy your youth before you are old and saggy, beaten by the oppressive every day of adulthood. Let this magical liquor intoxicate and transform you." Zack pushed himself away from the kitchen island. He licked his lips, holding up a bottle of tequila.

"I don't think so."

We each got a day to do whatever we wanted, and nobody else could complain or argue. Zack had waited patiently for his turn, being shot down on the first round. In truth, all I wanted was to go home.

"You've had enough for the both of us. You're starting to sound like Adam!" I yelled over the music—so loud it made my ears ring.

Z lifted his eyebrows, holding out a shot glass. Before I could deny him again, Adam snatched the shot from his hand and downed it. He spun, slumping down on the other side of the counter.

"I'll take another, thank you, Zaddy-daddy." He smiled earnestly.

Zack didn't find it funny. "Really? You want to play this game, Draco Malfoy?" He tugged at Adam's blond hair.

Adam yelped at his touch. "Oh, come on," he groaned.

"Bite me," said Zack. I caught the slight wobble of his foot as he launched himself at Adam.

Adam jumped aside. "Kiss my ass."

I shook my head. Those two were like giant toddlers. I had to deal with that level of unhinged every day.

Zack blew a kiss in Adam's direction before grabbing two new shots for them both. For me, he poured cranberry juice, winking as he handed me the cup. I reached across the table, digging my fist into a bowl of chips. As I licked cheese dust from my fingers, my eyes wandered around the house, further from the kitchen we'd occupied, and towards the party.

The air was thick with sweat and booze. I was trying to avoid my old classmates like some disease. As long as there's no eye contact, you can always say you didn't notice them. I would have *loved* to say hi, sadly I couldn't see a thing! Oh, what's that? You were standing two feet away from me? Well, what can I say? I wear glasses for a reason. I caught a few faces that made my memory tingle, but other than that, nothing major. I wasn't popular in school. I tried to keep a low profile and not step on anyone's toes. My antisocial behavior was probably the result of my hyperfixation on my studies, lack of communication skills, and the excuse of already having some—enough—friends. *Best* friends. Adam liked to mash it all together, and call it a superiority complex. Perhaps there was some truth in that, too.

It had been a long time since my last party. Ever since what happened, it didn't feel right. Lucas was so distraught he wouldn't leave his house. How could I party when my friend needed me? After a while, I think I just grew out of it. It was different for Zack and Adam. Especially Z. This was more his thing. This was how he let loose. Had his share of fun.

The kitchen gave way to the living room, from there easing into a dark corridor. The living room was more spacious that the other rooms of the house, therefore most people had squeezed themselves in there. I suspected the upstairs bathroom might've been a popular hideout too, considering that the line reached the top stairs. I felt a little sorry for the person who's house this was.

I sighed, but when I turned, I found myself facing an empty kitchen. Confused, I looked around, but Adam and Zack were both gone. Hopelessly disappeared from under my nose.

I staggered from room to room. It was so damn dark I couldn't even see where my own two feet were. I'd had two beers. Whoever had thought turning all the lights off was a good idea had clearly had more than me. I took it as a personal challenge. As I moved, I made sure to turn on a lightbulb here and there.

I passed through the living room and dining room. I went upstairs, but the bedrooms were locked, and the bathroom que was ever-growing. At some point I found myself opening a door into the garage. I gave up and started back towards the living room. Maybe I'd missed something, or they'd already circled back to the kitchen. *If you can't find someone, maybe you're the one who's lost,* said a sneaky voice in my head. *Shut up,* I told it.

I pivoted the corner, and almost walked right into Lucy Payne and her friends. I stepped back before she could see me listening.

"Sue me, Caroline, is it so unbelievable that I would actually walk away? He was acting as if I wasn't even there! Obviously, I took my shoes and left," talked Lucy. She pulled down the tight hem of her sparkly dress, only for it to slowly ride up again. "A woman who respects herself never runs after a man who wouldn't think twice about her. I wasn't born yesterday."

"Oh my god, I *hate* this dress! Jessica told me it was hot when we went shopping on Saturday, but I feel like a disco ball. It's clued to me, I can't breathe. Anyway, what was I saying? Oh yeah, never mess around with a basketball player." Lucy ran a hand through her long hair, revealing dangling diamond earrings.

She wasn't entirely wrong about the disco ball thing. And the fabric did look like it was suffocating her. How terrible for her. Queen snake and her little baby snake minions.

"You look amazing—like the night sky," complimented Arabella. She was wearing a baby pink poofy top, paired with light shorts, and a pink, silky headband. Her hair was almost down to her waist. Lucy and her looked quite strange standing together side by side. Bells was remarkable, as always.

The other girls surrounding them looked at Lucy like she was their goddess. Caroline—one of them—was another blond girl, but her hair stopped under her chin and came with bangs. Her nose and lips were thin, disproportional compared to her round, downturned eyes. Another girl had dark hair, glossy lips, and a comfortable smile. Freshmen, I was pretty sure. I'd never seen them before. It would make sense that they'd look up to Lucy.

Suddenly, Zack and Adam appeared by my side. I scrunched up my nose inspecting them. Was that sherry I smelled? Where would they get that?

"Dude, where'd you go?" asked Zack.

"You're the one who left me alone," I argued, but I might as well have been talking to a wall.

Z waved his hands, exposing us to the group of girls. Lucy's pupils dilated seeing him, but outright ignored Adam and me.

"There you are, finally." Lucy ran a finger firmly across Zack's arm. Even in the dark I could see her face redden, and the corners of Zack's mouth pull up.

Zack slid his hand around Lucy's waist, pulling the girl towards himself. "Can I get you something? A drink?" he spoke under his breath, casually playing with the straps of her dress.

"You can try," replied Lucy, voice like honey. She took Zack's hand, and then they were gone.

I exhaled. Hadn't Lucy been talking about some other guy just seconds ago? I supposed Zack was a premium member on multiple dating apps too.

"What? Why are you looking at me like that?" asked Arabella, eyes narrowed.

"Nothing," I said, pushing up my glasses. My cheeks warmed as I flashbacked to me searching her family up on *Google*.

"Hey, Bells, so, why don't you convince my boy Rafe here to have some fun? See how miserable he looks? You two would be perfect together." Adam's eyes widened as realization dawned. "Not that *you* are miserable. Not at all. Just a good match—"

I jabbed him with an elbow, horrified. Thankfully Arabella didn't appear offended. She was smiling. She was beautiful. The opposite of Lucy in every way that mattered. She was kind and humble, considerate. Intelligent.

"I think you got it."

"Yea-h," I muttered, falling over the word. "But hey, how are you?"

"Fine." She shrugged. "You?"

"Good," cut Adam in. I gave him the stink eye. One more word and I would not be responsible for my actions.

"Good. I've been reading a lot and just hanging out with the guys, some researching." I said before I could stop myself.

"Zero rizz, man. Zero," whispered Adam, bumping against me. "If I'm yawning, it's because I'm so fascinated by all your nerd talk."

I gave him a forceful shove, and if he wouldn't get the hint to shut the fuck up, then I'd smack him across the face next. Self-defense.

"Sorry," I apologized for my friend.

"It's okay," said Arabella, "what are you researching?" Her voice was sunny. She was radiant.

How do I put this? Your uncle. Your family. You, basically. Sounds about right. Questions? Maybe I could help with filing the restraining order?

"Uh ... serial killers." I gulped. She must've heard me gulp. "And mandatory minimum sentencing," I then added, just to spice it up.

Yeah, my critical thinking skills had left me hours ago.

"Oh."

"Speaking of which—" *Damn me.*

"Yes?"

"Wasn't your uncle—didn't they ... I mean, there were rumors." Once the words started to tumble from my mouth, there was no going back. I was overcome with the need to confess. To let everything pour out of me.

Arabella's expression didn't change. There was still a way to recover. I could salvage this. But first I had to shut up.

"I mean, you know, I saw some comments." I think I was sweating. It was hard to tell since I was also about to faint.

"Comments?" she asked.

"Yes. On an article I read."

She crossed her arms. Bad sign, that I knew. "You were reading about my uncle? Why?"

Where were Adam's snappy interruptions when I needed them? Why was it so impossible for me to stop talking? "Um, kind of. Just happened to see one. Or two. I didn't mean to snoop or be weird or anything. Sorry."

She took a step back, fidgeted with her hands. "Why are you researching my uncle?" she asked again. Her voice was clear, direct. Careful.

"Curiosity." I swallowed again, and if she hadn't heard it before, she definitely heard it now. I was butchering this conversation more and more every time I opened my mouth.

"You said you were searching up serial killers. You think he was murdered, don't you? And your dad is a cop, right? So you know some things," said Arabella in one breath.

"Well, I wouldn't put it quite like that." Dad rarely talked about work. He hated me knowing things.

The people around us had faded, yet it was feverish. At least we didn't have to yell. The music was quieter in that part of the house.

"No? What other reason could you possibly have?" she asked dryly. She stepped closer, sizing me up.

Again, no assistance from Adam whatsoever. My mess, I fix it.

"I'm sorry. I'll drop it. I didn't mean to be rude or insensitive. Sorry." I started to drag Adam away.

"Wait." Arabella had her hand on my sleeve, wrinkling up the fabric. I waited for her to say something, but nothing came. She let out a small breath of air, and I felt its warmth on my bare skin.

She released her grip in a flash, as if the fabric had burnt her. My eyes trailed her as she ran out the door. I was stunned.

The beginnings of a headache seemed to creep up on me. I found my way outside, to the porch. The crisp summer air cleared my head, as I thought about the mess I'd created. I took a deep breath, turning to find Adam right behind me. I was glad he'd stuck with me, even though he'd been no help at all. It wasn't his fault I had a gift for bad decision-making.

"I saw you two talking to Arabella and Lucy. What about?"

I yanked my head towards the voice.

Katie.

She gave a little wave with the tips of her fingers, a strict smile plastered on her face. "Hey there."

"What's it to you?" asked Adam. His body stiffened immediately. Always like wolves at each other's throats.

Katie shook her shoulders, ivory cardigan slipping and revealing delicate tan skin. "Just curious. You don't have to tell me though, I can guess."

If I hadn't promised Arabella I wouldn't investigate her uncle's disappearance a couple of minutes ago, I would've probably considered telling Katie about it and recruiting her. She had a sharp mind, detail-oriented. I knew that well. We'd been competitors enough times. Unlike my friend, that's what made me like her.

"Humor us, what is it that you think?" I asked, my back to the patio ledge.

Katie tilted her head, a mischievous smile playing on her lips, making the corners of her eyes crinkle. She'd cut her hair to shoulder-length a while back, and now it bounced around whenever she moved. "I saw how Arabella left. I don't know her that well, but I know you two. There's only one thing you could possibly be talking to Arabella about that would upset her like that. Don't get me wrong, I completely believe you're going to fail unless you have some help, but you guys sure dream big. I'll give you that, at least."

Adam snorted. "And let me guess, you're going to help? Swoop in and save us?" His blue eyes narrowed, sparkling dangerously in the dark. Cold air had sobered him up fast. Unless it was really Katie who had scared the devil out of him.

Katie leaned against a wall. "Perhaps," she said. "You still haven't pitched me your plan, but even without it I can assure you that you're barking up the wrong tree, not seeing the whole picture, digging up empty graves … whichever you prefer."

"Are we?" I asked. "Tell me, Katie, what is it *exactly* that you think you know which we do not?"

There are people who play to live and those who live to play. Katie was the latter. For her, everything was a game, a mystery to be solved, a puzzle lacking a piece. On a good day, I felt I was the same. On a usual day, I found all the pieces scattered around and the instructions missing. Life was a challenge for her, and no one had bested her yet.

Katie grinned, taking a step closer to us. "I know you're terrible at making the most obvious conclusions." She walked around, slowly, and deliberately. Solid footsteps against wooden panels.

"Conclusions like…" I waited for her to finish. I was getting tired of her beating around the bush. My head hurt and I wanted to go home.

"Tell me," she said, "don't you find it rather strange, that three people vanished three years ago, almost at the same time?" She turned to us. "Wouldn't you find it even stranger if these three disappearances weren't connected? And none—not even a single one—of the bodies was found." She bore into me, a wicked glint in her eyes. "You need Arabella, but you need me just as much. I want in."

"Cool story, but we've all heard the same conspiracy theories. Why would we need you?" said Adam.

Katie looked at me, expectant. I understood. Arabella knew things about her uncle. Things reporters didn't. And Katie—she knew things about Ophelia. The one who had disappeared with her passport. Her best friend.

My hands were cold, so I kept them in my pockets. It was just Adam and I. Zack had stayed at the party with Lucy. Katie had left in the opposite direction.

I didn't mind the quiet. The party had taken a toll on me, they always did. At least Adam had had fun. I liked my mind sharp. Drinking would make my thoughts dissolve and slip away. I didn't like playing catch with them.

I watched the street lights in the distance. The smaller streets weren't lit, and darkness pooled where light couldn't reach. I caught movement out of the corner of my eye. It was Joseph Graham, Ophelia's dad. He kept his head down, his walk cool and casual. He hadn't seen us, though we were in the middle of the street.

A moment later I caught another glimpse of someone. One of my classmates, Jeremiah Scott. He must've been at the party. I think he was dating one of Lucy's friends. Caroline, if I wasn't mistaken.

"Jeremiah!" yelled Adam.

Jeremiah relaxed when he saw it was just the two of us, and his lip curled. He kept his hands in the big pocket of his hoodie as he met us half-way.

"Were you at the party? I didn't see you," asked Adam. His words were a little stretched now that he'd relaxed again.

Jeremiah was sweating like he'd been running, but he wasn't out of breath. His dark hair dangled in front of his face, and he had to push it back. "Yeah, I was there, but it got boring, so I'm headed home. I have a family thing tomorrow, and my mom would kill me if I show up hungover."

"Where do you live?" I asked. "We can walk together." I was getting bored of counting the street lamps, and Adam wasn't much of a chatterbox when he was drunk.

Jeremiah looked around uneasily. "Can't. Sorry. I got to go." He dug into his pocket, scanning the street behind him, the dark road.

"Oh, it's okay. Don't worry about it."

"Fucking Jeremiah," said Adam when we were out of earshot. "That punk's been up my ass since nineth grade when I got six inches taller than him. He's out to get me, man."

I only rolled my eyes. What an Adam thing to say.

4/ Lucas

Are there no do-overs?

When I was five, my mother tried to teach me not to slouch. I was a bad learner. It was a miracle I didn't have any back problems. The cheap, gray fabric of the sofa itched the curve of my body where skin showed. I flexed my sweaty hand around my phone, tense from the posture I'd been holding for the last twenty minutes. My right leg bounced furiously against the carpeted floor. Rolling my neck, I found it a little sore after all.

Finally, I took a deep breath.

I scrolled through the contacts list until my thumb landed on dad. The line rang for a while, and I was half-praying he wouldn't pick up. I knew it was too much to hope for, though.

"Dad. Hey," I said, voice wavering. I sprang up, pacing around the room restlessly. There was no space to contain my nervousness.

This needed to be done with. I had to tell him. I swallowed, ignoring the pounding in my chest, and focused solely on my objective. Really, it didn't have to be a big deal.

"Lucas, how did the meetings go?" asked dad. "Did you get all the paperwork done? And the parts—I need that AC compressor first thing. John is getting impatient. I told him I'd get it fixed by Monday. I need to know if I have to drive to pick it up."

"Everything went fine. They'll send the things. Listen, that's not why I called. I need to tell you something."

I listened to dad's heavy and hacked breathing. It wasn't too late to change my mind, yet nothing could have made me do it. For years I'd wished for an opportunity such as this. Not only to see Ophelia again, but to be more independent and learn. My eyes latched onto the people on the streets below my window. How many parents clip their own children's wings out of fear of losing them? Dad was all I had. He was proud of me regardless of what I did. But then why was I terrified to let him down? He never had to clip my wings because I was too afraid to fly anyway.

"Okay, what is it then? Did something happen? You *are* still coming tomorrow?"

I pressed my eyes shut. "Yeah. No. It's not what you think. It's because of, well dad, I'm actually going to a wedding with a friend of mine. I won't be back for a little while longer. I'm sorry." I coughed. "Don't worry about me, I'll be fine. You trust me, right?"

"Lucas—"

A jolt went through me.

"It's all happening so suddenly. You'd like her, I'm sure. You won't even notice that I'm gone. I'll call you and stuff. I know this is sort of out of the blue. I certainly didn't expect this, but I also know you can manage things on your own for a bit longer." I sat down on the edge of the sofa, massaging my neck. I had to catch my breath for a second.

"I don't like this," said dad wearily. In his head, he was thinking of all the ways to make me change my mind.

My voice softened. "I know, and I'm sorry. But I promise to be back soon. I want to do this."

Dad didn't reply. At the end of the day, he trusted me. Because he wasn't just all *I* had, I was also all *he* had.

The inside of the car smelled like lilies and lavender. I'd noticed it the first time I'd sat in her car. Today she wore jeans and a pale-yellow top. We didn't speak much, but every once in a while, I caught her looking at me. My stomach dropped every time.

"There's something you should know," said Ophelia. "I lied to you a little bit. We'll probably stay for longer than I told you, but you can leave anytime you want. There just wasn't enough time to go through everything before. You don't have to stay until the wedding. It's not like I'm forcing you. But then we do have to think of an excuse

47

for Eloise and Jeanie. Some family crisis or an illness. They said to bring a plus one, but I'm sure it's fine if you must leave."

"What? When's the wedding?" This was not our agreement. I'd accepted because I thought it was a couple of days. Maybe a week if we were pushing it.

She ran a hand through her hair, her other hand loosely on the steering wheel. "In, like, a couple of weeks. Start of July. But I mean it, you can go. No worries."

"Weeks? How do you not know when the wedding is? Isn't there some sort of a date?" I'd never been to a wedding before, but even I knew these things were sorted out a lot earlier.

She sighed. "Well, Jeanie and Eloise are still arranging things. Some things are yet to be checked off the list. The, um, wedding is sort of a last-minute thing." She caught me scrutinizing. "They want my opinion, and I couldn't get off work earlier," she said with a shrug.

"You must be close then," I concluded. You wouldn't put a whole wedding on pause for one person if you weren't.

She looked at me again, sending a set of shivers down my spine. "Yes. I suppose so. If not for them, I don't know where I would be."

Somehow, that stung. I stared out the passenger window, but the closeness of our bodies made it impossible for me to ignore her completely. The car was becoming really, really confined. And I was starting to slowly suffocate.

Ophelia cleared her throat. "I'm sure you'll like them as much as they'll like you." She smiled, but it wasn't a real smile. I knew what her face looked like when it actually lit up.

"Yes, of course," I said bitterly. Suddenly I didn't want to talk at all. What had I got myself mixed up in?

"You're grumpy. What is it?"

I took a deep breath, and swallowed the rant I was starting to feel at the back of my throat. "Nothing. All good." I was sure she'd heard the irritation in my voice. I hated that I sucked at hiding my emotions. Especially since she seemed to excel at it.

"Uh-uh. Who are you trying to fool?" She paused. When she spoke again, her voice was gentle and low. "Tell me what's wrong."

It hurt how caring she was then.

"Why is it that they get to know you, and we never did? You left, and then you got yourself new friends and family, and I'm supposed to like them? I can't fucking believe this."

I'd meant for it to come out differently, but anger was seeping through my every word like love seeps through a bleeding heart. I trembled with it. My throat was throbbing, and I was starting to stick to the car seat. How dare she act as if she wasn't dead for three years? Flaunting with her new friends who didn't even know about her past.

"If you want me to apologize, I won't. You acting like a child won't make me any more sorry either." Ophelia's eyes were stormy, a troubled wrinkle on her forehead.

I cursed myself, letting my head fall back. She was right. We'd get nowhere arguing. She'd tell me when things settled.

"I'm sorry," I said, opening my eyes. I wasn't a petrified teenager anymore; I wasn't afraid of a girl. I slid my hand on top of hers. "I didn't mean to yell at you." I drew circles on her soft skin. It wasn't her fault I hadn't moved on yet.

She pulled her hand back, and it felt like a slap across my face. Everything was quiet.

5 / Rafael

I want your mess to be mine

"I barely signed up for one murder, now y'all are talking about three?" Zack threw his arms in the air. "How—just how—is this any fun? I can think of at least a hundred other things to do, and you go ahead and pick that one."

"Haven't you had enough of football and parties?" I asked. Enough of tagging along, it was my turn to choose what we did.

Z pointed at me accusingly. "Never. Besides, don't forget the booze. Never the booze. This is embarrassing. A real bruise to my reputation."

"Yes, how will you recover?" gasped Katie dramatically. "Anyway, three people is too much of a coincidence. Ophelia would have never run away."

Sometimes I forgot that Ophelia had been her best friend. Three years felt like a forever. It was tough to wrap my head around the idea that we'd once been completely different people. Some of us had changed more than others. Some of us had had to. I wasn't close with any of the people who'd gone missing, but there were some who were.

"What was she like?" I asked as we turned to Arabella's street.

She didn't hesitate. "She was always happy. A dreamer. She wanted to travel, get away." Adam gave her a weird look, and Katie stiffened. "That doesn't mean she ran away, you dipshit. She was loyal, protective. She'd never leave the people she loved."

"What about her parents?"

Katie kicked a pebble, then again, sending in hurling. "Her mom is a librarian. Her and Ophelia used to argue sometimes. Mrs. Graham always found something wrong with her. Little things, like how she dressed or walked or talked. And I'm sure you remember her dad. He works with Lucas' dad at the shop. I've known him a long time. When we were ten, he built Ophelia and I a small treehouse. Lastly, there's Ophelia's grandma. We're not that familiar, only ever talked to her a couple of times. I hear she's sick a lot, so she stays inside most days." Katie's eyes fogged. Like she'd been transported back in time. She blinked, and the haze was gone.

"We should talk about the night she went missing," said Adam. He fell into step with me. "Maybe she's still haunting the beach."

"If she were haunting anything, I think it would not be that beach. We might've been the last people Ophelia saw that night." She couldn't have died at the beach. The waves would've spit her back out if she'd drowned.

Katie said, "I walked home with her. She was fine. Her usual self, maybe a little distracted."

Zack flashed his teeth. "That's on Lucas, I'm afraid. He takes after me."

"I told him to shoot his shot." Adam shoved Z, both stumbling.

Arabella's house appeared at the end of the street. An ivory house with windows on each side. Flowers at the front, and a walkway leading to the door.

Zack pocketed his hands. "So, what's your grand plan now, detective *Scooby-Doo*?"

"Firstly, we need Arabella on our side." I'd promised her I'd drop the investigation. I felt more than a little humiliated to go knocking on her door because of it.

Adam patted me on the back. "You guys should've seen him at the party. Total fuck-up."

"Oh, come on. I can fix this," I argued, when really, I wasn't so certain.

Zack ground his jaw. "So, she opens the door, and you what? Apologize?" His emerald eyes pierced through me, turning my insides into goo.

Honestly, that was sort of what I'd had in mind. Zack had read me like a newspaper. He burst into more laughter. I ignored him. Let him be a pessimist if he wanted to.

We reached the porch. My hand was outstretched, ready to knock, but the door swung open before I had the chance. I took two steps back, surprised.

Lucy leaned against the door frame; hands crossed. My eyes shifted to Arabella next to her. A gentle breeze caught her long hair. She was studying me. As I felt her gaze crawl over me, my stomach did another flip.

Besides being gorgeous and popular, Arabella and Lucy had absolutely nothing in common. I couldn't fathom why those two would be friends. But friendships don't go unnoticed, and theirs was seen far and beyond. Lucy was always hovering close by. Even now, when she was not invited, and obviously not wanted.

"Just hear me out." I held out my hands.

"Well, what if she doesn't want to?" reasoned Lucy. "And would you look at that—he brought all his weird friends with him."

"Zip it, Barbie," growled Katie.

Lucy rolled her eyes.

"Look," I said, "I know this is asking for a lot, and that it seems impossible, and you know what? Maybe it is. But the thought of giving up before I've even tried makes me physically hurt. How will we ever know anything, if we don't try to make sense of this? Give it our best shot. You cannot tell me a part of you isn't interested. I see it in you, Arabella. The need. It's the same as mine. We can figure it out. Together."

"And I'll be there, so it can't be that bad." Zack gave one of his dashing smiles. He gave them out easily. They made him look fun and playful, and a little dangerous.

"I don't want to be disappointed," revealed Arabella, head down.

"Low expectations help." Adam was behind me, outgrown hair tickling my shoulder. He'd grown as tall as Lucas.

"Or you can come with us, and I promise I won't let you down," I said. It was a risky promise to make, but I took the leap of faith without fear.

"You truly think you can do it?"

There were only two options I had. A simple yes or a simple no. I knew which answer she wanted. Three letters, and she would be in on this, I knew it. There's nothing more powerful than determination, and it would lead me to my victory. All I had to do was take it.

"Yes," I said. My voice had gone raspy and I cleared it.

"So? Are you with us now?" asked Katie.

A long pause, long enough to make me erratic.

"I need to think. This is important. Big."

Nothing could ever work in my favor, could it? In my worst moments, I imagined the whole universe laughing at me as it forced me to put in twice the effort as everyone else. How come it always came so easy to other people, but I struggled with every small thing? If Arabella wouldn't change her mind, there was nothing I could do. The decision was out of my control.

On our way back, we passed Warren Repairs. Despite the scarce cloudiness, the air still felt sticky. I stopped in my tracks. There was still more questioning to be done. It was like therapy, a distraction to avoid my own self and focus my thoughts.

"Hey," I said, "let's go in and ask about Ophelia. Mr. Graham should still be here."

The inside of the shop stank like thick motor oil. I was no stranger to it, but every time I came around it baffled me anyway. Some of the ceiling lights blinked furiously. They'd been like that for years.

Mr. Warren was kneeling beside a jet boat's motor. Oily parts sat beside him on the ground, a filthy rag under them to not stain the concrete floor. He raised his head at us in greeting.

"Is Mr. Graham here?" I asked.

Dave rubbed his temple. "No. No, you missed him. Everything good?"

I inhaled slowly. "It's okay. We just wanted to ask him something. It's fine. We can come back another time."

Mr. Warren stood, wiping his hands with a cloth. "You boys sure I can't help?"

He was a bulky man with an incoming beer tummy. Gray eyes, cropped hair, tan skin. Lucas had his eyes, but not much else.

We exchanged looks. No one stepped in. "Okay, we wanted to ask about Ophelia."

His brows furrowed but if he found it strange, he didn't say so.

"How well did you know her?"

Dave rubbed his neck and did a head circle. "She came around sometimes for Joey. We didn't talk much."

"Do you remember the day she went missing? Did she stop by that day?" asked Katie.

Mr. Warren nodded. "I'm not sure what you kids are looking for. Is this about anything in particular?"

"Anything unusual. Perhaps you saw something, anything. Or heard."

"Well, I might have something. I told this to the police years ago when they asked me. What's this about?" He eyed us suspiciously.

"Go on," I urged him. Mr. Warren could be more useful that I'd thought. "We're just trying to remember her. To, uh, honor her memory."

He sighed. "It was a few days before. I remember that Ophelia rushed in, and they were talking in the back room—her and Joey. Actually, it was more like fighting. Ophelia was yelling, Joseph told her to be quiet."

"Did you hear what they said exactly?"

"No, no. I was in the other room. But eventually I got curious and took a peek. By then, they had calmed down. Ophelia picked up something from the table and came rushing towards the doors. I barely made it out of the way before she would have seen me." Dave dropped the now dirty cloth.

"What did she take?"

"To me, it looked like a phone. I don't know kid, maybe it was a box or somethin'. It was a rectangle shape. I remember thinking it was funny." Mr. Warren jerked his head. "I asked about the fight later, but Joey told me not to worry and that they'd already made up. He said Ophelia was just being silly."

"Did she come back after that?" asked Katie.

"If she did, I didn't notice. Sorry I can't tell you much."

I chased everything around in my head.

A few days before going missing, Ophelia had a fight with her dad. According to Katie, she normally got along with him. She took something, left. Then, she disappeared. The only thing I could make of that was that we needed to find Mr. Graham. Immediately.

6 / Lucas

A reminder to not forget about your towel

The car skittered to a stop, jolting me awake. It was midday, and sunshine tickled my cheeks through the car window. I rubbed my aching muscles.

"Look, you smell disgusting, and I'm exhausted. There should be a hotel close by. I don't want to show up looking like this." Her eyes slithered over me, and I shrunk in my seat. "It's not long anymore, but first impressions matter."

As we walked, I realized I had no idea where we were. I'd slept longer than I'd thought. Ophelia kept her nose down, navigating our way. My eyes shot up only when we stopped.

"This should be it," she said.

I followed her gaze up to a big glowing sign, and my stomach turned immediately. The building was literally falling apart. Like one of those places where they sell drugs on the street and black-market organs inside. The headquarters of Dark Web. I grabbed Ophelia's hand against her protests, pulling her closer to me.

"We are not going in there," I hissed in her ear.

She fluttered her eyes at me like I was crazy. "I'm sorry, did you expect something fancier? This is the closest place to us. Besides, it's not for long."

I didn't let go of her when we entered, but I did loosen my grip.

The beige paint on the walls was peeling, unraveling dark stains. The reception room stank of cigarettes and old books. No windows, no air conditioning, no clients, no nothing. Because the building was facing a wall, natural light was scarce.

Behind the desk sat a woman in her early forties. Her frizzy auburn hair was tied back into a low ponytail. The glasses on the bridge of her nose emphasized the bags under her eyes. Every inch of her skin was neatly covered; brown cardigan over a white shirt, long gray skirt, and brown rhinestone sandals. She was built more like a cartoon character than a real person. Her name tag said her name was Luna. I found it a fitting name—from a distance she could pass for an owl. Even in my head, that came out harsh. Her business was clearly suffering, and she seemed lonely. My smile dropped. Looking at her now, there was nothing funny about her.

Ophelia leaned over the desk. "Hi, can we get a room, please?"

Luna gave us a warm smile. "Yes, of course! How long are you planning on staying?" She inspected our intertwined fingers.

Ophelia ripped her hand away. "Just a few hours to rest. And, can we get separate beds?"

I bent towards her. "We don't have to stay. I can drive. It's not a problem."

"I apologize, um, we don't have any rooms with double beds." Luna fidgeted with a keychain. "I can offer you extra towels?"

"That's fine," said Ophelia while my sharp eyes dug into her. "We'll be fine. I just need a quick nap."

The elevator taking us to our floor was squeaky and rusting. It had a speaker where music had once come from and no longer did. I held my breathe until we reached the top.

The room was tiny and bland. Most of the space was taken by the bed, leaving none for anything else. The floor was covered with tacky gray fabric, and the timid blue curtains narrowed the room down. But for a couple of hours, it would do.

Ophelia grunted before throwing herself onto the bed like a toddler. She reached out her arms and legs, squirming. A high squeal escaped her. Something white fell from her pocket, gliding towards the floor and hitting it soundlessly. Ophelia's eyes blunged as I went to pick it up. "No! Don't look at that—"

"What is this supposed to be?" I held up the napkin. A dark blotch covered the front.

Ophelia's face flooded with bashfulness. She blinked slowly. "It's Kim Possible."

I widened my eyes in a dramatic manner. "Huh, and here I thought of something else. Why do you have a Kim Possible doodle in your pocket?"

"I only know how to draw Kim Possible. I thought I was her when I was little."

"Right." I rested against a wall; arms crossed. "Do you want to shower first or shall I?"

"Go ahead. You need it more."

I rolled my eyes, crouching to get my things from my bag.

Thankfully, there was warm water. The system worked a little weird, but it was straightforward enough to figure out. I felt tired, although I'd slept in the car.

I went to pick up my towel, but it wasn't where I'd left it. I growled, thinking I must've misplaced it. I wasn't about to ask for Ophelia's help, and give her the satisfaction. Reluctantly, I put my pants on and opened the door. I pushed my wet hair back, and found Ophelia staring at me.

"You forget to shower?" she blurted out after a long second.

I rubbed my neck and picked up the damn towel from beside my bag. "Forgot this," I said, waving the thing loosely in the air. My face was hot with embarrassment, but at least I didn't come off like a complete fool.

"Ah."

She kept staring, and I thought I caught a small blush. I didn't bother with the bathroom. I dried my hair, and pulled a clean shirt over my head. I'd be lying if I said I didn't like the fact I'd rendered the girl speechless. Maybe she didn't dislike me after all.

Ophelia mumbled something to herself.

I held back a smirk. "What was that?"

"Nothing. I should shower too." She jumped up from the bed so fast her body slammed into me, and we both tumbled back.

I steadied myself, catching Ophelia by her forearms. Her face was scarlet, mouth gaping. I met her eyes confidently, thrilling my way through her icy front. A little more and she'd open up to me.

"I could've driven too. We didn't have to stop." I whispered because speaking normally seemed wrong suddenly.

She swallowed a lump. "It's okay. I don't want you driving my car, but thank you for offering." She settled back on her legs, and I scooted over to let her pass.

I rolled my eyes. So untrusting.

7/ Rafael

The leftovers of his life

My movement sent glistening ripples into motion along the water's surface. Sunlight warmed my bare back. Droplets of water fell down my forehead and through my eyelashes. Soft splashes.

I looked back at Adam, whose feet tangled in the water, swaying back and forth. His pale skin was even paler in the light, almost luminous. His sandy hair matched his shirt. Zack and Katie were sitting on the ground, pulling out grass, taking in the distant forest across the lake. All three of them were deep in thought.

I swam towards the shore and climbed out. My absence left the water restless and void.

Tonight, we were going to question the Grahams. Couldn't afford to mess it up. What would they say once they figured out my plan? *If* they figured it out. Ever. Would they laugh? How ambitious of me, thinking I'm smarter than a whole police force.

My phone hummed beside me. It was a text from Arabella.

I opened the message with lightning speed and changed my plans just as fast.

"You seriously thought you could leave me out of it?" A sly smirk followed, as Lucy stepped aside to let us inside.

Adam crossed his arms and grunted.

"Come in. We have to hurry. My mom will be home soon," said Arabella, gesturing us forward.

Lucy slipped her hand into Z's. The rest of us followed in their trail.

Adam snuck up behind me. "Don't you think Barbie's a tad bit too excited to be searching a dead guy's room? Why is she into this anyway? We shouldn't trust her. She's a walking, talking liability. She could be a spy or a mole."

I rolled my eyes. "Adam, relax. I get not trusting her, but I also know you." He wanted to be rid of Lucy. I did too, but my gut told me not to act on it. Lucy and Arabella were a package deal.

I understood what an unusual and confusing group I'd assembled, yet every member was equally important. Katie and Arabella had their connections and information. They were both smart and diligent, vital to the investigation's success. Lucy was different, louder, and more vibrant. She could still surprise us. And of course, I needed the boys. There wasn't a thing I couldn't do with them by my side.

"I am innocent!"

I gaped over my shoulder and gave him the *are you really?*

We made it to the end of the corridor. The walls of Sheldon's room were dark navy blue, the floor dark wood. Papers were scattered, the desk cluttered, clothes lying around. Only the bed had been made.

"Do you and your mom come in here a lot?" I asked cautiously. It was as if a tornado had hit the room. If I didn't know better, I'd say someone had already turned it upside down.

"My mom cleans a bit sometimes, but she doesn't want to touch his things. It just doesn't feel right. I don't often come in here either. Honestly, I sometimes forget that this room even exists." Arabella fiddled with her hands. "I hate that I forget."

"How—*where* are we supposed to even start?" asked Katie, still by the door. She straightened her back, and let the door fall shut.

I took another look around. My hands moved unwillingly. One day this would be my job, better get used to it sooner than later. I'd always wanted to be like my dad. The good guy. I started with the desk, which seemed the most promising anyway. I opened every drawer. I left no chances, no possibilities to escape my mind. Dust had built up on almost all the open surfaces. The air tasted musty and dry, yet when I closed my eyes, I could easily picture Sheldon Rogers walking down these creaky floorboards. Dimpled smile and everything.

I skimmed through a stack of old files and checks, and even a bunch of sticky notes laying around. Nothing stood out.

"Did your uncle have a computer? Where's his phone? Anything we could look through?" I asked Arabella.

She shook her head. "He didn't want a laptop, although mom and I wanted to get him one for his birthday. I don't have the phone. I'm sorry. The cops told us they never found it."

I set my jaw. Rogers probably had the phone with him when he disappeared. Whatever happened to him, that phone had been destroyed a long time ago.

Lucy gnarled on the other side of the room. "What am I even searching for? This is so pointless!"

"It's not like you gave me a heads-up to think of something," I said, pulling out books from the bookcase.

"Oh, I'm sorry," replied Lucy sarcastically. "I thought you were supposed to be the smart one, but really, my bad. You're useless. All of you."

"Can you stop? You're giving me brain damage." Katie faced us both. "Let's just get this over with. If you find something suspicious, you'll know. And for the love of God, try not to make a bigger mess than we started with."

"Bells, did the police take anything?" I asked. *Bells*. I'd called her by her nickname. I smiled like I'd meant to do that on purpose, when really it just slipped out.

She cocked her head up from behind the bed. "Yeah, some stuff. Why?"

"Do you have it?"

"Maybe? It's probably around here somewhere. We have it all in a box. We stashed it the second they returned it. Mom didn't want to look at it."

I nodded. "Okay, but when he disappeared, did he take anything with him other than his phone? Was anything missing, or anything specific the police asked about?" Like documents.

She walked out from behind the bed and stretched her back. "Yeah, they asked questions. But it's not like I memorized them. My mom did most of the talking, so your guess is as good as mine."

I had another flashback to those first days in school after the disappearances. Everyone had been talking about them. Watching Arabella, whispering. All color had been absorbed from her face. For weeks she'd been a red-eyed picture of grief. She wasn't the only one, but it was different.

"And he never told you where he was going or when he'd be back?" questioned Adam.

"No, he didn't." Arabella sighed. "I'm sorry I can't be more of a help."

"What are these?" Zack was holding a cardboard box the width of his shoulders.

"Oh!" yelped Arabella excitedly. "Pretty sure those are the things police looked at."

We formed a circle, emptying the box. Wrinkled paperwork scattered and some personal items thumped against the hard ground.

Adam threw a stack of papers on the floor, right next to Sheldon's ID. "My IQ is not high enough for this shit. I'll let you Velmas of the world figure it out. Shaggy needs a rest." He stomped towards the window.

"Don't beat yourself up buddy. Some people are born with a lopsided brain. Embrace it," Zack told him cheerfully.

Adam grabbed a pillow and tackled Z. They both went sprawling on the ground. Dust got everywhere, feathers were in the air, and multiple hits were taken which would no doubt turn into tiny bruises later.

"Guys! Can you not?" I interwove.

Adam and Zack pulled apart, quiet chuckles between them. I picked up the things Adam had dropped, and something caught my eye. Four photographs emerged from between some of the papers, tied together with a yellow rubber band.

I flipped the first photo. Right away Sheldon's face stared back at me. A bunch of other people were there as well. None of them could've been much older than ten. I recognized Sheldon and Dave

Warren, but everyone else was a mystery to me. Some of them struck me as familiar, but not enough for me to connect them with a name. This was, what, thirty years old photograph?

Katie ran a finger over a short, long-haired boy. "That's Link Martinez." She moved her finger to the two on his left. "Dave and Joseph." The spooked girl behind them was Vivianne Reyes. I knew her from the police station.

I searched for my dad, knowing I wouldn't find him. He'd moved to Whitewood when he was in his twenties. Instead, I turned to the next picture. A family photo. There was only one strange face there. He was wearing a military uniform. It must've been Arabella's dad. She was only a baby in this picture, nestled in her mother's arms. She had her dad's beachy hair.

In the third one, Sheldon seemed closer to us in age. He was standing in a fishing boat. Either the picture had been taken from a funny angle, or the boat was tipping over.

In the last photo, five people were standing on the edge of a cliff: Sheldon, Link, Dave, Mr. and Mrs. Graham. They were older than us, I guessed somewhere in their early, roaring twenties. Esther held Joseph's arm; head tilted against his shoulder. Dave stood next to them, eyes on the camera, an easygoing smile on his lips. Link was looking somewhere to the side, and whatever it was that had caught his attention remained a mystery as it was out of the camera's frame. Sheldon's eyes rounded with crow's feet as he was doubling over.

"Hey, I think you guys should go," said Bells. "My mom texted me. She'll be home soon, and I think it's best if, um, she doesn't know we did this."

"Okay, then we go," I said, catching myself. "Wait. Shouldn't we interview your mom? Didn't she know your uncle the best? The longest?" We didn't have to tell her about the search, but a couple of questions wouldn't hurt.

Aarabella paled. "Er … I don't think she wants to be questioned. She doesn't like to talk about it at all. We should just leave it."

"Are you sure?" Her mom remembered more than she did.

"I'm sure. I don't want her to know. She wouldn't like it."

I couldn't help but wonder what secrets, if any, Iris Rogers knew? The police must've questioned her. The police must've questioned a lot of people. They collected evidence and alibis.

An idea was starting to take shape in my head.

8/ Lucas

Rich people are built different

It was another hour and a half before the house came into view—or should I say mansion? That sounds more accurate. The windows swallowed whole walls. A patio, and multiple balconies. So pristine and grand. Trees formed an alley and covered parts of the house from afar. It was like a puzzle revealed brick by brick.

Ophelia had told me little about these friends of hers. One of the bits being that they were wealthy. I think what she meant was rich. Nothing could've prepared me for this. Big money. Very. Big. Money. I'd never seen anything like it.

I closed my eyes to breathe in the salty air. Sea, somewhere in the distance. I couldn't allow myself to freak out.

We walked through endless rooms, Ophelia leading, and me following in awe. All sizes, shapes, and colors. A piano here, a pool table there. Walls of glass, and a tree in the middle of the room because why not? Every room was its own piece of art. All different and beautiful. Delicately designed and furnished.

I found myself on the patio.

The candles on the table flickered with every gush of wind. An older woman was lazing out on one of the cushion chairs. In her hand was a glass of red wine. She turned her head, and a lofty smile washed over her. Beaming, her cheeks warm and flushed.

"Oh, you're here! You made it!" She embraced Ophelia, slender fingers gently resting on her shoulders. "We've missed you! It's been too long, you should've come sooner!" scolded the woman, gray hair curling around her ears.

Ophelia chuckled. "Yeah, I know. I wanted to, but you know how busy I've been. It's good to be back."

"Let me look at you!" The woman pulled back, eyes devouring. "You're beautiful, darling. Eloise! Eloise, come look who came!"

I waited awkwardly for Ophelia to make the introduction, but I might as well have been invisible. Someone gasped behind me, and I whirled to see a short Asian woman rushing towards us.

"You came!" She hugged Ophelia. "Oh, my dearest!" Her dark eyes swelled with joy.

Again, my heart plummeted. They were hugging and smiling like they'd been starved of Ophelia's presence. They had no idea. Would they still look at her the same if they did?

"Lucas, are you staying with us until the wedding?"

My breathing hitched and I almost choked on my own spit. I focused my watery eyes on Eloise. She appeared friendly. And I must've looked pathetic. I cleared my throat. "Um, yeah. If it's okay. I wouldn't want to intrude." I'd missed the introduction, or maybe there hadn't even been one, I wasn't sure.

"Nonsense!" Eloise moved in for a quick hug. "We'd love to have you around."

"Oh, um, thank you."

We sat down for dinner. My mouth started watering as soon as I smelled the meat and steaming potatoes. Crispy on the outside, soft on the inside. I hadn't eaten since morning.

"What do you do, Logan?" asked Jeanie.

With delay I realize *I* was Logan. "I work in the family business."

Jeanie smiled cleverly. "And what's that?"

"Well, we repair cars and boats. Vehicles." I felt my cheeks heat.

"Ah." She grinned. "A repair shop. Of course. Your parents must be proud of you, Logan."

"Actually, it's Lucas—"

"What's your drink of choice?"

I searched around the table. The question had caught me so off guard it took me a moment to rearrange my thoughts. "Um, I'm not sure." Did she mean, like, alcohol? Surely not.

"Shame."

"Do you have to do that?" Ophelia asked Jeanie. "Be friendly."

Jeanie gave me one last pointed look, but left me in peace. For the rest of the dinner, I tried to avoid her if possible, worried I might end up on her bad side.

"How did you two meet?" asked Eloise.

Ophelia brushed a shiny lock of hair from her face before answering. "We went to the same school, practically grew up together. Lucas was hard not to notice. Small town."

"That," said Eloise, "is adorable!"

I fell into conversation with Eloise, who was anything but scary and mean. It was like talking to an old friend. She was a lovely lady, who radiated comforting warmth.

"Your house is amazing," I complimented. "It really is quite something."

"Thank you, that's very sweet of you, but it's more Jeanie's area of expertise. I only do so much here and there."

I fancied a quick glance at Jeanie. She seemed *almost* pleasant talking to Ophelia.

"They're lovely," I told Ophelia while we were walking down a long corridor towards our rooms. The day was coming to an end.

"You don't mean that," she replied. "I know you don't like Jeanie."

"What? I like her," I lied.

A smile tugged at her lips. "No, you don't. It's okay. You just have to get to know her better, she's very protective right now."

"So, what, she's testing me?"

"Yeah, something like that."

My brow creased. "What happens if I don't pass?" I startled myself, noticing there was real concern behind my words.

"You'll pass," she stated as a matter of fact, her shoulder brushing against mine.

"How can you be so sure?" As far as I knew, I'd already failed.

"You'll pass," she repeated, finally meeting my eyes. It struck me that she really believed it.

Stupid fluttery in my stomach. I cleared my throat. "How did you meet them?"

Ophelia sighed. "I met Jeanie in a cafe I used to work at. She introduced me to Eloise. Be patient. Jeanie will come around once she knows she can trust you."

"Why haven't you told them the truth?"

"Which truth? Yours or mine?" Her voice was strained, telling me not to push my luck. She needed more time.

We stopped, and Ophelia pointed at a door. "This is yours. Hope you memorized the way, because I will not be giving you a tour every day. Mine is there." She pointed to another door, a few steps from mine. "Good night, I guess."

I forced a smile down. "Got it. Night."

I stepped inside, closed the door behind me, and slumped against it. I took a deep breath.

How exactly was I supposed to show Ophelia that she could trust me? And why was it that I had to earn my right to know the truth at all? There had to be some way to get her talking. If only someone would tell me how.

9/ Rafael

Nostalgia

I knew the color of the Grahams' front door. It was red. Not bright red or dark red, but something of a muted one. It was the only house on the street with a colorful door, yet something about it felt like a warning. *Beware of this home.*

When I closed my eyes, I could picture myself knocking, hear the sound echo. When I opened them, Mrs. Graham was looking back at me. She was a small, fragile woman. There were cracks in her porcelain skin—not real cracks, but the invisible kind you know would be there if our deepest, darkest shadows were out for all people to see. Back when I was a kid, she wore her hair down to her waist, a funny bag on her shoulder as she walked down the streets. Even then she had that weird tiredness to her. She always did. All these years she wore her tiredness like an accessory.

Katie spoke, "Hello! We wanted to speak with your husband. Is he home?"

"It won't take long, swear it!" added Lucy, charming and chipper.

Mrs. Graham led us into the dining room where Mr. Graham was sitting, gripping a newspaper. He was confused at the sight of us, but the frown quickly morphed into a welcoming smile. He set his paper aside. "Boys." His eyes skipped to the others. "And girls. This is a surprise. Has something happened?"

"Sorry to interrupt," I said. "We found some old pictures." I shrugged my right shoulder sheepishly. *Let them underestimate you*, the voice in my head said, *that's all the advantage you're ever going to need.* Better to play it off coolly, so he wouldn't think much of our visit.

He chewed on his inner cheek. "I must say, you got me most curious. Staying for dinner?"

I looked back at Mrs. Graham, who had scurried into the depths of the kitchen. She was a mere speck of solid in midst the dark, ghastly eyes locked on mine. "Uh … sure." My voice wavered, and I backed it up with a steading smile.

There was more to that woman than met the eye. Something about Esther Graham made me uneasy. I could read most people fairly well, but Mrs. Graham was tough to make sense of. She didn't wear her heart on her sleeve or show her emotions too often.

I once had a teacher I feared. She wasn't particularly mean or cruel. She didn't punish me for getting an answer wrong—not that I ever did. She had a presence to her that emitted control and alarm. I think there are people we fear, because they challenge us the most. Like equals, but not really. They push you to be better and deep down you want to impress them. You fear their rejection because you crave their praise.

Esther Graham felt like an equal, despite me not particularly wishing for her support. I had to figure out why.

"We found these old photographs with you in them." I slid the pictures over to Mr. Graham. "That's you, right?" I asked, pointing to the figure I already knew was him. I didn't wait for confirmation before shifting to the next one. "And here you're all grown up."

"I haven't seen these in years." He quieted, turning the photos over and over.

"You seemed close," commented Katie from across the table.

Joseph grinned nostalgically. "Yes, we were. We were great friends. All our lives were knotted together. You lot remind me a of us."

I almost let out a snort. If he only knew. If I listened closely, I could hear faint chopping coming from the kitchen, a knife going *whick, whick* against a cutting board. Then, the sound stopped. Footsteps took its place instead.

"What happened?" asked Adam. He smacked his lips together and sunk deeper into his seat. His hair was fluffier than usual, recently washed.

Joseph's mouth hung open absently. His eyes flicked towards Esther, now in the room. The movement was so brief that if I hadn't been watching for a reaction, I might've missed it completely.

"I'll get the pickles from the cellar," stated Esther.

"We'll help," offered Lucy, Arabella standing up with her.

"Hey, I'll come too. I'll have you know I love pickles." Zack rubbed his hands together. "I also love olives. You wouldn't happen to have any, would you now?" I heard his muffled talking before they disappeared completely.

"Well?" I turned back to Mr. Graham.

Joseph sighed, setting one leg over the other. "Nothing. We grew apart. We fought, we disagreed. It didn't mean we weren't friends anymore, it simply meant we stopped trying to have the same opinion on everything. It was tough, but it was for the best. We were all busy with our lives anyway. Becoming adults."

"And this picture?" I pointed to the one where they were grown.

Mr. Graham stood and walked around the chair, leaning against it. "Twenty years ago. Our last road trip." He rubbed his chin. A sly smirk appeared on his face. "We used to take these trips every summer. We'd borrow a car or jump on a train—get as far from here as we could. Often, we were short on money, and had to sleep in the car or pack sleeping bags with us. It was only the bunch of us, sometimes girlfriends. We lived for those summer trips, and they are some of my favorite memories."

"And then you stopped being friends? Twenty years ago?"

He gave a bare nod. "It didn't happen overnight, but yes. I don't have bitter feelings. It was a long time ago. But I have to say, fight for what cannot be easily rebuilt. Dave and I have always been close, and I am lucky enough to work with my best friend. It's the friends who were left in the past I worried about the most. Right choices are hardly ever the easiest."

"One last thing," said Katie and I knew what she was about to ask. "Ophelia, she—"

Joseph inhaled sharply. "What about her?" he asked, turning. "What does she have to do with any of this?" He tensed, chest rising rapidly.

I'd made a promise to Arabella, and to myself. "But please," I begged. "Before she went missing, you fought—"

"No." His body rigid and voice strict. The windows gave a muddied reflection of him and us.

I should have stopped, but the burning desire in me wouldn't let go. I had to know. I was going to know. If he'd only let me get a full sentence out. I'd already decided I was going to find out the truth, and there was no stopping now.

"You fought. Only days before she went missing, you fought. Why?" I said louder. Katie mouthed me a silent *stop*. I ignored her. "Please, why did you fight? Tell us."

Mr. Graham shook his head silently, quarreling to hold back tears. "Enough. This is enough." He turned to us. His chest continuously rose and fell with an uneven pace, his lips were a thin, trembling line. "My daughter was everything to me. Everything. You knew her, but I raised her. You don't understand half the pain me and my wife have met. Do you think there has been a day I don't think of her? How dare you?"

"Mr. Graham, Sir."

"You've got what you came for. We're done."

A part of me wanted to apologize. A part of me knew I *should* apologize. The other part, the one I hated to admit was stronger, wanted to keep pushing. *What did you fight about? Do you know who hurt her and why?* But no, of course he wouldn't.

A net of sorrow had been cast upon the room. The air felt heavy, and we'd just lost our invite to dinner.

10/ Lucas

Do I smell ... cake?

I reached my hand out from underneath the silky sheets, blindly scanning for my phone. The screen was cold to the touch. I pried my eyes open one at a time.

Countless missed calls and unanswered texts—most from my father. Unsurprising, since I'd been ignoring him. He had too many questions, and I very few answers to give. Soon, I'd have to tell him something, though.

I put my worries aside for the meantime, and followed the echoes of voices into the living room. My sudden appearance must've come as a surprise, because Jeanie stood, dropping her magazine on the glass table in front of her. She sat back down, blissfully avoiding me.

I still sounded husky and raw; voice coated with sleep. "Morning." I flinched at that.

"Good morning!" greeted Eloise. "Have you eaten yet? I made cinnamon rolls. I left them out on the kitchen table."

I nodded. "Thanks, I'll check it out in a bit."

"How did you sleep?"

I opened my mouth to reply, but stopped at Jeanie's sudden hail.

"What? What's happening?" I squared my shoulders.

Jeanie stood again, positioning herself in a stream of light coming from the windows. "There's a scratch on my ring," she said in one disbelieving breath.

"The engagement ring? My dearest, not again." Eloise walked over to Jeanie, studying the ring over her shoulder. Her face was lined with concern, dark eyes wrinkled.

"I'm sorry. I'll get it fixed. It'll be like brand new. You don't have to worry, love. I'll have it done today." She took Eloise's hands in hers, squeezing them.

Eloise looked at me. "It's becoming quite a habit of hers."

"Twice. It has happened twice. And never again."

My panic eased. "How did you manage to scratch it?"

Jeanie huffed at me. "How am I supposed to know? I noticed it only a second ago."

Eloise gasped. "What time is it? We should get going if we don't want to be late."

Jeanie checked her phone screen. "Yes, we probably should, it's almost ten. Where's Ophelia? Still sleeping?" Her hand rested on her hips. She was wearing red trousers and a classy white blouse.

Eloise must've caught my confusion, because she stopped scurrying and explained. "We have a cake testing booked for today. You should come, there's room for one more. You can help us choose."

"Are you sure you wouldn't mind?" I glanced at Jeanie. She didn't argue, weirdly.

"You must come! We need your opinion. And find Ophelia, God knows where that girl is."

I couldn't say no to Eloise. Not that I would've dared to try with Jeanie breathing down my neck.

I didn't have to search for long. I knocked on Ophelia's door, repeatedly, before she grumpily opened it, hair like a bird's nest and dark circles under her eyes.

"What?" she asked, eyes narrowed. Her hand moved to her mouth, stifling a yawn.

"You have pillow lines on your cheek."

Ophelia rubbed her face, missing all the marks. "What do you want? And why are you dressed?"

I arched an eyebrow. "You want me to … undress?"

"Hm?" Her face turned maroon. "What? No. It's early, where are you going?"

"It's ten. Get your lazy butt out the door, we're going to eat cake. Jeanie said we're leaving in fifteen minutes sharp." I eyed her cherry-patterned pajamas. The upper buttons were undone, not enough to show anything, but enough to leave room for imagination. I swallowed, tearing my eyes from her.

She crossed her arms feistily. "What the hell are you staring at?"

I leaned against her door frame, feigning confidence. "I'm staring at you. You moving, or am I going to have to throw you over my shoulder and carry you?"

Ophelia rolled her eyes. "I am perfectly capable of walking myself. Will you leave already so I can get dressed?"

I *tsked*. "I don't know, it's not looking too good for you," I teased on. "Those PJs must be comfy." I looked her up and down again. Slowly, so she would notice.

"Don't you worry about my PJs."

I fought a wobbly smile. It put up a marvelous fight. "You're blushing."

"And you're about to have my fist in your face."

Ophelia and her threats. Always something violent with her.

"Worry about yourself. Excuse me now, I must brush my teeth." She took a step back, and slammed the door in my face.

The cakes melted together into one ooey-gooey sugary deliciousness that I couldn't get enough of. We must've had about twenty different cakes and we couldn't agree on a single one. I sat back and let the others bicker after the fourth. It wasn't my wedding; I shouldn't have had any say in what they served at all.

"Strawberry shortcake or red velvet?" asked Eloise. "Because I love strawberries, but red velvet is a classic and would surely be elegant."

"Red velvet. We are *not* presenting our guests with something as mediocre as shortcake," said Jeanie. " We're not getting married in a barn."

Eloise examined the two cakes, doing surgery with her tiny fork. "What do you think Lucas?"

I scratched my neck, thinking. "Both are good," I finally answered. Whatever they'd end up choosing, I knew it would be the best option.

"Well, I like the pistachio best, but most people would probably prefer chocolate. It's classy and one of the more popular flavors," declared Ophelia.

I set down my fork, finished with all my cakes. I really, truly, absolutely did not care which cake they chose.

Jeanie dabbed her mouth with a napkin. "That's my runner up. But perhaps we ought to stand out more? Chocolate can be such a predictable choice."

The shop was small, but the interior and the quality of the cakes made me think it must've been a high end one. All the furniture was rimmed with gold paint, and the walls were covered in art and plants. Some smaller cakes were on display, a few costumers standing at the front, choosing. For us, the cakes had been set on a big silver platter. Each one had a card description card.

While the women battled, I decided to take a breather and step outside for a quick phone call. As good of a time as any to deal with those missed calls, because the longer I put it off, the worse it would get.

As I was about to press call, the screen lit up with Adam's name.

"Hey, buddy, you okay? Where have you been? Your dad's worried and we haven't heard from you."

I exhaled. "I'm fine. Met a friend. She invited me to a wedding as a plus one. I'll be back soon, no worries. I can't leave right away; I've already created enough confusion."

"Uh-oh, who's the lucky lady? Your only she-friend is Katie, who, by the way, has been a menace since you left. We need you back, man."

I shifted around. I'd promised Ophelia I wouldn't tell.

"It's someone else. You don't know her." A promise is a promise.

"I see."

"Yes."

"So, who is it actually?" he asked after a minute. "I'm not leaving you alone until you tell me. What if you're kidnapped? I'll need a name for when the police come knocking. I'm not stupid, you gaslighting doofus. In fact, I've been told I'm somewhat of a genius, which means you can't leave me in the dark here."

I grinded my teeth together. Yes, a promise is a promise, but best friends don't count when making promises, right?

"Okay, fine, yes." I slumped against a wall. "It's Ophelia. She's alive. I met her in New York, and we talked, and she invited me to this wedding she was going to, so I didn't lie about that. I couldn't say no—not after everything. I can tell she's holding back. Clearly there are things she's not comfortable talking about. I wish I could earn her trust somehow, but it's bewildering when she keeps pushing me away. Also, the house is beautiful. These people are crazy rich. I swear to God, I've never seen anything like it. You'd love it."

"What the fuck, Lucas."

"What?" I crumbled.

"What do you mean *what*? Are you shitting me? Tell me you're fucking joking, man."

Oh. He didn't believe me. "I'm not kidding you, I swear. It's all true. You know I wouldn't lie about this."

"You have no idea what this means, do you? Listen, we're doing a little something back here too. Anyway, if the Ophelia you're talking about is the same one I'm talking about, then this is fucking crazy. What a coincidence."

"First of all, how many Ophelias do you know? And secondly, I don't think she hurt anyone. She seems guarded."

"You have to be our spy," blurted out Adam. "You have to! She's hiding something. You can figure out what exactly."

"Adam, no. This is a terrible idea. I don't want to snoop. I don't want to do this." This could not be good for my nerves. I wasn't a spy; I wasn't a good liar.

"Don't you want to know the truth?"

"Yes, of course, but sneaking around? It feels wrong. I'm sorry." I had to stay focused and gain her trust. It was the only way. And what would happen if she found out I was going behind her back? She'd be furious.

"Please. We need this. All you have to do is look around, keep an eye on her. Ask her some questions if you get a chance. But don't scare her off! Think about how important this could be. Do you even remember what the town was like when she went missing? This changes everything. *Everything*. I didn't believe Rafe before, but now?" Adam whistled. "I have to tell the others."

I swallowed the lump in my throat. He did have a point. I felt a weird, twisting fear take root in my stomach. What if she was lying? What if she was hiding something big? I couldn't trust myself when it came to her. Three years had done nothing to erase my feelings for her. I cursed her for leaving, and I blamed myself for caring. There was no going back now.

"Okay, I'll be your damn spy," I agreed reluctantly. "But you have to promise me you won't tell people about her who don't absolutely need to know. Inner circle only."

Adam breathed out happily. "You're an angel. Try not to spook her."

I went back into the shop with my head held high and all the intention of making Ophelia confess all her little deceits to me. The talk with dad was long forgotten. A trouble for another day. He could wait a little longer. It was fine.

It was no secret how I felt about Ophelia, but Adam had helped me realize I couldn't trust myself when it came to her. And more importantly trust her.

Ophelia walked past me and turned a corner. I decided to follow her.

"Hey." I grabbed her wrist, dropping it once I remembered she didn't like me doing that.

"What?" she asked. "Can't a girl pee?"

"Sorry. I wanted to talk."

She peered around the passage we were blocking. It was quiet. We were alone. "Go ahead."

"I want the truth. We've been playing this game for days, and I think it's time you finally told me the real reason you left town." I was willing to wait for her as long as she'd let me know that eventually she'd trust me enough to talk. Pushing her wasn't my goal, but I couldn't be patient if I had no idea if she was ever planning to be honest at all.

"Didn't I tell you to leave it alone?" She strode past me.

"Where are you going? You do that a lot. Leave."

She came to a halt in front of a cleaning supplies closet. Fire danced in her eyes; eyebrows tightly knitted together. "Oh boy, here we go. That's why you've been such a brick, because you want to punish me?"

"Ophelia," I said with strain, "I'm not trying to punish you. I want to understand you, but you make it so damn difficult. What could possibly be so bad that you can't tell me? You hurt me a lot. You hurt everyone. I thought I meant more to you than that."

"I don't understand what you want from me. What was I supposed to do? Bring the whole town with me?" She bit her lip. She knew what I wanted. She was just making it difficult like always.

"No, but if you didn't want anyone to know you were alive, you could've at least made sure we knew you were dead." I didn't notice myself pressing closer to her. A piece of paper couldn't have fit between us. "Not knowing was the cruelest thing you could've done." Up close I could feel her heartbeat as if it was my own.

I focused on her watery eyes, tracing her soft face. Closer and closer until there was nowhere else to go. My mind was screaming at me, but feeling her breath on my skin felt like she was breathing life into me. I was weak around her. She made me weak and I kept letting her.

"You think I killed them, don't you? Those two men." Her voice was sad, quiet, and distant. "That I'm the reason they are gone."

I searcher her eyes frantically.

"Sorry to disappoint. I'm not the murderer you want me to be." She wiggled under me. "But you—you must stop with this obsession. I don't want you to ask again. Ever. Do you understand me? You can't control everything. Sometimes you have to let go. I've let my past go; I've moved on. It'll only hurt us both more if you keep poking at it. You don't have to be perfect for everyone else. You don't have to live life the way other people expect you to."

"I don't do that," I replied.

"Yes, you do. It's all you do. When are you going to realize, you owe nothing to the world? Are you ever going to just be your own person? Their rules are not yours to follow."

"And what is so bad about living a normal life? Having a home, a job, and someone who loves you enough to be selfish with you? I guess you wouldn't know anything about all that, though. All that talk about freedom and letting go is just a lie. You tell it so good you've started to believe it yourself." There was another reason. The true reason, she didn't want me to know.

She walked out of my grip and reach. "See? You're doing it again, bringing my choices into this and turning them against me. That town was holding me back, and if you looked at yourself, you'd see it's holding you back too."

I shook my head. She was wrong. All wrong. She didn't understand me at all. Maybe she never had. We'd been acquainted with each other briefly, so perhaps it was entirely my fault for expecting more. I'd deluded myself.

Ophelia knew who she was. She knew what she'd done. And she knew how it made me feel. She'd just decided she didn't care.

11 / Rafael
The card of truth

The soggy Cocoa Puffs had lost almost all their color. I floated them around in the breakfast bowl, occasionally scooping a few onto the spoon, and then drowning them in milk again. It was tough finding appetite when there was so much to do. One thing about working as a team was that if I wanted them to be invested in the case, I had to be confident and ready to lead them. The talk with Joseph Graham hadn't exactly proved me a great leader. We shouldn't have asked him about his daughter, but in my opinion, his reaction had been more than a little dramatic.

The notifications on my phone made my stomach lurch. The voice in my head kept whispering things. Stuff that made me question everything. I was chasing ghosts not people. Too much was left for blatant theories and wild possibilities. Quite overwhelming. We'd tried to start somewhere, but I felt like we'd untangled the wrong end of the yarn. I'd made a promise to Arabella, and to myself, that I'd try to figure this out. Now, not far into the investigation, I was already doubting my own skills. I wasn't a professional, I knew that, but surely having spent my whole life as the police department chief's son, I would've picked something up.

I pushed the bowl away, sighing. It was too late to give up anyway. People were counting on me.

I flipped my phone around, and picked up the mail, which had been collecting on the kitchen counter. I skimmed the letters, tossing them aside. That was until my eyes landed on one addressed to me. I leaned forward, elbows resting on the cold marble. I never got mail.

I ripped the envelope open, the sound of tearing making me shake in my shoes. I pulled out the paper inside, checking to see there wasn't anything else along with it. The letter itself was thin. A blue-striped paper that could've been torn from any notebook. I didn't think before flipping it open.

The note read: *Stop looking or I'll stop you. This is a warning.*

For a moment I was paralyzed. Who would send such a thing? Who knew? A stupid thought. We'd gone around the whole town, asking questions, and digging up old stuff. I'm sure it wasn't difficult to guess why. Mr. Graham could've easily sent it to keep us from asking more questions about Ophelia. He wanted to scare me away. I rotated the paper around in my hands. I didn't recognize the handwriting, so it wasn't Zack or Adam. It could've been any one of the girls, though. A prank. A stupid joke to make me mess up or scare me because they thought the whole investigation was an embarrassment. No matter who'd sent it—or why—it made me shiver either way.

There was no time for doubts. After loitering around the house for another short while, prolonging the inevitable, I finally opened the messages.

I gathered quickly that everyone was at the lake. I grabbed my keys, and stuffed the ugly letter in a shoebox in the back of my closet, where no one would see it. I was sure it was a prank, either from the girls or someone who might've heard me at the party.

When I got there, a storm was ready to blow up in my face.

Lucy's hands were curled into small fists, her cheeks heated. She was soaked from hair to toe. "What is wrong with you? Where the hell have you been all day? I don't have time to sit around waiting for you!"

She was wearing a red bikini, tight to her curves. The water still drawing circles where she'd crawled out of it. I looked away, but my eyes latched onto Arabella instead. She blushed and rubbed her wet arms to warm herself.

I drew a sharp breath. As I spoke, my eyes remained on Bells. "Yeah, um, sorry. I was busy," I lied. If the letter had come from Lucy, I wasn't about to give her the satisfaction of showing fear.

Lucy crossed her arms. "Oh, really? How cute. Thank you for sparing a minute of your sparse time for us. I know how tough that must be for you." She rolled her eyes.

Adam stood between us. "Okay, alrighty. Let it go." Adam had actually got a slight tan, because his arms and shoulders were turning a little red. His shirt hung over his shoulder. He scratched his bare side absently, a worried pout on his face.

Everyone was there. They'd all been waiting for me. No. That's not true. Not everyone.

"Where's Katie?" I asked.

Katie's house had high ceilings and a tiny potted palm tree in the middle of the entrance way. The living room was an open space. A huge brick red carpet, bookshelves, a TV stand filled to the brim with weird junk, and a dark couch in the center of the room.

Zack and Adam were sitting on the floor, a little boy facing them. The boy reached for Zack's hand, and snatched a yellow *Lego* brick from him. He didn't lift his head as Katie and I walked in.

Katie exhaled. "That's Otis, my brother. Ignore him. I'm on babysitting duty."

I sat on the couch whilst Katie picked one of the armchairs, swinging her legs over the side. "Okay, let's talk yesterday," I prompted. "Any thoughts?"

Adam slouched in the other chair. "They were both weird, but Esther gave me serious heebie-jeebies. Am I the only one who thought she might float through the walls like a ghost? She was always hovering behind me. I got chills. It was like she saw right through me."

Zack stood, slumping next to me. "Isn't she always? Weird, I mean. And hovering."

"That's what I'm saying! She's not normal. I didn't hear her say a single word all night. I don't think she's a human."

"Hold on," said Katie, heading towards the kitchen. When she emerged, she was holding a small bowl of chocolate chip cookies. She passed the bowl around until we were all like chipmunks, our cheeks full.

I licked melted chocolate from my fingers. "According to Mr. Graham, the whole group used to take annual road trips. Then, suddenly, they stopped. He said they grew apart."

Katie, crumbs in her lap, gave a cookie to Otis. "He is hiding something, that's for sure. They were friends for ever, and all of a sudden, they *grew apart*?" Katie drew air quotes.

I believed it. Katie didn't, but the way Mr. Graham had spoken about the trips, I'd believed him.

"What else did he say?" asked Lucy.

Adam answered. "We tried to ask about Ophelia, but he said we were disrespecting him. Quite evasive. Honestly, didn't you guys feel the tension at all?" Adam cleared his throat, suddenly a little white in the face. "Actually, talking about—"

"What do you mean, caveman?" shrieked Lucy. "You do realize that when you question someone, you're supposed to actually *question* them, right? That means *get answers*."

"Did you not see the guy at dinner? How were we supposed to question him like that? And don't pretend like you know everything, princess." Adam's shoulders strained as he glared.

"You can't let a few tears confuse you! But then again, you are incompetent, I'm not even surprised you failed." A satisfied smirk appeared on Lucy's face. She ran a hand through her tangled hair.

"Why are you attacking me? I didn't even ask the questions, Rafe did." Adam waved a hand in my direction.

Both looked at me, and I wanted to disappear between the couch pillows.

"What the hell Rafael?"

"Sorry," I mumbled. "He started crying. I didn't know what to do." I pushed up my glasses. "I tried."

Lucy threw her hands in the air. "Great. He tried."

"Luce," calmed Zack. Almost adoringly.

"Oh, and guys," said Adam, "there's something you—"

"How did it go with Esther?" asked Katie. She pretended not to hear Adam groan when he was cut off. On purpose, I imagined.

101

Arabella answered, "Pretty much the same. She was upset." She fiddled with her long braid, twisting, and tugging at it. "She didn't know about the fight Ophelia and Mr. Graham had. She seemed almost surprised when we told her. Called Ophelia very temperamental. I couldn't tell if she misses her daughter or not."

"Guys—"

That wasn't right. "That's odd. Joseph made it seem as if they both really miss her." I shot Katie an eyeful, a question etched behind my eyes.

She sat up straighter. "It's not like she's wrong. Ophelia certainly had a personality. Everyone knew that."

Adam fidgeted in his seat, mouth closing and opening, mumbles spilling.

"What?" I snapped. "What is up with you today?" The constant movement and anxiousness was getting on my last nerve.

"Has," he said.

"What?" Adam wasn't making any sense.

"Ophelia *has* a personality."

I was about to repeat myself again like a broken record, but he didn't stop there.

"I talked to Lucas. He met her in New York, they're together right now too. He's keeping an eye on her. I tried to tell you guys."

My eyes flew open, a jolt in my chest. It took me a good second to scoop my jaw off the floor. She was alive. How was she alive? Could the others be alive too? Did Ophelia know what happened all those years ago?

Was she the one who sent me that letter?

Then, I realized with embarrassment that this wasn't about me. I think we all did, at the same time, because all eyes in the room turned to Katie. Her face was perfectly blank. Not even a hint of joy or distress or anger or anything.

"I don't believe you. He's wrong. He's lying or he must've understood wrong," she said. She shook her head, resolute. But then, something changed, and tears began running down her tan cheeks. They fell silently. "Why are you all believing this idiot? It's someone else. It can't be her. It's not her." Katie was shaking, wiping snot from her nose. When Arabella wrapped her arms around her, she flinched.

"How is this possible?" asked Zack. The dreariness on his face had vanished. "Are you sure?"

"Positive. And how should I know? It's not like I had time to ask him much. He was in a hurry. But to be fair, I don't trust her for a second, and I told Lucas that much. He's now officially our spy."

He must've been oblivious to the havoc in the room, because he refused to look Katie in the eye. The girl cried, and he was watching everyone but her.

"This is insane," said Lucy. "How could they just run into each other? Especially now?"

Adam shrugged. "I'm not complaining. It's better for us. The Universe works in strange ways."

"Where are they? New York?" I asked.

Adam clapped his hands together. "OK, so what if I told you I forgot to listen during that part? Something, something. Pretty house. Rich people. Wedding, I think? I could swear he mentioned a wedding. I think he's her date."

"Of course you'd not pay attention to the most important part!" yelled Lucy. For once, I agreed with her.

"Hey! That's not very nice of you."

Lucy stuck a finger in his face. "*Shh*, I'm talking. Adam, you need to get your shit together. You're like a toddler. Even Otis is smarter than you, and he is five."

Otis, upon hearing his name, raised his head.

Zack tugged on Lucy's hand. "Question. if Ophelia is alive, then what about Rogers and Martinez? There weren't any bodies."

I pushed up my glasses. "Maybe. But I don't think so. It's highly unlikely." This revelation changed a lot. It opened doors to new possibilities. Ones we didn't have before.

I glanced at Arabella, to see how she was adjusting to the idea of her uncle being alive. She stayed quiet, letting Katie lean on her.

"Will I get to see her?" asked Katie, voice husky. Her eyes were distant, the warmth she usually radiated sucked from the room. Her weak whisper made the blood drain from my fingertips because no matter how badly I wanted to, there was no way to comfort her. Nothing I could do to undo the fact her best friend had lied to her and left her.

"I don't know," I admitted.

Maybe it was better she didn't see Ophelia. What if it only hurt her more? There was little we knew about the situation and what had happened. I understood that Katie wanted closure. I got that. But what if closure wouldn't be easily given? If revisiting those memories only provoked more pain?

Katie stood, and dragged her feet towards the bookcase. She knelt, picked something up, and then sat on the ground in front of the glass coffee table by the couch.

"What are you doing?" asked Zack, pulling out a pack of cigarettes.

"What does it look like?" hurled Katie. "Also, I don't want you smoking one of those in my home." She scrunched her nose.

Katie started shuffling tarot cards.

"Fine. Whatever." Zack put the pack away, but one cigarette still remained in his hand. He didn't light it, just toyed with it.

Lucy leaned forward. "Are you truly a witch?"

Katie snorted. "Yeah, sure, I'm a witch."

I shifted uncomfortably. This was a waste of time. I didn't believe in the superstitious. People forget that coincidences don't stop existing when they hold a deck of cards in their hand. Those pretty pictures don't mean anything, although people often love to believe that they do. They are just cards. Plastic. Fake. Besides, our eyes already play enough tricks on us. They betray us more than anything else in the world.

"So? What do you see then?" asked Lucy impatiently.

Katie had placed three cards in front of her.

"First is The Fool. The Fool represents innocence and beginnings. Pureness. Encouragement to move forward, though there are challenges ahead. The Fool doesn't care about them yet, because he is too focused on the start of his journey. It's as if he only exists in the present, and is blind to everything else."

I shook my head, amused, but no one noticed.

Without much fuss, Katie turned the next card. "Okay, so, this is Ten Of Swords. Painful endings, betrayal, crisis." The low tremble was gone from her voice. She really believed in all of this.

On the card, there was a man. Face first in dirt, with ten swords in his back. His demeanor tired and waiting.

"Ten Of Swords is about accepting the outcome. It may be harsh. It may be a betrayal. It may seem like the worst of all. But it will also bring solace. Even in times, when the darkness looms, there is peace and calm to be found."

"This is so cool. How did you memorize all the meanings?" Lucy was glowing. Not literally.

"They just stick with you over time. In most readings, you would pick more cards. I always do three. It's more specific, in my opinion. The most important stuff. All I have to do is understand the message."

"Anyone planning a big betrayal? Confess now," teased Zack, the cigarette finally finding its way into his mouth. One warning from Katie made it drop into his lap for the final time. "Not much to go off on, little witch. You might want to flip a few more cards."

"Yes, Katie, do tell," encouraged Adam, "where are all the juicy details? Too much left for the imagination." He smiled lopsidedly.

"Shut up, both of you. What do you know anyway? Nothing. You know nothing." Katie returned to the cards. "The cards have no reason to lie. But sadly, a beautiful lie is easier to believe than a harsh truth. I take what I get, and if anyone has a problem with that, then please, the fucking door's that way." Her eyes glimpsed over Otis, but he wasn't paying us any attention.

Katie's fingers lingered on the last card before she turned it over, as if dreading. Her tears had tried, her skin still plump and pink.

"Death card," said Arabella in the deafening quiet.

"Yes," confirmed Katie, "But death isn't simply black and white. It's about endings and beginnings. Change and transformation. We die each night and are reborn each morning. Death spares no one. It's unpredictable, merciless, sudden. It can be beautiful, quiet, and give life meaning. But Death can also be the opposite. It's the worst card, I believe, because it will never tell you which it is going to be. Death, death, death, it is always."

Death, death, death, it echoed in my head.

Didn't matter if the cards were liars or not, they were ruthless either way.

12 / Lucas

My heart burns so much I think it's just constantly on fire

Searching Ophelia's room was like looking into the deepest corners of someone's soul, knowing you have no right to. Like seeing someone type out their password and not glancing away. How I could ever look her in the eye again I did not know. My fingers were tingling, this spontaneous idea becoming something very real.

I'd have to be stupid not to take what might as well be my only opportunity at uncovering some of her secrets. If not for the sake of myself, then for my friends. They'd been relentless since I'd told them about Ophelia, annoying me with questions and tasks. They'd only succeeded in making me realize how big of a mess they were truly in. They didn't even notice it themselves. I was the only one who could get them out now. Just like when we were children, I was the one to fix everything.

I was expecting Ophelia to burst in at any moment, screaming. In that case, no apologies could fix the already gaping ravine between us. She'd never forgive me; we'd never be the people we were once upon a time. I didn't know what I was looking for, hopeful to recognize it when I saw it.

Ophelia wasn't a messy person. Her bed was made, her bookshelves were organized, and her suitcase was neatly at the end of her bed. I sunk my hands into every drawer, case, and crevice I could find. I checked under the bed and the mattress, even stopping to check behind the headboard. I plucked every book from the shelves, skimmed them, and placed them back. I searched for hidden compartments in the floorboards and the desk. I opened the suitcase, then packed it as it had been. I did everything in hurry, because despite the fact that no one else was home, I could not stop panicking. How much time had I already spent on this or that?

I moved to her desk. The drawers were empty, but her laptop was open. I sat down, guessing at her password.

I tried Ophelia's birthday. I tried the names of her family members and her childhood pet. Her favorite food, band, book. Everything I could think of. I experimented with numbers, with lower case and capital letters. I must've spent twenty minutes just guessing in a dazed frenzy without any luck. Finally, I unclenched my jaw. There was no way I could figure it out. Despite wanting to, I didn't know her well enough. How much of what she'd told was a lie and how much of it true? The password could've been related to anything or nothing at all.

I got up from the desk and took in the rest of the room. What else was there? I walked over to the shelf next to the window and surveyed Ophelia's trinkets: a model car, a cactus, some more books, a rabbit plushie, jewelry, perfume. I smelled the perfume—a hint of lavender. She never liked too sweet things. I didn't remember how she'd smelled three years ago, if it was the same or not. Some things fade over time, and you don't even notice them leaving you.

Suddenly it occurred to me, and I rushed back to the laptop. Her favorite childhood TV show. We'd talked about it. How much she'd resonated with the main character. How she'd watched it every morning before school whilst eating her breakfast. When the password didn't work, I typed it in again differently. This was my last idea. I grabbed a piece of paper from Ophelia's desk drawer, scribbling down some of the possible variations.

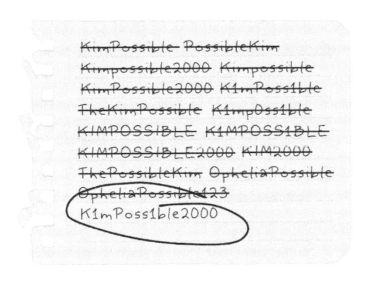

With the last one, a loading sign appeared. I blinked in surprise. *Holy shit, I'm in.*

I stared at the desktop and the folders there. I rolled my shoulders, and started clicking through them. The first one was labeled *Pics*. I opened it. The folder was full on pictures, almost all from old family vacations, a few newer ones with Jeanie or Eloise in them. A picture from when Ophelia was a little girl, her tiny hand draped around her father's neck, a wide grin on both faces. Her and Katie at the beach, building sandcastles. Since it didn't seem important, I closed the folder and moved on to another one named *Junk*. That was how she organized her old school papers and presentations, mixed with job applications. I looked at the other files on her desktop. Nothing. I opened the trash pin, but it had been emptied. Ophelia didn't have a lot on her computer, which I took in with relief.

Next, I opened her browser. Her search bar suggested Taylor Swift music videos and a *10 Books To Read This Summer* post, but nothing suspicious. I couldn't tell if it made me more anxious or relaxed. If she was guilty, the snooping would be justifiable. But if all of this was for nothing, I would feel absolutely awful. I clicked the top right corner and opened her search history, scrolling further back.

She seemed to search up Whitewood a lot. All the local news sources. She'd searched up me a few times, not to mention her family whom she'd been stalking on a daily basis. A wide range from old articles to a couple days old. She'd stalked my social accounts. Katie's.

Could it be that Ophelia had been telling the truth all along? There was nothing to hide. All this time I'd been refusing to believe her, too stuck in my own head. Now I was the fool. Why wouldn't she search up her family if she missed them? I would do the same. There was nothing sinister about it, nor was there anything else in her room to suggest otherwise.

But then why let everyone believe she was dead? Why run so suddenly? There had to be something. A lie. A deceit. Some crack in the story.

I barely made it back to make room without collapsing. I opened the balcony door, and stepped outside into the fresh air. I needed that—air. My head hurt from thinking, dizzying with thoughts I was too afraid to say out loud.

My head and heart were screaming at one another.

13/ Rafael

This might not be exactly legal, but who cares?

I took a deep breath, in and out. "We're going to split up today. I have this plan I've been thinking about. The girls will talk to Mrs. Graham again. Find out how she really feels about Ophelia's disappearance. We have to sort the inconsistencies out." My eyes narrowed at Lucy. "Be casual," I added. "Zack, Adam, and I will go to the station. There is information we can't get on our own, and since my dad would never willingly give us any of it, we'll have to obtain it differently. I don't like it, but it's the only way, if you get what I mean."

I'd mulled it over in my head, coming to a conclusion that taking a risk might just be the one thing to set us on the right path and speed things along. If we got caught, it would be over. There would be consequences. It was my plan, and if anything happened, I'd take the blame. Luckily, I was confident enough that it wouldn't come to that. I knew the place inside and out. I could do it.

"Hold up," protested Adam. "I don't agree to this."

I quirked an eyebrow. "Do you want to go with the girls?"

"Not particularly, but also I don't want to find out what prison food tastes like." He wiped grass off his pants.

"Those are your only options. Sorry, I overrule you." I shrugged.

The plan didn't necessarily require three people, but I'd already played it out in my head that way and, honestly, I just needed my best friend by my side. If anyone insisted, I would never force them into anything. But for now, I played the boss card.

Adam's eyes darkened as he looked towards Katie. "Never mind, I'd rather be a criminal. I hear there are splendid desserts in some prisons."

Katie smiled from ear to ear. "Try not to miss me much in there."

"What makes you think I'd miss you?"

"Are you sure about this?" asked Lucy. "I thought you were supposed to be the good guy, Rafe. Do you really want to go that far? We could figure something else out. There isn't any need to do this. This could end badly." For the first time I think I saw something close to concern on Lucy's face.

"Luce," said Z, pulling the girl under his arm. "Rafe has never been much of a good guy. Believe me, he'll do anything to win. He always has." His lips pursed.

He wasn't wrong. I *did* want to win. And I *would* do anything for it. My old pops had raised a winner not a quitter.

Lucy scrunched up her nose. "I don't think this is a good idea."

"We'll be fine," I assured her. Piece of cake. Walk in, get the stuff, get out. It wasn't even a complicated plan. It didn't need to be because at the station, I was part of the family, and no one would ever suspect me to go behind their backs. Besides, nothing remotely crazy ever happened in Whitewood. Except for the triple vanishing, of course.

"Be careful," whispered Arabella quietly.

"We'll be fine," I repeated, softer.

Lucy was right. We didn't have to do this, but in a way, we needed to. The police had stuff we needed. I had to get my hands on them.

My stomach hurt, my eyes and lips were dry, and I had this irresistible need to throw up. I was actually doing it. Committing a crime. Me. Worst of all, behind my father's back.

"There isn't anything specific we're looking for, is there?" asked Adam almost to the station door.

"Any data the police have; interviews, evidence, analysis. Pretty much anything will do. The truth is, all we have are theories. We need facts. So, we find them."

"Ah, got it—steal everything." A nervous laugh.

We stepped through the automatic doors. I imagined myself doing just that a thousand times before. No one knew what we were up to. All we had to do was act normal. I hid my sweaty hands in my pockets. *Stop twitching,* I told myself. Adam was better at pretending than me. He'd been so distraught before, but he put on a magnificent act. Blank face, open palms, comfortable pout. Cool as a cucumber. He was too good at hiding his feelings.

My main worry were the CCTV cameras. The ones in the corridors and in the archives would catch us snooping. After some time, the footage would be deleted, and I knew there wasn't anyone constantly watching us, but that didn't really make me feel better. I wanted the cameras gone.

"Morning, Miss Reyes." I gave the lady as cheerful of a smile as I could muster.

The receptionist's small wrinkles tightened. "Rafael, it's good to see you. Your father isn't in his office right now, but he should be back soon." Vivianne tucked a strand of dark hair behind her ear. "And you've brought friends! I'm glad to meet some of them finally."

"Yes. Great, thanks. We'll just wait in his office, if you don't mind. And, um, it's good to see you too. You look great." That made her smile. Always the friendliest face to see. Pops must've thought the same thing when he'd asked Vivianne on a date at the start of the year. They were going steady so far. I hadn't really decided how I felt about it yet.

We walked past the desk, down the corridor towards pops' office. We had to get the archives keys.

My glasses were starting to slip off my nose because of the sweat, and I pushed them back up. One of the CCTV cameras in the corridor made me want to hide under a rock. We didn't have time to figure out how to get to the control center and turn them off. The only choice I had was to leave them be. Damaging the cameras wasn't good either, and would most definitely raise questions. It was not a reliable option, so it was no option at all. I prayed there was no one on the other side of those CCTV cameras.

I opened the door to my father's office, walked towards his desk. Adam and Zack were waiting by the door. I knew exactly where my dad kept his copy of the keys. I opened the bottom drawer, searching under a mountain of papers. A quick glance towards my friends, back to searching.

Found it.

Out the door, to the flight of stairs taking us underground. Down the long corridor, then right.

Not a place you accidentally end up at. I took another shaky breath. *This was a bad idea. Bad idea, bad idea, bad idea.* Dread turned my insides into knots, stomach heavy with it. Breathe. So far so good.

I hurried us inside and closed the door behind us. I could've locked it, but it didn't matter. It would be easier to explain.

I took a quick peek around. All these years I'd never been to the archives. The walls were dark, matching the gray carpeted floor. The shelves—dark metal. I struggled to keep my eyes open against the blinding lights. The walls devouring it hungrily.

"Okay, start looking. Find the right sections first," I told Adam and Zack. "Anything on Sheldon, Link, or Ophelia. They probably looked into her the most, because she was a high-risk case. Take as many pictures as you can, we'll piece it together later."

"Maybe I should guard the door, and you guys do your detective thing?" proposed Adam. He'd been calm coming in, but I could see the pressure getting to him.

"Fine," I agreed, sweat covering me entirely. We were lucky no one had seen us yet, but who knew how long we had before someone would.

Zack and I got to work. First, I went to the shelves marked with the letter *R*. Zack started at the front, with *G* for Graham. There weren't many files under *R*, and finding the right one was easy. Good, it had to be easy, and we had to be quick.

And there it was, the box I was looking for, with *Rogers* at the top in small print. I rushed to open it; my breath hitched. I knelt on the ground, speeding through the evidence, taking pictures of what I could. Blurry fingerprints and reports with half the letters falling out of the camera's frame. I skimmed through the interviews, taking photos of any I found interesting, making sure to at least be careful with those. So many files and evidence, yet it had never led the police anywhere. How could that be? What must it be like to dedicate your life to finding bad guys, only to fail after all? It was an honorable, rewarding job, but sadly I found that not all people took it nearly seriously enough. That was why I'd decided, long ago, to become a police officer, and show everyone what it meant to be committed to it. I'd make dad proud.

"Hey."

I jumped.

"Sorry," said Zack. "I finished with Ophelia's files. Did you get everything?"

"Yeah," I replied. "Now it's just Link Martinez left."

This was going well. We'd made it inside, unseen. We'd already found two out of three files. One left and we'd be out of there.

Together we hurried towards the overflowing *M* shelf.

Zack was coming towards me from the left side while I moved from the right side.

"Guys, hurry!" hissed Adam, sweat glistening at his hairline.

"Shut up, I'm trying," said Zack.

Where is it?

"There!" Zack pointed his finger.

And yes, there it really was. At the very top. I reached both my hands towards it, stood on my tippy toes, yet it was out of reach.

Zack managed to hook a finger behind the box and pull it forward. It plummeted down, opening mid-air, and spilling its contents all over the floor. Paper skittered across the carpet and under the shelves. The box was left on its side. There had been some heavy things inside, and I hoped no one had heard the bang.

Then, I got to work. I scooped up as much as I could. Zack did too. Handfuls of files and a couple of Ziploc bags. Some of the photos I took came out terrible. I didn't have time to worry.

"Guys, stop," said Adam. "Stop, damn it! Someone's coming."

Yes. Yes, I could make out the faint steps of someone on the other side of the door. My hands were sticky, clutching evidence. There was a camera right by the door, red light blinking. As quietly as I could, I started shoveling everything back into the box. No one was entering, but I could hear muffled talk. Someone on the phone. We heaved the box up on the shelf. I wasn't even thinking. All I knew was that we needed to be out of there.

"We have to wait here until they leave," I told the guys.

"Shit, do we hide?" asked Zack.

I looked around. There was nowhere to hide besides the shelves. ."Come, let's stay behind this one." We moved behind shelf *J*. It was the second-row corner. Hidden, good lookout. There were enough boxes there to cover us. I held my breath.

The door flew open a couple of seconds later and a clean-shaved man walked in. His body build was like a bamboo stick. His eyes were glued to his phone one minute, the next he was swearing under his breath and pushing it into his back pocket. The man moved between the shelves, stopping at *P*. He grunted and reached for a box, pulling out a person's file, holding it under his arm.

He squinted a bit when his eyes slithered over us. I didn't breathe. He took a poised step forward.

"Excuse me, I think I'm lost. I'm looking for the bathroom," said Adam loudly, stepping out from behind the shelves.

I wanted to scream at him, but it was too late.

The man startled. He opened his mouth, scratching his chin at the same time.

Adam took another step forward, turning only slightly to look me in the eye and mouth *'wait.'*

[Sticky note: NO MATCH!]

POLICE DEPARTMENT
Y STATEMENT FORM

e / time occured: 06/12/2015   Date
Incident location: Fairfield Avenue, alleyway next to the hardware store
): Officer Lawson
Witness address: 2466 Overdale Way
-5120

SWORN STATEMENT

I was walking my dog yesterday when I heard two people whispering. It was around 9:30 AM, and they both sounded angry. I stayed behind a wall, listening. I realized that the voices belonged to Joseph Graham and Sheldon Rogers. I couldn't see them, but I heard Graham shove Rogers so hard he hit the trash cans. I know it was him, because when I was leaving, I caught sight of Rogers wiping dirt off his pants. Graham also told him to get the money or it would be over. Frankly, I was quite frightened by his tone. Then Graham walked away and I left shortly after. It was a miracle he didn't notice me. Rogers stayed behind. Before I could get too far I heard him swear to himself.

CONTINUE ON THE BACK

I hereby swear or affirm that the facts contained herein are true and correct to the best of my belief.

WITNESS SIGNATURE: WCandice   OFFICER WITNESS SIGNATURE: DATE SIGNED: 06/13/2015

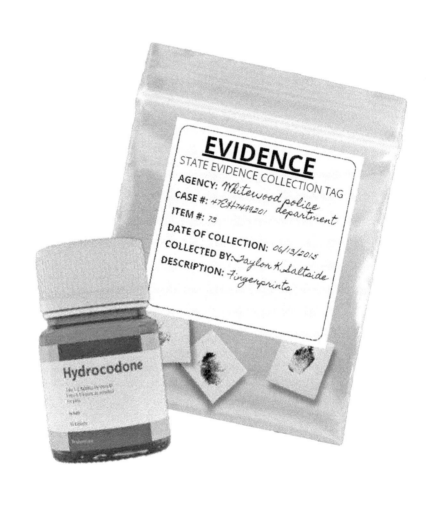

14 / Lucas

I most definitely will not dance with you

It was raining when I found the library. It opened with grand doors and rose with high ceilings, carefully constructed carvings along the walls. The room was massive. Tall windows, and white, dustless bookcases.

I dragged my finger along the chiseled wood of the shelves, tracing the spines of many books. A chandelier was hanging from the mural-painted ceiling. I felt as if I was in a fairytale. My gaze was pulled back down to a nearby table, where Eloise sat with a book in hand. Her eyes were watching me, trailing as I went.

"This place is stunning," I told her. Much like a museum. How wonderful it must've been to live there.

Eloise snapped her book shut, setting it down on the table. "Thank you, dear. Considering how long it took to build it as I saw it in my mind's eye, it better be." She smiled, lost in some memory. "There's this architect you remind me of. One of my beloved friends. I can't quite put my finger on what it is exactly. He constructed this room and the guest hall as I imagined them. Jeanie can have a specific taste when it comes to interior design, but she let me have my fun. He's a talented man, my friend. A professional." She coughed.

My eyes fell on the book, on the trembling hand there. The diamond on Eloise's engagement ring sparkled like a star. "I don't think I ever thanked you for you letting me stay here. You have been awfully kind. I know I'm a stranger."

Eloise swat with her hand. "Don't say that. We're happy to have you. And even after the wedding, we'd love to have you around whenever you want to visit. This house is too quiet anyway. Not nearly enough people to fill these lonely corridors."

"Thank you," I muttered, not knowing how else to show my gratitude in the face of earnestness.

"I was so thrilled when Ophelia told us she was bringing someone with her. Jeanie expected the worst, but I knew you were going to be better than that. After everything, Ophelia deserves happiness. She's had enough misfortunes."

"Um, yeah ... lucky me." I shuddered. What exactly had Ophelia told them about us? And what about her disappearance? Whatever she'd said, Eloise obviously had got the impression that there was more to the story. Perhaps she was just too considerate to inquire more, seeing as Ophelia wasn't much of a talker.

"And you grew up together! I think that's simply perfect! Are you planning on studying creative writing too?"

"Writing? No, no. That's not for me. Actually, I have no clue what my plans are. I've applied to some schools, but my dad would rather me stay near home and help with the business. I don't really fancy the courses in my local schools. That means that if I wanted to study something I'm interested in, I'd have to move, and my dad's not excited by that." I hoped I wasn't boring her with my silly troubles.

Eloise's face scrunched up. "Oh. I'm sorry to hear that. But let's say you could go anywhere, do anything, where would you go?"

I opened my mouth, ready to say I wasn't sure. That I didn't know and hadn't given it much thought, but then it occurred to me that it would be a lie. In the back of my mind, I'd imagined me doing things. Silly dreams I hadn't thought could ever become reality. So, I'd ignored them. Cast them aside.

"I was thinking architecture, but maybe that's too ambitious of me. I don't have much talent." I scratched my neck. "I considered engineering ... that sort of thing. Figured dad wouldn't mind that. It's a backup plan. Architecture might be out of my reach. I probably don't have what it takes anyway." Why would I? I was brilliant at math, physics, and I happened to enjoy the creative aspect of the field, but that was all the skill I had. No college would want me when there were so many better candidates out there.

She took a deep breath, taking her time with a response. Wording it carefully. "Well, I hope your father comes around. But if he doesn't, let me tell you to go for it anyway. People who love us don't hold us back. And if it matters to you in the slightest—I believe in you. No dream is too big."

Though her words didn't erase my worries, they did lighten my heart.

I still hadn't called dad. Leaving the library, I decided it was time. I'd promised Ophelia I wouldn't spoil her secret, so I only gave him crumbs of what was really going on. About NY, about going to a wedding with a friend. Bits and pieces to keep him happy. He told me he was holding up fine, but I heard it in his voice how much he missed me.

I texted Adam, and he told me about their investigation. He sounded cheerful, until he got to the part where they'd almost got arrested. I asked him if they were okay, if they needed me back home, but he assured me it was nothing. I worried one day their luck might run out if they didn't stop playing games.

I ventured around the house, in rooms I had yet to see. The first floor had everything a person could possibly dream of; the library, two offices, a game room with a pool table, a garage with three different luxury cars. The kitchen, worthy of a Michelin star restaurant, with wall-length pantries and a kitchen island bigger than my whole room back in Whitewood.

On my way upstairs, I walked by a parlor. Hearing music coming from there, I decided to investigate.

It was Ophelia, sorting board games on a case by the open window. She hummed softly along to the music, swaying on her feet. She didn't notice me.

I leaned against the doorframe, watching her work. Sensing my eyes on her, Ophelia turned. She startled, dropping a small box. It fell flat on the floor.

"Sorry." I leaned to grab it, a game of Boggle. "Your shoes," I said. They were untied.

Ophelia stuttered awkwardly, ogling her undone shoestrings.

I set the box down and bent over.

I tied her shoes.

Soft light was coming from the window, backlighting her. A breeze ruffled the thin curtains. The hairs on my arms rose as Ophelia looked down at me. It was like turning on a light in a dim room. Suddenly I wasn't just looking at her. I saw her like every human dreams of being seen. Like she was a poem only I could comprehend.

I stood, reaching behind Ophelia to put the game back on the shelf where it belonged.

"Thank you," she said. The song ended, and another began. Ophelia shot me an edgy take. "Do you dance?"

Dance? I had two left feet.

I shook my head, probably looking like a tomato, red and flushed.

"Why not?"

"I'll step on your toes. You'll have bruised feet for the wedding." I scratched my neck—something I found myself doing often when worked up.

"I'll survive," she replied with an airy-laugh, eyes traveling to my lips. "Sorry about the other day. I shouldn't have snapped at you. I guess I'm still figuring things out myself."

My breath caught in my throat.

Ophelia sighed, moving past me, but stumbling. I caught her, holding her up by the elbows as she tried (and failed) to regain her balance. Just like back at the hotel. She stared at her shoes, which I'd sneakily tied together. Every time she tried to take a step, her body fought not to slam into the floor.

"I will get back at you for this," she said, blushing.

"Go on then." Had she run out of remarks? No more snide comebacks? Nothing? "Funny, how I'm always there to catch you."

"You're the reason I keep falling in the first place!"

I smiled at her. I backed away, hardly capable of tearing my eyes from her, stopped at the door.

Ophelia was only gawping at me, her face unreadable.

"What?"

The corners of her mouth perked up. "Your eyes look like storm clouds and I love rain."

15 / Rafael

Burned

I stroked Ivy's white fur coat as she lay in my lap. It was an automatic gesture, because really, I was focused on my phone screen, greasy with fingerprints and chipped in the corners.

You can end this. Stop looking and leave the past alone. This can all be over.

I swallowed the tightness at the back of my throat. This didn't feel like a joke or a prank anymore. No one I knew would send me something like that. But who else could it be? Maybe the Grahams had figured out what was happening, or the man at the station had pretended not to realize what we were doing there. I thought we'd done a good job sneaking out of the archives, but perhaps Adam's web of lies didn't work as imagined.

A jitter went through me. I'd faced bullies before, but never threats like that. I had no way of knowing how serious they were. What they knew, what they didn't.

Real or not, the messages made it crystal clear that I had to stop investigating, or something might happen. Then again, knowing myself, I would not accept such blatant threats. With a stutter the realization dawned on me that I was doing this no matter what. It was about the truth. Nothing else. Not me needing to prove myself. Not me needing a purpose, or even to satisfy my curiosity. There were people I owed the truth to. Not the ones passed long ago, but the ones alive and waiting for justice. The ones who were counting on me.

Nothing bad would actually happen. Even if there had once been a killer in town, they were long gone by now. These messages were only to scare me, so I'd stop asking questions.

I put Ivy down, and sauntered to the bathroom. My eyes felt like sandpaper, yet somehow clued stuck. My hands found the switch, and I got to the sink, splashing cold water in my face. Tiredness was like a fever, shifting and leaving my body. Closing the tab, I grabbed a towel. I opened my eyes, wild.

There, on the mirror: **What would your father say?**

I sucked in a breath, the towel slipping from my hand.

They were in my room, my bathroom. They were there. They stood where I was standing. They were in my home. My vision went black. My gut twisted, and my chest began to rapidly pound. I turned on the spot, again and again. *No*, I reminded myself, *they are gone. It's just paint, they are gone.* They'd been in my room. They'd touched my stuff. *They could do it again.*

It was real. It was happening. I'd made an enemy of someone.

That was when I realized it was not a prank. For a hot minute I stood unmoving. Every dark shape became a monster come to get me. I was entirely chilled, blood turned to ice and spikes. I watched the red paint on the mirror, my horrified face flashing between the letters as if they'd been written on my skin. Carvings of menace.

I stepped closer to inspect the message. I was careful at first, unsure and fearful. There didn't seem to be any fingerprints left behind. The paint was dried and cracked against the smooth mirror. It had been there for a few hours at least, I assumed. That meant someone had painted it while I was breaking into the archives.

With trembling hands, I took pictures of the threat before cleaning it all up like it had never even been there. My chest was tight all the while, breaths dissipating. *They won't come back*, I convinced myself, uselessly. They wouldn't, because I would catch them first. Provoking me was a bad idea on their part. I wasn't one to yield easily. I was scared. No, terrified. But that wasn't the end of the world, was it now?

My new plan was to catch the person who so desperately wanted me out of their way. Surely that meant they knew something about the case. I could handle them. I could take care of everything—as I hid a knife under my bed and clutched a pepper spray in hand.

I was exhausted, but that night I didn't sleep at all. Not even for a minute. I was now the monster in the dark, waiting for another monster.

I groaned, falling head first onto my bed. It was utterly pointless trying to reach anyone so early in the morning. It was almost six, and my friends were still asleep. I'd been up all night, itching to crawl out of bed. I was ready now. I didn't want to waste more time. I put on some proper clothes. I ate proper breakfast. And then I went to Link's house, like a proper detective.

It was chilly, the sky a bleeding misty color. The grass was covered with cold morning dew. Birdsong followed me farther down the dusty road. The ashes of a house came into view. With one half blackened and trashed—the other intact, yet inevitably rotten and falling—it was like something out of a horror movie.

I jumped at the sudden buzzing fracturing the air. My phone. Deep breaths.

"Hello? Hello?" I asked twice without a reply. I checked the screen again. The call ended. *No Caller ID.*

This was getting old real fast. Prank calls? That was a huge step down from breaking in.

When the phone rang again, it was Zack's name on the screen.

"You called. What's up? Did I miss something?" His voice was scratchy with sleep.

"Um, no. Sorry." I took a deep breath. "I'm at Link's house, though, if you want to come. I'm not exactly expecting to find anything, but it's worth a try. Three years ago, police were up and down this place. I know it's early."

A ruffling of sheets sounded on the other side. A moment passed. "Yeah, I don't think I can make it. I have to work today." I thought I heard a giggle, and it definitely didn't belong to Zack.

"OK, I'll, uh, call you later?"

"Yeah, I'll call you."

I could barely manage a bye before he hung up. Great.

I'd looked Link's house up on the internet beforehand. On the pictures it was still as it used to be. Wildflowers and weeds around the house and down the road. The windows had been covered in spiderwebs, dust, and pollen. I mean, they still were, but the feeling of a home was gone. The walls used to be white, a wind chime by the door. Now they were dirty with soot.

The fire had come out of nowhere. Sprung on its own.

It had happened shortly after Sheldon's death, and scary stories were quick to spread. The murderous Martinez. The crazy man who'd killed his friend and then himself. For a while, everyone blamed him. It was a ghost house in a ghost town. A place for children to tell tales about. They'd dare each other to go near the house. Who could survive the murder house? I remembered kids in school talking about it. Walking past them as they gossiped. Thankfully, I'd been too old for it, or else I might've been tempted to go along with it. Sometimes it was easy to forget he once lived. That he was once a real man with dreams and hopes. Who mourned him? He had no family. He didn't even have friends. Now he was just a scary story to tell on Halloween.

I rattled the door, and the whole thing almost fell apart. Carefully, I stepped around the mess, inside. My heart skipped a beat or two when I tripped over the cardboard which covered the floor in an uneven gray blur. The walls were grimy, the green wallpaper peeking out from underneath it. Whenever the wind howled, the house soared with it.

I made it into the living room, where cords hung from walls and furniture had been torn up. Some trash had made it inside. Maybe the children had left it there. Almost like a weird offering. This was the part of the house that would not crumble at a touch, saved from the worst of the fire. The officials said the long grass behind Martinez' house might've caught fire and lit the house. It had been a hot, dry summer. When the police and firefighters had arrived, it had been already too late. They couldn't find Link's remains. No body or burned bones. No ashes. They thought the wind might've carried them away, or they'd washed it away extinguishing the fire. Talk of wildfire made people forget the incident within months.

I walked around, inching towards the kitchen. I had to use my phone for light. This time when it buzzed in my hand, I wasn't alarmed.

"You called," stated Adam.

"I'm at Link's—"

"We'll be right there."

I didn't ask who was *we*.

The kitchen was burned to the crisp. The fire must've started there. Another wisp of air blew in from the window. It was hard not to imagine Link Martinez' bright blue eyes, reflecting the flames eating him alive. Had he screamed as his flesh bubbled with the heat? I once read that some people don't make a sound. I kept looking. The house only had one floor, and I was left with the bedroom and the bathroom. I went for the bedroom first. Any thought of Link's death I left behind with the scorch marks.

The light from my phone was bouncing back on the cracked mirror above the dresser. But there was something *on* the dresser. Something silver. I took a few steps towards it, when suddenly my foot slipped through the wooden planks as if it was water I was stepping through. A blinding pain split me in half. I fell, grasping for my leg. My ankle was stuck between the planks, a hole where I'd went through. Plummeted like a rock. The wood must've been rotten and torn with age. I should've been more careful. I wasn't bleeding, and I didn't think anything was broken, so I attempted to tug on my leg gently. It came with a yank, pulling more of the floor loose.

I sat there, rubbing my hurting ankle, and narrowing my eyes at the hole in the planks. Where there should've been dirt under the wood, there was instead something leathery. I got to my knees, picked up my phone, and shone the flashlight into the darkness. There was some kind of a book in there. I pulled it out, and flipped through the stale pages. Not a book, I surveyed. A journal, or some kind of a diary. The dust on the cover stuck to my sweaty fingers.

"Fuck," I mumbled, turning the book around.

Was this Link's? If so, I'd just hit jackpot.

April 30, 2015

I bought some new paints. I've been feeling the need to pick up a brush again, after so long. I painted some flowers around the house and I was surprised they didn't turn out completely terrible. I think I pulled something, because today my neck is a little sore. I'll keep practicing.

May 17, 2015

Yesterday Evie and I met at our usual spot. It was an especially delightful day. No wind, the water was glistening. I felt enthralled to paint it. Evie only rolled her eyes at me for constantly gazing at the trees and the lake. She laughed, so perfectly. She's carefree when she's with me. At first, I worried, but this predicament isn't so bad. Evie is special to me, and sometimes I do wish I didn't have to hide it. I suppose this is for the best. Occasionally, I am undone by her existence. I explode. Like yesterday, when she looked at me while the world was in full bloom around her.

<u>June 13, 2015</u>

I haven't written in some time, forgive me. The truth is, I wouldn't be writing now either, but I need to distract myself or else I won't be able to stop myself from opening the door. She keeps knocking. She's outside. I can't involve her. If she knew what I saw ... it's too big of a burden to lay on someone. It haunts me. Those eyes, fear reflecting mine. God, save me, save her. It's hopeless. Who would believe me? Besides Evie, no one. Yet she's the one person I refuse to tell. It was awful enough to witness, she shouldn't have to feel that pain as I do. I don't know what I'm going to do. I need some time to think.

I heard a click behind me, followed by slow footsteps. I got to my feet, ankle still hurting. I grit my teeth, putting weight on my other leg as I reached for my pocket and pulled out my pepper spray. I took a step back, so there'd be more space between me and the door. The footsteps quieted, but I could still make out faint breathing outside the bedroom door. My body shook, ready to leap.

The door opened. I let out a weak war cry, and stormed forward, ignoring the splintering pain in my leg.

"Stop! Stop! God, what are you doing? It's just us!" Adam was waving his hands, Katie huddled behind him. "Are you trying to kill us? I swear I'll hit you back."

I breathed out. "Shit, you two scared me."

Adam looked me up and down. "Mhm, you don't say."

"I found Link's journal." I showed them the leather-bound. "I fell through the floor. He must've hidden it there."

Adam was still cautiously holding his hands in the air. "Right. That's cool. Are you going to put that weapon down now? You're freaking me out, man."

I pocketed the pepper spray. "Sorry."

"You don't look too good," said Katie.

"I haven't slept, and now my ankle hurts. I need a shower."

"Did you break anything?" Katie stepped out from behind Adam. "Can you walk?" She was wearing a short-sleeve checkered shirt over a tank top.

I waved her off. "I'll be fine. I just need to rest for a bit." I leaned forward, resting my hands on my knees.

I remembered seeing something silver on the dresser before, but there was nothing there. I must've imagined it, or it was another reflection bouncing off glass. For a moment I thought about telling them about last night, but hesitated. Why scare them? It was better this way. I'd deal with it. A hot shower, coffee, and back to business.

We left the house behind us. For a minute there I thought I saw someone at the edge of the woods, but on second glance there was no one there. I was going insane, running on fumes. I needed sleep, but how could I sleep if any minute someone might break into my room?

Adam and Katie offered to walk me home. I couldn't ride my bike without it hurting too much, so I let them. It was good to have company.

"You should've waited for us. Why did you go alone?" asked Adam.

"No time to wait."

He shook his head. "You have to sleep, man. *Scooby-Doo* club can wait." He bumped my shoulder playfully. "Can't have our lead detective falling asleep on the job, can we? Batman sleeps too when he's not defending Gotham."

We were turning a corner, when I heard someone crying.

A girl with short, dark blonde hair was sitting on the ground, bawling. She was a bony little thing. Pale. But when she met my eyes, they were big and round. I'd seen her a few times at the station. She brushed dirt off her knee, then cupped it tenderly. Her sobs stopped when she spotted us. Wearily, she got to her feet and heaved up a purple bike beside her.

"Are you okay? Do you need help with that?" asked Katie, nodding at the girl's leg.

"No, thank you," answered the girl. She sniffled, rubbing her red cheeks.

"Your name is Maya, right?" I asked.

It was as if she was seeing me for the first time. "Y-yes. You're Rafael. I know your dad."

I smiled. "I know your mom." She was Vivianne's daughter. Sometimes I saw them talking. Maya Reyes. Younger than me by a year or two. Weird that our parents hadn't introduced us yet.

Maya smiled at Katie. "I'm sorry, I didn't mean to cry. I feel like such a baby now. I'm okay, really. I just ran over a big rock."

"Don't apologize. Are you sure you don't need a hand, though? Where are you going? It's so early."

Maya adjusted her grip on the bike. "Home. I stayed over at my friend's house." The wind caught her short hair, drying her tears.

"We could walk you," offered Adam, shrugging.

Maya shook her head, blushing. "I'm okay. I was just surprised. Thanks, though. I should go now." She clapped her hands clean and glanced at me briefly.

"Okay, well, be careful," wished her Katie.

Maya nodded and got on her bike.

She disappeared down the road.

16 / Lucas

Her smile makes my day

Already, my first time at the estate felt like lifetimes ago. Stepping out on the patio, seeing the dishes on the table; stir fry and salads, I was suddenly reminded how time had flown. At least I wasn't a nervous wreck anymore, though I was a curious.

We were having a guest over for dinner.

Eloise, quick on her feet, brushed past me and took seat at the edge of the table, next to a man with a thick, graying beard and glasses. Ophelia, on her right, waved at me to sit as well. Being the last one standing, that saved me a spot next to Jeanie, across from Eloise.

"Lucas, I want to introduce you to someone," said Eloise, her cheeks flushed. On her left hand, a ring of diamonds and rubies.

My eyes shifted to the stranger beside her. His suit was as gray as his hair, yet he didn't look older than 45. He stretched out his hand, which I accepted hesitantly.

"Benjamin Howell. Pleasure to meet you."

"Hello. I'm Lucas."

"I've heard a thing or two about you from Eloise. I'll get straight to the point. You're into architecture, right? If you're serious about it, I might be able to help. How about an interview at Northenview? Unless you have other plans, of course. Then, the best I could offer is a handshake and the promise to put in a good word for you." He showed off pearly white teeth.

"Benjamin is such an old friend of ours. We met both fresh out of college when Jeanie darling introduced us." Eloise's eyes sparkled, sighing as she reminisced about the past.

"Do you work there? At Northenview?" I asked, trying to make sense of things.

Jeanie dabbed her mouth with a napkin to hide a smile.

"I suppose so. I like to think I run the place." Mr. Howell's deep brown eyes glinted.

"Oh." I shuddered. Of course he did. "Why would you want to help me?"

He leaned forward on the table. "Eloise asked me to give you a chance, and I am. I trust her judgement. And if she's right about you, then I'm sure you'll be an asset to the school. But you must decide for your own if this is something you are interested in and whether you wish to pursue this. Here, let me know as soon as you can." He handed me a business card, and I tucked it quickly into my pocket.

"Thank you." I hesitated. "Sir."

Ophelia snorted and Jeanie twisted her head away. Ophelia touched my arm. "Do you want to go on a little quest?"

I nodded, no idea what that meant.

We walked inside. When we were out of earshot, Ophelia whispered to me, "Eloise made souffle for dessert, but I'm much more in the mood for brownies, which we so coincidentally happen to have in the kitchen."

"I see. You want to steal snacks behind her back?"

She bumped my shoulder. "It's an adventure. Come on."

I hadn't actually been in the backs of the kitchen yet. Technically, you could count it as a separate kitchen wholly, because the first one was for everyday use—for Jeanie and Eloise— and the second was more for professionals. Caterers and cooks hired for parties and such. A proper kitchen. Expensive.

Ophelia knew exactly where to find the brownies. She opened a cupboard, pulled out the goodies, gleefully. "We better make our escape now and eat these precious ones somewhere else, lest we leave crumbs of evidence behind. Would you fancy a walk?"

"Sure." I wheezed.

I had to admit, Ophelia knew her way around the house impressively well. She snuck us out through the back door in the kitchen, meant for deliveries and staff. Then, and only then, did she offer me a brownie. We walked for a couple of minutes, munching, and talking about the moon shining bright above us. It, too, was smiling for people lost and found.

Ophelia cleared her throat. "I have a gift for you."

"A gift? Why? For what?"

"Come on." She dragged me along.

We sat down on a bench, setting the empty brownie container on the grass.

"I wish this night would never end," she murmured.

I tucked a piece of loose hair behind her ear. "Yes, it is rather heavenly," I agreed.

A flash of confusion crossed her face. "No. Well, that too, but I meant that Eloise seems better today. Didn't you see her before? She's glowing."

"Better how?"

Her lips parted. "Do you not know? Did they not tell you yet?"

"Tell me what?" More secrets?

"Lucas, Eloise has cancer. Did you not know? Jeanie makes sure she goes to her appointments and takes her medication, but it wears on her. The sickness. I thought you knew. Weird." Ophelia looked at me pitifully.

My jaw went slack.

This entire time. Poor Eloise. I knew I was a stranger to them, but I'd imagined we had an understanding. Everyone knew. Everyone but me.

"But why?"

"I'm sure they didn't want to worry you. Come now, don't think about it. It really isn't that bad. And, like you said, it's a heavenly night. Let's enjoy it. Eloise is in good hands."

I nodded grimly. Put it off my mind for the moment, no matter how shocking the news were. Surely everything was okay. Jeanie wouldn't let it be any other way. As for not telling me, I couldn't really be upset with them for that. Having someone close to you be sick, it's easier to pretend they aren't rather than talk about it. I understood that well. When my mom was sick, I used to sit at her bedside, reading to her. In my mind, I always figured she'd eventually get better. As if it was common cold she was sick from.

But if Ophelia was right and Eloise was doing well, then it was cause to celebrate, right?

We sat side by side, Ophelia's hand occasionally brushing against mine. Our thighs touching. I, too, wished the night would never end. "So, what was this about a gift? Or were you just looking for an excuse to get me alone, thief of sweets?"

She laughed. I loved to hear her laugh, even more if I was the cause of it. It made me forget everything she'd done and everything she hadn't done and how strange that none of it mattered suddenly. The years spent in waiting fell away as she leaned in to kiss me. Her lips were warm and soft, her tongue prying mine open. My hands were on her cheeks and the nape of her neck and then her hair. She grabbed hold of my shirt, gripping the fabric. I didn't care about the wrinkles it would leave. It was dizzying to have her so close to me and still want to be closer. I could forget everything.

When we finally broke apart, her lips were pink and luscious, her eyes sparkling like the stars above us. "Your gift," she said.

I kissed her knuckles absently. "Maybe you should make me gifts more often."

She chuckled. "Maybe I should."

Ophelia was like electricity. Like snowflakes on hot skin, or warm rain in summer.

She was spectacular. But most of all, she made all my worries turn to dust.

17 / Rafael

Sweet things

I didn't know how long she had been staring at me for. Bells, approaching carefully like a cat hunting for pray. Footsteps soundless yet sure, hands tucked behind her back. Long, thick waves of hair resting over her shoulders, framing her face. Pointed chin lowered, eyes observant.

"M&M?" I offered.

She nodded, sitting cross-legged on the ground to face me. Bells popped the candy in her mouth while I continued to categorize the rest by color.

I coughed. "I like to sort things. I want to know which color I have the most of." So far, the majority seemed to be orange but there were still ways to go.

Arabella took another M&M and, without saying a word, began to sort the blue M&M's from the brown.

"Where's Lucy?" It didn't happen often that I was first to the lake, but on the days I wasn't the last, I got to see the two of them arrive together. Unlike now.

"She's with Zack. They went to see a movie yesterday and she slept over. They'll probably be here soon. Look at that, blue wins." She smiled, showing off soft dimples.

I counted the candy. She was right. "Go ahead." I encouraged with a headshake.

She reached for a blue piece.

"How you've been?" I asked. "This isn't all too much for you? Everything good with your mom?" Bells had worried about her mom finding out about the investigation, so much so that she'd made everyone promise not to mention it. Was the cat out the bag? Or was Bells still tiptoeing around her mother? I supposed I wasn't one to speak, since pops still didn't know either.

"I'm fine. She's fine. It's weird, is all. When we're doing all—" She waved her hand around, pointing at everything but nothing at all. "—this, it's almost like I don't think of him as my uncle at all. He becomes just this guy who's missing. I feel sorry for him but it's different. Then I go home and remember that it's real." A scrawny finger poking at the candy, pushing them around. Arabella shrugged. "It's life, I guess. Nothing anyone can do. Heck, does that even make any sense to you?"

"Yes," I croaked. "We'll find out what happened, don't worry." I stuffed my mouth with brown M&M's. Brown ones were my favorite—felt like less food coloring, though I knew that wasn't true. Really, I shouldn't have been making promises I wasn't sure I could keep, but I couldn't help myself. Something about Bells made me want to promise all kinds of things.

Arabella smiled, but her eyes didn't sparkle. She poked me with those same scrawny fingers, An acceptance of my promise. A deal. "Are *you* okay?"

Should I tell her? This was the perfect opportunity to tell her about the messages I'd been receiving. Arabella was trustworthy. If I wished it so, she probably wouldn't blab about it to the others too. But if I did tell her, it would only add more stress on her, and she already had too much going on. It wasn't as if she could help either. Telling her would do no good for either of us.

"I'm okay."

I poked her back.

Just then, Adam's loud laughter echoed through the woods. Time for a meeting.

18 / Lucas

Moth to a flame

I woke with a start. Reaching over to the bedside table for my water bottle, my lips dry and in need on refreshment.

In my dream, my mother was alive. A ship in the distance only I was allowed to board. Before I could beg the man with a navy suit and to let her pass, we sailed off. My mother left standing on the pier.

I kicked the sheets aside, a speck of water still on my chin. A stupid dream.

I got ready hastily. It was Ophelia's fault I was distracted. Having her back in my life was such a shock, I'd surely be recovering from it for a while. How the dead came back, yet they didn't. God, what a weird day, and I hadn't even had breakfast yet.

I went down the cascading staircase, through the corridors. From the kitchen, I grabbed a banana, eating it as I moved. My appetite wasn't much, and I blamed that on Ophelia too. That kiss had left me feeling aa kinds of mixed things.

I was supposed to be watching her. I was supposed to gain her trust and find out the truth not fall for her. My friends needed me.

"Good morning," said a voice. I turned on my heel. "But is, though? Good. Step out of bed with the wrong foot, hm?" Ophelia searched my face.

"Just peachy."

"Well, then, maybe I could help you with a game of pool? Might take the edge off." She smiled, already moving past me to the game room.

My interest was piqued, and so I followed her towards the pool table, where the game had already been set ready, waiting. I'd played only a few times before, and could barely call myself average.

Ophelia and I took place at the table, the balls in a perfect triangle at the center. She swallowed, touching the tip of her tongue to her bottom lip in concentration before making her move. I observed her, the perfect flush of her skin, long eyelashes downcast, blinking slowly. I thought about our kiss, and if another might follow sometime. I should've forgot about it and moved on, but I didn't want to. I wanted to keep doing whatever it was we were doing.

"Will you tell me what's on your mind?" she asked.

I scrunched up one eye, twisting away. "It's nothing." When she didn't press on, I felt myself wanting to tell her anyway. The quiet was tempting. "Your reappearance has made me doubt everything. I think about home, and I think about my father. How I miss both yet don't. I want to see the world more. I think about college and I think about my mother and my friends. About you. Always about you. How you left and how I found you and how confounding this little adventure has been. Our kiss. Both kisses. How I hope there might be a third." I could very well feel the wash of heat turning me scarlet.

Ophelia seemed amused by my outburst. She watched me with those big green eyes of hers, mouth turned up. "You worry about that? Easy enough to fix." She reached up on her tippy-toes, pressing her lips against mine.

How could she be so infuriating and reassuring all at once? Witch.

I lifted her against the table, her thighs digging into my biceps, already melting under her touch. Like a damn moth to the flame, always drawn to her.

Ophelia stopped abruptly. She hugged me, my arms stuck between the two of us, so I couldn't move. "Lucas," she spoke, face pressed against my torso. "I missed you too. I have doubts too. I've made decisions I'm not sure were right, or even mine to make. I understand how you feel, and I want you to know that you'll be okay. You will get through it. There are always better days to come."

She released me from her grip, jumping off the table and taking a step back. "Did I ever tell you that you're such a sorehead?"

I rolled my eyes.

"Fine, but did I ever tell you that you have the most beautiful, deep eyes?"

"Storm clouds. And you love rain." I grinned.

"Yeah. I do." Ophelia blushed. "Should we finish the game?"

I told her we should. After all, we didn't yet know who would win and who would lose.

19 / Rafael

The dead man, his lover, and his enemy

"You should have seen his face." Adam mimicked my scream, his dimples like two holes in his face. "Knock, knock, who's there?" He screamed again, the end morphing into laughter. He fell in the soft grass.

I rolled my eyes. "Ha-ha, funny. You're hilarious."

"Ooo … are you embarrassed? Guys, I think he's embarrassed." He cackled. "Oh, how the mighty have fallen. I should've taken a picture; your face was priceless. Such a great day!"

I glared at him.

Lucy and Zack, too, found it funny. They wouldn't have, were they the ones with an angry egg-sized bruise on their leg. I'd been genuinely afraid when Adam and Katie burst in.

"It was rotten, I think," I said as coolly as I could. "At least I found the journal. I heard your giggling on the phone, by the way."

Lucy's face turned hot pink, like the bow in her hair.

"How's your ankle?" asked Bells, touching my shoulder like I was a wounded puppy.

I rubbed my bruise. It was an ugly shade of purple. For a couple of days, flip flops weren't an option. "Fine. Nothing's broken."

"Did you read it?" asked Katie. "The journal?"

"Most of it, yes," I answered, then remembered something. "How did it go with Esther? Did you find something?" The journal was a mess. Reading it, I'd had to go back and forth many times just to make sense of things. A lot of it was nonsense, or simply irrelative, but I think I might've found the reason Martinez died hidden between the pages too.

"I don't think she was ever pretending to be sad; I think she *was* sad. I think she's trying very hard to make people believe her heart is made of stone." Katie sighed, turning to Adam. "Any news from Lucas?"

"No. Nothing. Not after he searched Ophelia's room. He managed to get into her laptop—she's been keeping tabs on her family. That's all. Feels like he's avoiding us," answered Adam, the lake glistening behind him. He studied the water, forehead wrinkling, but then shook his head as if detaching for his thoughts.

Katie huffed and stood.

Secrets. Secrets everywhere.

Esther Graham worked at Whitewood Public Library, and she had a secret no one knew of.

Well, someone might've.

When I'd read it in the journal, I hadn't believed it right away. But the more I thought about it, the less surprised I was. It made perfect sense. For the first time, I felt like we were getting somewhere and that the puzzle pieces were slowly starting to fit together.

Mrs. Graham lifted her head, eyes dulling the moment she realized we weren't there to borrow books. "Are you going to patronize me every day? I have already talked to you twice, and that's twice too much."

"Yes, well, both times you failed to mention your relationship with Link Martinez."

Her eyes grew wide, whipping around to see if anyone had heard me. Luckily, the library was empty this early in the day. "How did you—"

"Find out? Sorry, no telling. But if you want to avoid that third visit—or is it technically fourth?—I think it would be wise for you to just fill in all the gaps this time." I smiled. "Please."

She chewed on her cheek. "Fine, but this better be the last time. And be quiet about it. The next time I see you I will be calling the police and your parents."

She wouldn't. Unless she wanted to explain to them what we knew. "When did it start?"

She smoothed out the wrinkles in her skirt. "Around March, three years ago. But nothing happened until the end of April. Am I right to believe you haven't told my husband?" Her eyes were searching, a lively twinkle there that hadn't existed before.

I hadn't even thought of that. "We haven't said anything to anyone, but if it stays that way depends entirely on your willingness to answer our questions. So, March. Did Ophelia know?"

She scrunched up her nose. "Of course not."

I angled my head forward. "You don't think she might've figured it out? Suspected it?"

"We never called, never texted. We only ever left each other little messages here and there and met up from time to time. Why on Earth would she have suspected a thing? One thing you need to understand is that a mother always knows everything. So, when I say my daughter had no idea, I mean it."

And Mrs. Graham had just hinted that her husband didn't know either. I believed her.

"But why?" asked Arabella over my shoulder. Her voice was like honey, coating my ears.

Esther gave her a long, troubling eyeful. "I love my husband. Right now, you don't know a thing about love, but one day you will. It's complicated. You can't fit it inside a box. It doesn't have rules, it doesn't bend to your will. You don't understand, and why would you? It's all empty, meaningless words to you, but one day … one day you might be where I am. If you don't have any more questions, then I must ask you to leave. I have work to do." She turned in her seat.

I held up my hands. "Wait, wait. We're not done yet. How often did you meet Link? Where?"

She crossed her arms. "Once or twice a week. Sometimes we were at his house, but usually we met at this lake. It's by the—"

"We know where it is," asserted Lucy, in hurry. Irritated.

None of us liked Esther Graham much. She was a body of eerie darkness. Shadows. You never knew what to expect from her. But for the first time, she'd told us the truth. She appeared less like a ghost now and more like a human.

"Did you meet there on the 14th of June?" I asked.

Mrs. Graham narrowed her eyes. "What are you suggesting?"

"Answer the question, please."

"No, we didn't. We were supposed to, but he never showed up. I wouldn't even remember such a thing if it weren't for that terrible accident. I found out a few hours later. I've thought about that day over and over."

"What time were you going to meet?"

"Around twelve. That's when I have my lunch break. It was always either lunch break or after work." Esther visibly deflated. A bit of gray was woven into her reddish hair.

Lucy leaned against the desk. "And you didn't go looking for him?" she asked.

Zack watched Lucy quietly. Fierce green eyes jumping from her hair to her mouth to her eyes. Compared to the rest of us, he was taking everything extremely chill.

Mrs. Graham shook her head.

She slammed her fist against the countertop. "Bullshit! You must've wondered where he was."

"I didn't go after him! If he didn't want to come, fine. It was a crazy day for everyone, talking to him was the last thing on my mind."

That, I did not believe.

"Are you really saying you didn't worry where he might've disappeared to? Especially on a day like that, crazy for everyone. One might think to check on their secret lover, make sure they are okay."

We were doing so well, why lie now?

"Not that day. If you must know, I went over to his house the next night, but he didn't want to see me. The TV was on, I knew he was home. I left. I think he was angry with me, because I'd ran late. A stupid misunderstanding. I got to the lake maybe fifteen minutes later because there was a small mess at work I had to fix. I don't know why he was upset about it. I wanted to talk it out."

I massaged my temple. "On your way to the lake—you didn't see anything or anyone?"

She squinted. "Of course I saw people. In the middle of the day, how could I not? What do you want me to say? I wasn't walking around looking for suspicious activity." She grabbed a stack of papers. "Now, I ask again, are we done? I have work to do."

"Last one," I replied. "Did Link keep a diary?"

"A diary?"

"Yes."

"He loved poems, but he wasn't a teenager. People don't keep *diaries*." She made a face.

How sweet. "Right. Thank you."

We left the library, as promised. It was already past nine, and heat was starting to build in the air. All the light made my eye sockets burn. I could literally feel the weight of the dark circles under my eyes. All those nights staying up, reading under the covers, were catching up on me. But it was better than fighting for sleep I knew wouldn't come.

Zack said he was parched and that we should stop by the corner store. It wasn't too far from the library anyway, ran by a friendly Chinese woman. When we were kids, Zack and Adam once stole all the pennies from her donations jar. The next time we went back there, it had been replaced by a bowl of candy.

We entered, and the little bell on the door announced us. Sometimes I heard that bell in my dreams, way back.

I grabbed a cold bottle of water. The kind of cold that bites your fingers and makes them numb. I thought of Lucas. Suddenly I missed him a lot. He should've been there, spending the summer with us.

"Rafael!" chirped a voice. It was Maya, her arms full of groceries.

"Maya, hey. Didn't expect to see you here. How's your leg?" I asked, stifling a yawn.

She blushed, long lashes fluttering. Her eyes were familiar, like I'd looked into them before but not quite. Her mom, probably. "A little blue. Thank you for the other day. I don't know why I cried."

"It's alright. And hey—" I rolled up my pants to show her my blotchy bruise. "We match."

Katie, hearing our chatter, came over to say hi too. "I love your outfit."

Maya stared down at her white dress. "Thank you! I'm getting lunch for my mom. She forgot to take food with her in the morning, so I'm bringing something over to her. She's been so busy lately."

"That's nice of you," said Katie.

"How is Vivianne?" I asked.

It wouldn't be long now until the footage would be deleted. We'd get away with it, crazily enough. Hopefully I could soon forget about it too. We'd been insanely lucky not to get caught.

"Good." Maya's big eyes glinted. She was glowing, happy and light.

Mr. Graham was standing across the lot when we returned outside. He held a hand up to his face, squinting.

What is it? Run into everybody day? My social battery was draining fast. I'd half-hoped to get home soon, so I could devise the next step of my plan. Plus, there was so much new information to process.

"You kids doing okay? Haven't heard from you in a bit."

I held up the water bottle. "Yeah, just grabbing some water."

Mr. Graham's T-shirt stuck to his skin, and he jolted it free. A breeze crossed the empty parking lot, ruffling his dainty hair. He didn't look too good, old and exhausted. Did we do that to him?

"How are you?" asked Katie, not just out of courtesy.

"I'm fine, you kids worry 'bout yourselves. A lot has happened. The photos you showed brought back a lot of memories, that's all."

My stomach hurt. We'd reminded him of his dead daughter and vanished afterwards. The man was frail and sad there was no way he'd thought to send me those messages. "Sir, we're really sorry about that. The questions, I mean. We crossed a line. I'm sorry," I stammered.

He waved his hand. "Honestly, I could have handled it better too. Hey, tell you what, why don't you kids come over for dinner? We'll start over."

"Really? Are you—"

Joseph's phone rang. He fished it out of his pocket with a scowl. He took one look at the screen, turned, and took a couple of steps away before answering. There was muffled talking, then he closed the back of his truck, and drove off without waiting for our answers.

"We should have told him about the affair," said Katie when the car was out of sight.

"No, it's not for us to tell," argued Adam.

"Yes, it is! We are the ones who know about it, and he doesn't! Imagine it was you—wouldn't you want someone to tell you?"

"First of all, my wife would never do that," he said cockily. "And believe me, if she did, I'd know about it." He smirked, hands in his pockets.

Zack whistled.

"Yeah, sure. Whatever." Katie's eyes flashed with disbelief. "But it's clear he doesn't know, and it's wrong not to tell him. I feel like a liar."

"How do you know he doesn't know?" asked Z.

"Because why would he still be with her? Also, Esther just told us he doesn't. After three years you'd think he'd have said something. Divorced her, maybe. We should do the right thing."

"Sorry, I don't speak stupid. Do you truly want to get involved in that? It's their family drama, I say let them deal with it on their own. Martinez is gone anyway, why stir up more trouble? Leave it, Katie." I'd never heard Adam so commanding. So serious.

"Fuck you, Adam, I'm not scared." She crossed her arms.

He huffed. "You should be." Adam stepped closer to Katie, both their faces red.

"Go to hell," she whispered.

"Maybe I'll drag you down with me."

Katie gulped, blinking multiple times. She had a sense of right and wrong. No matter the consequences, she would always choose the path harder to walk. How many of us could say the same?

Could I?

Lucy stepped forward, deciding to be the grounding force. "Guys, this is ridiculous! We can't—"

"Shut up Lucy!" yelled Katie. "I don't want to hear it! God, you always make it about yourself. We didn't invite you here, you decided to be part of this."

"*No,*" said Lucy harshly. "I am not going to shut up! Sometimes, being a bitch is good. Like right now, when I'm trying to tell you we need to talk about this, but everyone is acting crazy."

Impressive, I had to admit. And surprising, coming from her.

Zack's face twisted until he couldn't help but crack up. He covered his mouth with both hands, strangled laugh bubbling, catching attention. Quiet the entire day, but now.

"What's so funny?"

"I'm sorry. Sorry," he said in between the bursts, "keep going."

Lucy took a deep breath. "Firstly, we have heard plenty about what you two think." She pointed her finger at Adam and Katie. "Now, what about everyone else? Bells?"

Arabella blinked once. Twice. Three times. Then shrugged. All wide, innocent eyes, and a pleasing smile.

"Rafe? What is up with you?" asked Katie.

I looked at her, confused. Had she been talking to me?

"Even when you had your ass stuck in a hole you didn't look this terrible," said Adam. "I wasn't going to say anything, but since y'all already mentioned it…"

"Thanks," I muttered. "I haven't been sleeping well."

"Why?" Lucy fixated her caramel eyes on me.

Because I was worried there might be someone watching me. Because I couldn't stop my thoughts nor the memories replaying in my mind. Because my mind would not stop even if I wanted it to.

"I keep thinking."

"About what?"

"Everything. I can't turn it off until we're done. We have to finish this. I think our best bet is to keep the information about the affair and Ophelia to ourselves right now. We can use it to our advantage. Not to mention, I just promised Esther I wouldn't tell her husband, and I'd rather her not call my dad." I chortled, then choked. We had to put it off for a little while. Katie could spill the secrets later if she still wanted to.

Zack bobbed his head along, lighting a cigarette and putting it between his lips. His messy black hair was getting longer. It dangled in front of his eyes. But even with all that, he didn't come off as dark and mysterious as he used to. And I think the reason had something to do with the pretty blonde beside him.

"Fine. But promise me that one way or another, we'll do the right thing eventually," said Katie.

"I promise."

———————

"Mrs. Graham, these potatoes are excellent," complimented Adam.

Did he just? No—but he did. Did Adam come from a Jane Austen novel?

Esther huffed and puffed. She was bitter about us questioning her and then showing up for dinner too. I almost felt sorry for her. She couldn't shake us.

"More salad, anyone?" asked Mr. Graham enthusiastically.

As the dinner went on, I couldn't help but get the impression Joseph had something to say, but wouldn't in the presence of his wife and mother-in-law, Mary. He'd stare and cough as to begin speaking, but never did. I was the only one to notice out of the four of us there.

Adam, Katie, Arabella, and me.

I excused myself before dessert to go to the bathroom (I lied). Instead, I went into Joseph's study. It was like breaking into the archives all over again. I'd done worse, no reason to be nervous now. He was hiding something. I had to know what. Maybe there were clues that would tell me whether he'd been the one to break into my room. Would've been nice to have a face to go along with my invisible stalker, although just hours ago I'd been sure it wasn't him. Okay, so maybe I was confused. The fight before had made me speculate if Joseph *did* know more than we thought.

There was only so much time I had before they'd start wondering what was taking me so long. I started going through the drawers, first stopping when I found some paperwork, but they dated back long, so I put them back and moved on to the other drawers. I hadn't told anyone I was planning this. In fact, I'd come up with it minutes ago at the table while chewing on a pickle. Spontaneous was my middle name.

I came upon some of the documents from Warren Repairs. I slid my eyes over the payments, hoping to catch some discord. I opened a file, the papers clearly thrown inside in a hurry. One fell under the table. I went to fetch it, but something else caught my attention, and my hand halted mid-air. The bottom right drawer was slightly ajar, something blue peeking out. It was a box. I opened it, inside were a bunch of unused brown paper bags. I grit my teeth. Why was this so testing? Every single time I had to do something illegal, it could never be made simple for me. If I was a bad guy, where would I hide my things?

A sound across the room startled me.

"Despite of what you seem to think of me, I am on your side."

I pushed the drawer closed as I stood, coming face to face with Mr. Graham.

He walked closer, slow, and careful, hands behind his back. "Tell me, what is it you think you're doing in here?"

I had to remind myself he wouldn't hurt me in his own house with seven witnesses in the other room. It didn't help to ease my rattling heartbeat. "You have been threatening me. Why?" I asked, ignoring his question. I had to get the upper hand. He had this sneaky look in his eyes that told me I'd been right all along. I tossed the theory out there, hoping he'd just tell me if I was right or not.

"And you have been asking around, showing up with old pictures. You thought I wouldn't realize you're snooping?"

I swallowed hard, but stood my ground. "You don't deny it?"

"Deny what?"

"That you're the one behind all of this! You killed Sheldon Rogers, and then you killed Link Martinez after you found out about the affair. Now you're threatening me 'cause you know I'm onto you! Oh man, you're going to be locked up for this." I smiled coldly, but my victory was brought to a quick end when Joseph burst into laughter.

"You think I'm a killer? Oh, I'm going to be locked up? Good luck finding evidence, you little shit!" he said, then cleared his voice. "I haven't killed anybody. I haven't been threatening you or anyone else for that matter. I want the truth as much as you, but you don't see me going around accusing people, or going through their offices. By the way, that's illegal. I'd expect you out of all people to know that. Why should I believe a word you say? You're trying to frame me! How do I know you're not lying? Damn me for believing we might've been able to help each other for even a second." He rubbed his hands over his red face.

"You're lying. It must be you who has been threatening me."

"If someone has been harassing you, boy, leave me out of it. I haven't done anything to you. All I wanted was to talk."

What? I stared at him. "Is that what you have been hiding all evening? You knew about the investigation?"

"Yes. I was waiting for an opportunity to talk about it, that's why I invited you tonight. I know you went to see my wife today, and before that Dave told me you asked him about Ophelia. But now I see you're playing detective, and nothing more."

But that made no sense. A cheating wife was the perfect motive. But then what about Sheldon Rogers? Could he have seen something? Or Ophelia? What did she have to do with any of it?

"Why should I trust you?"

"You want me to prove I'm innocent?"

I raised an eyebrow. "Can you?"

"No, actually. But if you think I would hurt my own daughter, then you might not be as smart as you think you are." He took a step forward, and I took a step back. "Now tell me why I should trust *you*?"

The office door opened.

"Is everything okay?" asked Arabella. "I heard yelling."

I found comfort in her hazel eyes and could breathe easier. "Yes," I replied. "Coming."

She nodded and closed the door behind her.

If what he was saying was true, then there was still someone out there watching me. Someone very careful, who knew how to not get caught.

Three years ago, cops arrested Joseph Graham. We knew that from the files from the archives. Then they let him go.

Was that because he'd been telling the truth then too? Or because, like now, he was very good at covering his tracks?

20 / Lucas

Candlelit strangers, dazed by spins

I heard the buzzing of guests as I corrected my tie, fawning over every imperfection of my suit. I took a deep breath, steadying myself. The day had come sooner than I'd thought.

The lights were dim in the corridors and almost the same in the hall. The decorators had spent a chunk of the day hanging up flowers and plants, lights. Jeanie had the house done like royalty. I felt like a peasant in a king's court, small and unimportant. The wedding venue was massive; a big shade built on the grounds, only for this occasion, to fit all the guests. It was a bit chilly outside, so everyone gathered inside before the wedding would begin. I'd imagined Jeanie might book a venue elsewhere, but Ophelia told me Eloise had wanted to do it home. I supposed it was fine when you lived in a mansion with achars of land.

I moved past the guests, focusing on the gold-framed paintings covering the dark walls. Jeanie and Eloise had been collectors for years, but guests could buy them, if they'd like. Jeanie and Eloise were donating the money to an organization of their choosing. They hadn't yet told us who. Weirdly, it had been the one thing they hadn't squabbled about.

I'd sneaked a look at the cake before. It was enormous, with edible flowers and fancy frosting detailing. It wasn't exactly white, more of an ivory tone. The edges had been sprayed with glitter and gold. Three kitchen staff members had fussed over it, visibly worried they might drop it.

Eloise was wearing a laced dress with a long tailing skirt, her shoulder-length hair curled and dosed in sparkles. She smiled brightly, warmth radiating off her more than ever before. Maybe Ophelia was right and she was doing better. I hadn't yet had the courage to ask her about her illness and I didn't want to cause her more stress right now. I'd been watching her more closely these few days since I'd found out.

Jeanie was just as gorgeous as her bride. She wore a minimalistic white suit, and a low bun. She didn't glitter, but the diamond earrings she wore sure did. And if Eloise was the sun, then she was the moon. She greeted guests, shaking hands and kissing cheeks. Jeanie's hand hung lazily on Eloise's waist. They tittered over something, eyes lighting up when they looked at one another.

Someone bumped into me, making me turn. My eyes landed on top of the staircase, nailed in place.

I stood my ground, soaking up the breathtaking view of Ophelia descending the stairs. Holding myself back from stealing her away from the party before it could really begin. Dark blue silk sat snug at her waist and pooled around her like she'd risen from the depths of the ocean. Her green eyes were piercing. Magnificent. Her eyes met mine, rosy lips parting slightly. Chills covered me.

What made falling for her terrifying was that never did I know if we were falling together, or if I, alone, was plummeting into heartbreak. But after waiting for so long, I decided the fall was worth the risk.

"Lucas! Dear, you're so handsome," observed Eloise from behind me.

With dismay, I turned, but my eyes kept darting back to Ophelia. It was hard to focus. I hugged Eloise gently.

"Yes, not too bad at all." Jeanie smiled. It was the first time she'd said something nice about me. Or smiled in my direction.

"Thank you. You both look absolutely radiant." I pointed around. "Not to mention, everything looks great. Must be the best party I've ever been to."

Eloise squeezed my shoulder. "Have fun, and make sure you try some of the appetizers. Oh, and you and Ophelia are sitting at the front. If you see her, let her know. We'll begin soon. People should start gathering outside."

I promised I would.

The music stopped, and Jeanie blossomed with excitement at once. "Oh! It's time for my speech!" She kissed Eloise's temple and rushed off.

She waited for everyone to quiet before speaking. I searched around for Ophelia, but I'd already lost her in the crowd. I would be lying if I said it didn't make me deflate a little.

"Firstly," said Jeanie, "I would like to thank every single one of you for being here on this very special day. Eloise and I are extremely thrilled to share all of this with you." She gestured around with her hands, finally resting them on the microphone.

"Secondly, we've been impatiently waiting to tell you, that we have chosen to donate the money from the purchasable art pieces to helping more people survive cancer and live long, fulfilling lives. Both me and Eloise feel strongly about the topic, so let this be our gift to the world.

"Lastly, I would like you to raise a toast with me in honor of this glamorous night. As Atticus once said, *'I hope to arrive to my death, late, in love, and a little drunk.'* Well, I hope none of you are feeling unwell quite yet, but that all of us are a little drunk, and deeply in love." She lifted her glass, and so did everyone else.

Clapping echoed, and Jeanie met everyone's gaze. Bravely, and gleaming with joy.

Ophelia and I sat at the front as told. I placed my hand on top of hers and laced our fingers.

Through the tent roof, it was impossible to see stars, but I knew they were out there. Fresh flower petals covered the floor all the way to the altar, where Jeanie was already waiting. Fairy lights swirled the thick, white columns at the front, and vines curled, falling from the top like curtains of greenery. The night smelled sweetly. So sweetly it made me feel drunk.

The music began, and everyone snapped their heads towards Eloise as she began walking up to the front. Jeanie leaned in and kissed Eloise's knuckles. Eloise's hair caught the firelight, shimmering. Neither of them looked at all nervous. The rest of the world fell away.

When the time came for vows, Jeanie went first.

"Ever since I first met you, I knew I belonged by your side. You lift me up when I'm down. You tell me when I'm being unfair, even when I don't want to hear it. I love that you're not afraid of being honest. You are the light making my days shine, and I promise to spend the rest of our time making sure you are the happiest person in this world." Jeanie teared up, her voice breaking slightly. "And when you should leave me one day, for that day will come for all, I'll pack up my heart and send it with you, because I love you. You are my life, and I am immensely lucky to have you by my side." She released a heavy breath, touching a hand to her hair, making sure it was perfect as she finished.

Eloise's grip on Jeanie tightened. She smiled, assuring. It was her turn.

"My mother used to say that the people who love us also challenge us for the better. Every day with you has been an adventure—you challenge me. I love you, especially the parts you try so hard to hide from everyone. Know that you are beautiful and loved, and adored. I promise to never, ever give up on us. This love is burning fiercely. It is strong, it is extraordinary. I want you; I want all of you, and this is just the beginning of our story, I promise." If a smile could say a thousand things and mean another thousand—that was how Eloise smiled, looking into Jeanie's eyes. Like they had their own language no one could ever comprehend.

Many of the guests cried. Happy tears, I hoped. The celebrant pronounced Eloise and Jeanie wife and wife, and everyone clapped in a thunderous unison.

The servants started to pour out of the house, bringing platters of food and drinks and appetizers. We sat in two long table rows, feasting on stuffed, crispy duck, grape mousse, pesto-chicken sprinkled with sea salt, and washed everything down with expensive red wine. And then, when I thought I couldn't eat another thing, they brought out the cake. I always have more room for cake.

Once the feast and ceremony concluded, guests moved back inside for snacks, drinks, and dancing. The night was getting cold, and even with a jacket on I felt the chill creep into my bones.

I stumbled upon Mr. Howell on my way inside, and we fell into conversation. I'd spent a restless evening weighing the pros and cons of his proposal. Finally, I convinced myself there was no harm in trying out Northenview. I might not even get in. Mr. Howell promised to set everything up for me regarding the school and admission's interview.

I made my way through the people, searching for a sign of blue silk. I was hoping to find Ophelia, since we'd got separated leaving the outside venue.

And then I saw her. She was standing in the middle of the dance floor, misplaced, and lost. I smiled to myself, walking towards her.

"Lost?" I asked.

"Just waiting for someone to sweep me off my feet." She curtsied.

Something tugged at my heartstrings. The truth was, Ophelia Graham had captured my heart a long time ago, and I never got it back.

I took her hand, holding her firmly against my torso, my other hand resting on her hip. I gave her a dashing, close-lipped smile. "May I offer my services?"

She nodded and we began our dance. I looked down at her from my full height, moving to spin her.

Ophelia leaned in close, and whispered in my ear, "You smell like aftershave and pine, did you notice?"

"You clearly did."

Too long had we been playing this cat and mouse game. I was sick of it. Let it end now.

I eased my hands to the small of her back. Our bodies molding together into one.

"Do you ever miss home?" I asked.

Her parents, her childhood house, her friends, school, the town.

"All the time," she answered.

All the time.

I kissed the top of her head, watching the couples dancing around us. Seeing Eloise smile and Jeanie grin. An old woman rested her head at an old man's shoulder. A little girl dancing with her father.

I looked back at Ophelia. "I missed you," I said.

"I missed you too."

Although I'd heard those words before, this was the first time I really listened.

Our dancing was more swaying from side to side than actual dancing. I was a terrible dancer, that was partly it. I planted a kiss on the side of her mouth. Her eyes fell shut. It had never been clearer to me how much I needed her. And I wanted so much more. I wanted everything with her.

"Enough dancing." I practically dragged her out the door, and up the stairs. Ophelia only giggled, letting me do whatever.

The music and talking were muffled on the second floor. No one else had any place there. We were alone.

Ophelia's breathing was heavy, cheeks flushed. Her hand slipped beneath my shirt, untucking it. Her nails carving out my muscles. Her skin against mine.

I opened the door to my room before lifting her against a wall and pressing myself closer. Her eyes bore into mine. "I feel like you've been avoiding me tonight," I said hoarsely, kissing my way up her neck and running my hands over her body. That thin, silky dress. Her warmness underneath it.

She shivered, legs wrapping around me. She wiggled out of her heels, letting them drop on the ground. Her eyes were closed, she swallowed. "I haven't. I'm sorry if it seemed like that."

We had much to catch up on, but for the time being, *talking* was the last thing neither one of us wanted to do.

I kissed her furiously, and she kissed me back even harder.

We'd been different people when we'd met, but now we were exploring the people we'd become over the years.

Our kisses became frantic, our hunger insatiable.

Blue silk fell to the floor.

21 / Rafael

My eyes on you and your eyes on me

Pops never asked about my absent-mindedness. Why I slept on the living room couch more than in my own bed (as if bad things couldn't touch me there). He was clearly worried, but never asked why I looked so exhausted in the mornings. Tired during our grocery runs, half asleep when we watched football together. I didn't feel safe, even at home, unless I was with him, so I took every opening I got to spend some time together.

Is fear alive? Worming inside your body, molding it into something you do not recognize. Stones in your belly, pulling you down and making you shrink.

I'd been brave. I'd tried to be strong. I'd imagined that if only I was fearless and smart, I could catch the person threatening me, and life would be normal again. But when the adrenaline wore off and I was tired and sleepless, more so every day, the hero in me disappeared too. We'd made progress. We were getting somewhere. But then why did I feel like shit? Why did fear start to creep up on me?

The office door opened softly.

"Detective Porter? Sonya asked me to deliver these to you. She isn't in today. Can I just leave these here?"

Pops smiled. "Yes. Yes, come in." He straightened in his chair, smoothing out his gray-tipped hair.

I stared out the window, still seeing pops' and Vivianne's happy reflections on the glass. Outside, it was cloudy, but it didn't seem like it would rain anytime soon. The pavement in front of the station was bone dry, the leaves on surrounding trees wilted.

Vivianne walked in and stood by dad's desk. She leaned over, hand playing with her necklace. The way she blinked with her long, dark lashes made me want to wash my eyes with bleach. Neither one of them noticed my discomfort. The only woman I'd ever seen dad flirt with was my mom, but that was a long time ago.

I rolled my eyes when Vivianne left, receiving a scolding glare. My phone beeped as dad investigated the paperwork, and I tucked my head to look at the lit-up screen.

A new message from an unknown number. A photo looked back at me.

My friends and I at Link's house.

A cold, icy, shiver slithered down the back of my neck. A throaty whimper almost escaping me. I snapped my head up to make sure pops wasn't watching me. If he'd seen my reaction and sudden change of mood.

He wasn't. He hadn't.

I'd felt someone following me that day at Link's. I'd even imagined seeing someone in the woods. I'd thought it was nothing. A hallucination.

I kept my walk casual, straight to the bathroom, even though all I wanted to do was run and keep running. I locked myself in, unable to stop shaking. No matter how much I inhaled, it wasn't enough. No air enough to satisfy me, my breath catching in my throat. My insides burning liquid, spreading like wildfire, screaming for an escape. My heart was going to stop, my lungs would give in. Legs buckled under me, trembling, and I wiped cold sweat from my brow.

I sat on the bathroom floor, the picture in hand, staring like any moment it would transform into something else. I'd realize it had been a trick of my mind, that it was something entirely different I was truly looking at. Seconds ticked by, yet nothing changed. It was like being cold and burning up at the same time. There I was, walking, my head turned towards Adam. Smiling awkwardly, unaware I was being watched. *Photographed.* I was snowballing down a slope. Everyone was counting on me; it was already too late. How could I give up and go the rest of my life knowing there was someone out there who'd watched me like a hawk?

Please, please, please, please don't hurt them, I prayed.

How could I know what was the right thing to do? How to protect my friends? Giving in to the threats would never keep anyone safe, and I could never live with myself knowing I allowed a person like that to live in freedom. Continuing the search, I wasn't sure I was strong enough. No matter what I chose, everyone would be in danger.

At some point, when my breathing had calmed and my eyes no longer stung, I felt steady enough to stand. I couldn't hide in a bathroom stall all day. Pops finished up soon after, and we could finally leave. Suddenly the station didn't feel as safe as I'd stupidly though it was. The thought made me well up with angry tears. I didn't let them fall.

Pops and I didn't go home, no.

Vivianne was waiting, bag in hand, at the door for us. Her shift was over, as was my dad's. Naturally, pops had given me no heads up. It was a ten-minute walk to Vivi's house, and when we opened the door, Maya was already waiting. She saw us and smiled.

"Mom, you didn't tell me we were having guests over," she said.

Vivianne blushed, fumbling with her handbag. "I'm sorry, honey, it must've slipped my mind. Why don't you show Rafael your room while I get dinner started?"

So they were finally introducing us.

Maya stared at her. "Uh … sure. Come on." She didn't wait for me to follow. I liked Maya, but not enough to want to be her brother.

"Do you want to go outside? We have a new porch swing," she said like it was supposed to impress me.

I nodded; I didn't care. She could've taken me wherever. In my mind I was still lying on that dirty bathroom floor, soaked in tears, clutching my phone like I could somehow fix everything. How could I save my friends if I couldn't even tell them the truth?

Maya opened the porch door for me. We sat on the swing, side by side. I looked up at the moon, half covered by wispy clouds, letting the air cool my hot eyes.

"It's weird that our parents are … you know," said Maya.

"Yeah. How do you feel about it?"

Maya's mouth fell open, head tilting from side to side, like she wasn't sure how to best respond. I eyed her sideways. "No, no, don't get me wrong. You're great, and your dad is super cool. It's just that it's been me and mom for so long, I don't know how I'd feel if the house was full of people all the time. It's a bit overwhelming to think of. Scary." Her cheeks turned pink.

"I get it," I said. It was the same with me and pops.

"Can I ask you something? Would you mind if I sometimes hang out with you and your friends?" Maya's voice quivered, her hands nestling into her lap anxiously.

"You don't have friends? But the other day you were coming from a sleepover, weren't you?"

"Um, yeah. I have some friends, just not that many. Can I? I don't want to be annoying or anything. And I'm sure our parents would like that."

"We're kind of, er, busy." Solving crimes. Getting threats (as most people do). I didn't want nor need her anywhere near all that.

Maya turned away. "Right, but if you happen to have time. I have lots of fun ideas we could do."

"We'll see," I said. There was no easy way to put this. "What do you usually do while your mom's at work?"

She tucked her hair behind her ear. "I go to school, duh. And on Thursdays I have chess club. And sometimes, after school, my friend Tilly comes over, but lately she's been acting weird." She shook her head, stopping herself. "I paint. I watch movies. Mom lets me borrow her camera to take pictures sometimes."

I felt sorry for her, because her life sounded a lot like mine. At least I had my friends, but Maya was lonely. "What about your dad?" I couched. "Sorry, you don't have to say if you don't want to."

"No, it's okay. He didn't want me. He was kind of a major asshole." She laughed, but it sounded a bit cracked and sad.

I smiled back, just a little.

We sat on the swing until Vivianne called for us.

22 / Lucas

You shall not have which you desire most

Part of me wanted to stay and never leave. But Jeanie and Eloise would soon head out for their honeymoon, and it was time for me to pack my bags.

Standing on the threshold, leaving felt like a forever kind of thing.

"Try not to forget us," sniveled Eloise. "And you must visit some time." She brushed my arm softly, pouting.

"I won't and I will," I said, hugging her. "Enjoy your trip, I'm sure it'll be great." Before she could part, I pulled her close, and whispered in her ear, "I know that you're sick. I don't understand why you didn't tell me or why you didn't want me to know, but I'm here for you. We don't have to talk about it if you don't want to, but you call me if you ever need me. I will be there."

Eloise looked stricken, but eventually she nodded.

I kissed Jeanie's cheek. "Call me if something happens to her. If you need help, if something is wrong. Promise me."

She pulled away, tucking away my flyaway hair, and smoothing out the wrinkles in my shirt like a mother would. If my eyes were closed, I could imagine it really was my mom. I remembered so little of her. She was a distant memory engraved on the back of my skull. "I promise," she said.

I angled my head towards Ophelia, to whom I hadn't said a word yet. Eloise gave me one last goodbye, squeezing my hand before she and Jeanie left to give Ophelia and I some space. I had a couple of minutes left before my Uber would arrive.

I took her hands in mine. "If I asked you to come with me, would you?"

I knew her answer before she even parted her lips.

"I can't." She scrunched her face at our intertwined fingers. Her hands were ice.

Ophelia had made her mind up a long time ago, and I just had to accept the fact that I was going to lose her all over again. Just like three years ago. All this time, my feelings hadn't changed. All this time only for it to end the same fucking way. I never learned, did I?

She slipped her cold hand from mine. "I'm sorry, I can't."

"You mean you won't."

She stopped fighting, finally looking at me. "*I can't.* I need to move forward, and my past must stay behind me. There's nothing there for me."

"You have me. You have your family. Your friends. Please, Ophelia, please. Don't do this." *Not again.*

"I'm sorry."

Hopeless would be the only way to describe what I felt—weirdly similar to the feel of a breaking heart. "Is there nothing I can say? Nothing I can do to convince you?"

I didn't stop her as she stepped away from me. One step, two steps. Three.

Like a stab in the chest, I cracked. "One day you'll regret running, and on that day, you'll realize what you've lost. There will be no one beside you and you will be truly alone. Even I won't find you then."

The quiet stretched between us like a rubber band. Looking at her was like looking at a dream you never fulfilled, a wish that never became true, all the time you lost and will never get back. That's how it felt to look at the person who you cared about but to whom you were never enough.

"Let me know if you ever come to visit. I'll try to be here."

I watched her leave. Gravel crunched under her feet.

I ran a hand over the nape of my neck, feeling the cold sweat. I had no right to be disappointed. I was the one who'd given her a hammer, and now I was in pieces. She'd done this before; I should have seen it coming. *I'm such an idiot.*

Uber was running late. I sat down on one of the benches lining the driveway. It would've been better if I'd never met her. If she'd never kissed me, or so much as talked to me. I could never explain to my friends why I was drawn to her. Maybe there are people we are simply wired to love. Every time I thought of her, I thought about all the things we could've been if she'd only let us. What if I hadn't glimpsed into that bookstore that day in NY? If I hadn't been there at all? My soul had leapt after her, down the abyss of our stolen time and future *maybe*s.

As I let my eyes fall shut, it was as if I'd time traveled back into that night under the stars with her lips on mine. Sitting on this very same bench, two warm bodies clustered together. I took a deep breath, a ray of sunlight tickled my eyelids, coaxing them open, stealing me from my bittersweet dream.

I kept reliving the past, hoping for a different outcome. Knowing it wasn't going to happen, but being disappointed all the same.

Maybes was all I had, but at some point, I had to let them go. They were a fantasy, and I had to live in the real world where love wasn't always enough.

Some of the white paint was peeling off the bench, and I dug at it with my nail. Other than the paint, the bench was surprisingly sturdy. I wanted to remember it, the moment we'd shared, even if she didn't. One day I could think back at it and not feel pain. My leg was bouncing against the bench's edge. It jabbed the grass and kept hitting the wooden leg. The paint was falling on the grass like snow. I wished it had been snow, cold like my lover's heart, cool against my feverish skin.

A weird crinkling sounded from below me. I leaned down, knowing I was clinging to my last moments there, scrutinizing for a reason to stay—literally, apparently. My ride was pulling into the driveway. My ticket home.

All shits and giggles until my fingers actually caught on something.

A piece of plastic was taped to the back of the bench's leg. A ziplock bag. Inside the bag was a phone. I didn't pull it out, afraid to touch it as realization hit me like a truck out the dark. I felt it travel along my skin, turning into fear. I was holding someone's secret in my hands, and there was only one person who had secrets to keep. I released a shaky breath. How stupid could I be? I'd believed her when she'd promised me she had nothing to hide.

I pushed myself up. A jog turned into a run, a run into a tired, panting search. I marched through the house. Eloise and Jeanie were nowhere to be seen and I was half-angry about that. She'd been lying to them too.

Ophelia was on the patio. She rose abruptly, as if sensing what was to come. She met my gaze straight on, wide in confusion. Her mouth fell ajar.

I shoved the bag in her hand. "What is this? What did *you do*? Was everything a lie? All just a fucking game to you?"

Ophelia stared at me, still as a statue. She looked terrified. For the first time in all the time I'd known her, Ophelia Graham looked terrified.

"Say something!" I yelled, feeling the veins in my neck expand. "Tell me I am wrong! Tell me you didn't do what I think you did!"

"I can't—I ... how did you find this?" Her voice was small. Fragile, even.

"Does it matter? It was *you*; it was always *you*, and you lied to me when you told me you were—" My hands were red and hot. I knew my face was the same. Neck bulging with angry veins.

"I didn't! Don't you dare say I lied when you know nothing!"

I threw my hands in the air. "Then tell me! Ophelia, if you don't tell me the truth—the whole truth—right now, then I'm going to the cops, and I'm telling them everything I know. I'll give them this burner phone and then they can figure out whatever goddamn shit is on it that made you run."

"You think I murdered them," she said, voice breaking. "How could you think that? I told you I didn't do it! I thought I meant more to you than that." She was on the verge of tears.

"What else am I supposed to believe? You have been lying to me this whole time," I replied dryly. "I don't even know who you are." I kept my voice indifferent. It was unchallenging when looking at her stirred up way too many feelings for me to comprehend at the same time.

"I didn't do it! Please believe me!" she screamed at me.

"This is your last chance to convince me." I tensed. "Tell me the truth, otherwise I never want to see you again. I mean that."

She was crying uncontrollably. I waited for her to say something, but she just stood there like a small, scared girl. I waited for what felt like ages. Eventually I had to accept that it was over. She'd probably started to believe her own lies, and perhaps truth had simply become something too foreign for her.

My anger had vanished as quickly as it had come, and now there was just pain left in my body. Everything hurt and ached. Everything felt like it was breaking. From my toes to the last strand of hair, my nerves were screaming.

Ophelia tried to reach for me, fruitlessly. "Please. Please don't." She sighed through sobs. "I'm sorry, I'm so sorry. Please, you can't do this. Trust me. I swear I had a reason." Her eyelashes were dark and clumped together. I wanted to wipe her tears away. I hated myself for it. "I swear I didn't do anything, please believe me. You can't tell anyone. You know I care about you. I'm sorry for all of it. Please."

It had always been doomed to end one way or another. No one actually finds love when they're 15, right? I'd given her endless chances to explain, and every time, without fault, she'd chose no to. Everyone would know what she'd done.

"Goodbye, Ophelia."

No matter how much I wanted to comfort her, I couldn't. This couldn't go on any longer.

I turned, and I didn't look back.

Ophelia's distant sobs haunted me all the way home.

23 / Rafael

Father and daughter

"What is going on? What did you do?" demanded Adam accusingly.

Katie smiled cheekily, warm eyes flashing. "See, why do you assume I did something?" As if she hadn't called a meeting first thing in the morning. At Warren Repairs of all places.

"Because usually when something happens, you happen to be the culprit." Adam returned the smile, more taunting than genuine.

Katie rolled her eyes. "You're such an asshole."

Adam towered over her, thinking of a reply. He thought about it, paused, thought again. Nothing funny or snarky came to mind. He stared at her, blue eyes unmoving.

"Alright, why don't we move on now? Why are we here?" I asked. "Katie?"

She took a step back from blondie, turning. "Because of Mr. Graham. I saw him yesterday and he told me to bring everyone—that he'd already talked to you about everything."

Murmurs echoed. I hadn't told them about what had happened in the office the other day. Only Arabella might've guessed something, but even she didn't know the full story.

Mr. Graham had denied it, but I knew he was my stalker. Who else could it be? He had motive to murder. Yes, true, a couple of things in my theory were still blurry, but I would figure it out in no time. In his office, he'd been trying to confused me, throw me off the tracks. What if I was getting close to the truth? It was all an act to throw me off my game.

Now he was coming. This was exactly what I'd feared.

There was the sound of steps on gravel. "Good. You're here." Mr. Graham cleared his throat.

"What is going on?" I asked cautiously.

"Relax, kid, I'm not going to eat you." He sniffled. "I thought you should know the whole story before you do something you'll regret. You wanted to know about my daughter, didn't you?" Mr. Graham turned away, shifting his weight from one leg to the other. He was jumpy. Eyes glossy and red-rimmed.

"But that was weeks ago," said Katie.

"And what do you mean by *something you'll regret*? Detective *Scooby-Doo*, please explain." Adam pinned me.

I pressed my lips shut and shrugged.

"Kid, you've got heart. I like it. But next time, don't go through my stuff. Now, Ophelia—where do I start?"

I polished my glasses with the hem of my T-shirt. "Why do you want to cooperate all of a sudden? You've wanted nothing to do with this since the very beginning."

Was this some kind of a trap? He'd hated us for asking questions, now he was practically begging us to. What kind of a stalker was this man anyway?

Mr. Graham moved closer, visibly shaking. "So you'd leave my family alone. I'm sick of hearing about your new little theories every damn day—one day I'm some killer, the next you say I'm sending—"

"Okay, okay," I snapped. One wrong word from his foul mouth and I was done for.

"Does that mean we have a deal? I answer your nosey questions, and you leave me and my wife alone. Unbelievable that I once thought you might prove to be useful." He shook his head. All flattery and pretenses were off the table. For once, I think I was seeing the real Joseph Graham.

"Deal," answered Katie. "You and Ophelia had a fight before she went missing."

"Yes. Did Dave tell you that too?"

"Does it matter?"

He shrugged. "Not really, but would be nice to know."

She crossed her arms. "Well, we're not going to tell you."

"What did you fight about?" asked Arabella.

She'd been much quieter lately and I hoped it wasn't because of me. Maybe the pressure was getting to her. The stakes were higher for her. Her mom could've found out. She never argued or complained. She did what she was told. I should've been paying more attention to how this was affecting her.

"Nothing. Evil spirit must've bit her. It was as if she'd woken up on the wrong side of the bed." Mr. Graham moved around, kicking at air. "Then again it was unfair of me to expect her to understand what it's like to be a parent. Kids never realize when you're trying to protect them."

"Why was she upset with you?"

Joseph sighed, rubbing his eyes. "She thought the same thing that you do. Obviously, I told her that I haven't done a goddamn thing. Are you seeing the similarities? I've told you that a million times too." He scoffed.

Adam shifted. "But why would she think that at all? Did she see something? You must've given her a reason."

Joseph's mouth turned into a thin line. "No."

"You're hiding something," stated Lucy as a matter of fact. A blind cat could see he was lying.

Joseph Graham had wanted to talk to us. But now he was holding back. People accuse you of murder once, they might be wrong. People accuse you of murder twice, you must be guilty of *something.*

Mr. Graham stopped pacing. "Understand that there are certain things I can't tell you and you'll just have to take my word for it. Now, that doesn't mean I'm a bad person. I have a right to privacy, you know. You have to listen to me; I don't know what's going to happen when—"

"You invited us here. You said you were going to answer the questions. Now you go on about *privacy?*" Lucy pointed at him with a nail, one hand on her hip.

"You can ask whatever you want, but there are some answers I cannot give. Sorry, kids, it's the way it has to be."

"Yeah, sure, whatever." Lucy's chest deflated. She whispered something to Zack.

"That day you and Ophelia argued, she took something with her. What was it?" I asked.

"Again—how do you know that? It was my phone. My old phone. She had it in her hand while we talked and when she walked out, she was still holding it. That's all. See? Nothing criminal here." His eye was tweaking and he held a hand to his chest like an honest man. Except he wasn't one.

"I don't believe you."

"Then don't."

I needed to try a different approach. "You told me you invited us to dinner because you knew we were investigating." The others stared at me.

He exhaled slowly. "It's stupid. I thought since you might've known my daughter, that maybe you knew something. I thought we could help each other out. I told you I'm on your side, but then you went through my things anyway, so you'll excuse me if I have my doubts about trusting you."

Fair enough, I supposed. "Why won't you tell us why Ophelia was accusing you?"

"Nothin' to tell."

"And your wife?" prompted Katie.

"What about her?" His eyes glittered. His smile was smug, and I wanted to punch it right off his face. He wasn't even going to try and hide it. Bet he wouldn't even deny it.

"Ask him. He knows. Ask him about her," I told Katie.

It took her a moment to understand. She gasped. "Mr. Graham? You know about your wife's affair, don't you?"

"Do I? Doesn't ring a bell."

"You've always known."

He sighed. "Yes. Yes, I have."

"But how could you—why—"

"It doesn't matter. It's over now." Mr. Graham's face relaxed.

Katie's eyes were about to bulge out of their sockets. "Why didn't you do something? Don't you care?"

"You don't get it, kid."

"Don't call me a kid! And don't tell me that I don't understand something when you haven't explained it to me!"

"She's my wife." Mr. Graham's voice was soft, tender.

Love really was blind.

"Unbelievable," muttered Katie.

"She doesn't even know that you know. This family is confusing," said Adam.

He sniffled again. "Yeah, well, I like it that way."

Arabella handed Joseph a napkin. "Did you ever tell Ophelia?"

"Bless you," he thanked, blowing his nose. "No. She never suspected a thing."

Of course there was the possibility that, after all, she might've known. Dead people must know all kinds of secrets. Mr. Graham continued to remind us that he expected us to never ever (under no circumstance) talk to him again. Which we had to agree to.

After the questioning we set our steps back to the front of the shop where we'd left our bikes. The doors were open and Dave was already stepping outside to say hello.

"Were you looking for me?" he asked.

"No, not today." Adam smiled. The tired version of a smile.

"Everything okay?" He uncapped a water bottle, but didn't drink straight away.

"Yes, everything's good."

"Did Lucas tell you that he's comin' home?" Mr. Warren raised the bottle to his lips.

"Yeah, he called yesterday," confirmed Z.

Mr. Warren nodded. "So, who were you looking for?"

"Joseph Graham. We already talked to him," I replied. I was tired too. We all wanted to get out of there already.

"About Ophelia?"

"Yes. About the fight you told us about."

Mr. Warren nodded. "Right. Did you ask him where he was that night?" Seeing our faces, he scratched his head. "I didn't tell you? Ophelia asked him that. Joey was out and about when Rogers went missing. That's what she asked him."

"Fuck," I swore, and suddenly we were all running back to where we'd come from. Around the corner, behind the building. To the garage doors.

But it was too late, Mr. Graham was gone.

24 / Lucas
Bittersweet

I drifted off as soon as my back hit the soft blue fabric of the bus seat. Staying awake meant thinking about Ophelia, and I was sick of letting her consume me. Every second I wasn't keeping myself occupied, my mind wandered to her, questioning everything. Most of all, I hated how I'd left things. Not knowing the full story. The lies, the secrets, and the twisting of things polluted every memory I had of her and every moment I'd spent with her. I no longer knew if any of it had been real. Ever.

Since I slept all day, I couldn't even close my eyes now, which meant that my rapid mind was constantly drifting around aimlessly from subject to subject, and face to face, and all I could do was keep it from the one that caused me most pain.

I watched the familiar dusty roads slip into view, the bushy and sandy terrain forming before my eyes. I'd missed home, the smell of it. I'd missed all constant and familiar. I'd missed my friends, my dad. Missed their voices and teasing jokes. For once, my life didn't feel like it was cursed, because I knew everything was as it should be and where it should be and it would all be all right if I would only let it fall back into its normal rhythm. It was bittersweet accepting that nothing was ever going to change, knowing the rest of your life before living it. But at least there would be no more ugly surprises.

The forest neared. Behind it was a shadow of the sea. No. Not the sea. The lake. I'd nearly forgot it. Old memories flashed before my eyes, their echoes loud enough to force my eyes shut just to not hear them.

I wished that kiss had never happened.

As I began to relax a little more, I felt the familiar buzz of my phone in my pocket.

RAFAEL: @LUCAS When do you get here?????

                                          Haha almost there, give me a minute

RAFAEL: We miss you!!

                                                           I know. I miss u too

ZACK: The bromance is bromancing

ADAM: They are in love <3

                                        We are getting married in June

ADAM: Whose best man am I going to be?

RAFAEL: Adam you'll be serving cocktails at the door

ADAM: Only if I get to mix my own drinks

    That's dangerous. I think we should put him on toilet cleaning duty instead

25 / Rafael

What keeps a person from shattering?

Zack dug the heel of his shoe into dry dirt. The burning cigarette in his mouth was almost out. He sighed, checking his phone.

We didn't need to say it out loud to know that we were all missing Lucas. We weren't complete without him. But today, finally, he was coming back. Minutes couldn't tick by quickly enough. Time dragged on and on.

My forehead prickled with tiny pearls of sweat, some of them racing down my neck. Sunlight caressed the asphalt. Melting. The sky was spotless. Not a cloud in sight. I hid a yawn, playing it off as a cough.

I worried Lucas was upset with us for asking him to spy on Ophelia, but then I figured that maybe he'd ended up in a ditch of old lingering feelings. If that was the case, I had no idea how to go about it. Gently, because he might be hurt and vulnerable? Or firmly, because he might need a steady hand to guide him? I was unsure, but Lucy wasn't. She was a predator waiting for her moment to strike. Lucas had intel, and Lucy was going to viciously bombard him until she got her answers. It unsettled me seeing her so composed. But I had to hand it to her, her dedication was inspiring.

Thick dust swept into air as the bus squeaked to a slow stop. The doors opened and it didn't take long before my friend's tall frame came into view. Lucas tossed his bag down, a wide grin stretching over his face. Z, Adam, and I ran, hugging and tackling him aggressively.

"I really missed you guys," said Lucas, familiar gray eyes taking in all our faces. A spark of curiosity traveled across him, seeing Lucy and Bells.

Z nudged Lucas. "Ah, man, you look terrible. Can't wait to hear all about your little adventure." The cigarette was gone, disposed of. He still smelled like smoke, rosemary, and something sweet.

"Don't be shy now, spill the beans," urged Lucy.

Lucas looked away. "It's a long story." He cleared his throat, thinking. "Tell you what, why don't you guys go ahead? We can meet up at the lake in an hour. I should go home and change. Grab a bite. Dad's been freaking out, and I should sort it out." He smiled weakly.

"All right. Don't leave us waiting." I pat his arm, attempting to go for the gentle approach.

"I won't," he replied, his lips quivering only slightly.

I could pretend for Lucas' sake that everything was fine and there was nothing to worry about, but that would've been a lie. Beautiful lies mask ugly truths, but eventually the beauty will peel off like cracked paint. I wasn't good at all that emotional stuff. I could barely handle my own.

I tipped my head, watching Adam fall behind as we left the bus stop. He reached out a slender finger to poke Katie in the ribs.

"I saw you blush. Don't tell me you're crushing on my best friend," I heard him tease.

"I am not."

"Well, then you like me, because you're still blushing." Adam poked her again. He was grinning from ear to ear. I had to hold back a snicker. How guilty I felt being thankful for him never changing. Always remaining the same, like a pillar I was leaning on.

"What's there to like about you? And get your sticky fingers away from me, you stupid." Katie sped up, storming past me with hands swinging at her sides and her face turning five different shades of red.

Adam pat his mop of a hair, whistling a soft tune.

Lucas slumped on the ground. "I found something. I, uh, I'm pretty sure it's something important." He bit the inside of his cheek.

He held up a small, wrinkled plastic bag. His face morphed into disgust he wasn't doing too good of a job at hiding. He tossed the bag towards me. I hesitated before picking it up.

"What is that?" asked Zack with no response from anyone.

Adam and Lucy were puzzling alongside him, but Arabella and Katie seemed to have drawn the same shocking conclusion I had, rendering the three of us speechless.

"Is that—" I started to ask, but the words got stuck on my tongue and withered away. I already had my answer. I knew it in the marrow of my bones, *this* was the reason.

"Yes. A burner phone. Ophelia's big and scary secret," explained Lucas bitterly.

"Did you turn it on?" I touched the cold screen through the thin plastic. The buttons. There could even be fingerprints there!

Lucas huffed. "She hid it. I only found it by accident. It was a coincidence I stumbled upon it at all. I haven't touched it, and to be honest, I don't care what's on there. She told me she wasn't involved, and then I found this. Anyway, I guess you can have it. I asked her about it, but she didn't tell me anything. Sorry, I wish I could've been more helpful." His eyes fixated on the grass he was bunching up between his fingers.

"Rafe, what are you waiting for?" spoke Lucy, "turn it on!"

"What? No! We can't. We'll get fingerprints all over it." Now that wouldn't be good.

"Then use gloves," she hissed back. "Who knows what she used it for? It might be, like, incriminating."

Lucas' eyebrows creased. How many times was Ophelia allowed to hurt my friend? To me, love was like a stone in a shoe—annoying, distracting, and more painful than you'd think. Obviously, Lucas did not share the sentiment. If he did, he might've saved himself from heartbreak.

"Maybe she had an accomplice and they used burners to communicate," proposed Katie. If this was hard for her, she didn't let it show.

"Ooo, that's a good one!" agreed Lucy happily.

"Or maybe she just stole the goddamn thing, and it's not even hers." Zack shrugged. "Mr. Graham's old phone, remember?"

"You've got a point," I muttered. "But then she would've had to have a good reason to take it and hide it. But why would she steal evidence intentionally unless she herself was also connected to the disappearances? We know she didn't have anything in common with Martinez or Rogers."

I couldn't exactly picture Ophelia accidentally slipping it into her pocket. Surely, she couldn't mistake it for her own. Mr. Graham had said it was his, and she'd taken it accidentally. But why keep it? Why hide it?

Katie gasped, hand flying to her mouth. My eyes shot to hers, realizing what she'd pieced together before me.

"Of course, yes. How could I not see it?" I mouthed to myself in one breath. "We have to go." I stuffed the burner into my pocket. I was up and moving while the others were still trying to catch up.

"What do you mean? What's happening?" Lucas searched our faces like a lost puppy. There was so much he still didn't know.

"Tell you on the way," I yelled over my shoulder.

Mr. Graham had a habit of dodging us and then showing up when it was convenient for him. I didn't have time to chase him around the town, this needed to be addressed now. (No, I hadn't forgot my promise to leave him alone).

We were heaving and choking on saliva by the time we arrived at the workshop. We used Lucas' keys to get in through the back door. Mr. Graham was alone, working. He didn't bat an eye when we stormed in.

"I take it you kids aren't here to help me change these tires?" He gestured with his hand. Though he smiled, his eyes betrayed him by constantly flicking towards the door. Who or what he was hoping to see I could not tell. "I thought we had a deal."

"No," I said sternly, "you left something out of your story yesterday. We're here to clear it up. The deal was that you tell us everything." I gave a stiff smile, and his eyes narrowed in reply.

"When you fought with Ophelia, she took something from you. A burner phone, and we happen to have it. She wasn't *just* upset. No, she was angry, wasn't she? Angry with you. Protecting you. And the other day at the parking lot, you got a call. I didn't think much of it then, but it was another burner, wasn't it? You have a new one. You were almost surprised when it rang, and then you turned away, so we wouldn't see or hear you talking."

Mr. Graham heaved a breath, almost laughing out right. His nostrils flared; face still puffy. "Why would I—"

"Lie? You tell us. And, I'm sorry, are we bothering you? You look a little pale. Are you waiting for someone? Your accomplice, perhaps? We'd be happy to meet with them too."

Adam coughed like I'd said something outrageous.

Joseph crossed his arms. I noticed his nails were dirty and a little blue. "You done? Because I got work to do and very little time to do it."

"Funny," said Katie. "I don't believe anything you say."

I wanted to hug her for being snarky. Mr. Graham needed an attitude adjustment. I was happy to provide one.

"*God*, I am sick of this! You want to know? You really want to fucking know? Rogers was buying pills. There you have it. He was in pain and the doctors wouldn't give him anything, so I got him some medicine. Just once or twice." Joseph turned his back on us. "Sorry to disappoint again, but I'm not in the habit of murdering people, especially my old friends. And what do I have to fear? You won't go to the police; you're scared shitless yourselves. What would your pa say, Rafael? Who knows, I might even tell him about you going through my office, like the little thief you are. How many times do we have to have this conversation? I haven't hurt anyone. I'm tired of trying to convince you. Just stay away from me."

What would your father say?

I swallowed.

He was right, he could turn this against us. I had everything I needed. I just had to play my cards right, or else. "You should be afraid, Mr. Graham. Your daughter hid this for you, I'm sure of it. I'll make sure you get what you deserve. Ophelia knew you weren't home the night Link Martinez died. I don't know yet what you did, but I will. Soon. And when I do, I'll be back."

He couldn't have been selling pills then, seeing as Rogers was already gone.

Maybe those same pills killed him.

He bobbed his head. "Go ahead, and try. You think the police are going to care about anything you have to say? It's your word against mine. How do I know you aren't trying to frame me?" He nodded towards the door. "Go. Now. Leave my family alone. If I ever see you come near me again, I'll have a word with all your parents. How does that sound? Fun enough?"

I had all the evidence I needed. And if he could lie, I could lie too. He couldn't prove I was at his house, but I had the phone and I had the threat messages and I knew he wasn't home that night and I knew his motive. I knew *enough*. Ophelia was protecting him. He wasn't getting away with it, not ever again. Now I just had to put together a plan for the police. Tomorrow the footage at the station would be wiped, and I'd make Joseph Graham's word against mine mean nothing. I had six people backing me up. He had no one.

I didn't notice how angry I was until my teeth hurt from gritting. I should've been too tired to be angry, but I'd let Joseph Graham get under my skin. We left and I let myself get lost in thought.

Pills. Pills. What kind of pills?

We were barely down the road, when we heard the anguished scream. I hardly had time to look at my friends before we all bolted back to where we'd come from, like last time. The door wide open.

I was the third inside.

Dark crimson blood was making its way towards us, a whole river of red. I followed the trail to Mr. Graham, face down on the ground. It was his blood, coming from his slashed-open head.

I stepped back, pulling Zack by his sleeve with me. Mr. Graham's eyes were strange and lifeless. They were still open. Blood was oozing from the wound on his temple, smeared on his clothes and the floor. Red streaks in a funky pattern. It was dripping from the car door next to him, meaning he must've hit his head. I stood paralyzed, letting the warm iron smell devour me and wrap me in another nightmare. The scene implied he'd been dead for weeks, but it had only been a minute since we'd spoken to him.

Lucy screamed at the sight, tears streaming down her waxy face, turning splotchy with pink. Adam was puking outside, the sound of him heaving strangely echo-y. I stared in horror at the blood reflecting my face, and at the man kneeling before the corpse. It had taken me a moment to register him, so quiet and still.

"Dad, was that you who screamed?" asked Lucas, rushing towards Dave and helping him up onto wobbly legs.

Mr. Warren didn't lift his eyes from the corpse. "I came in, and I thought he'd fainted or got hurt. I didn't see the blood. How is this possible?" He inspected his own hands, tainted with red.

"Oh my god, we have to call the police." Lucy couldn't control her tears, even as Zack wrapped her in his arms and led her outside under the sun, both shaking. He kept her from looking back.

"What happened?" I asked, holding onto all the steadiness I had in me.

"I don't … I didn't see anything." Mr. Warren was still watching the blood slither across concrete, glossy, and fresh.

"Come on Dad, we have to get out of here."

My eyes were clued to the body. It was sickening. I'd been so sure that I was right. For a moment it had been over. I'd had him and I'd been angry but it had been the satisfying kind of anger. I'd had him.

Did he kill himself?

It looked like a murder scene. Everything smelled like blood.

"Rafe?" Arabella placed a hand on my shoulder and I flinched at her touch.

"Sorry." I met her soft eyes. "Are you okay?" I asked, holding onto her hand, needing to feel her warmth.

She nodded. "Come." She squeezed my hand as we walked out, but I couldn't keep myself from looking over my shoulder one last time at the carnage.

I'd got everything wrong. I was wrong. Always wrong. How could I protect everyone if I had no idea who I was supposed to be protecting them from?

"This can't be happening," Lucy said through sniffs. Her mascara-running face had found comfort in the nook of Zack's rigid shoulder. She pressed herself closer to him, hands around his neck.

Arabella wrapped her arms around herself. There was no one to comfort her. I let my head slump, tugging her closer. There was nothing strong or brave about me. I was crumbling, legs shaking, and on the verge of panic. She held onto my shirt, crying silently. For a short while, I could pretend to be someone I was not. For her.

Adam wiped his mouth. "I'm done, you hear me? Done. Somebody is *dead* because of us." His eyes jumped to Mr. Warren, but he was harmless. He wasn't even listening, instead focused at his scarlet hands.

Lucy broke into louder sobs. "There was so much blood, oh my God. Did you see his head?"

Arabella's hold on me tightened, swallowing salty tears. I didn't know how to comfort her. How to comfort any of them.

Katie rubbed her eyes, her whole face red. She sniffled, tucking hair behind her ears.

He was gone. Skull cracked open. The smell of fresh blood was crisp in my memory, gooey and dark against the gray stone floor.

My phone buzzed.

Now you know just how dirty I can play.

26 / Lucas

The great war of head and heart

It was easier to slip back into my old shoes (metaphor for my life) than I'd thought. Time away from home felt like a hazy dream. I could pretend it never happened at all.

But, of course, I was never good at pretending.

Rafe had the burner now and he would know what to do with it. I didn't want to look at it or touch it or even think about it. It would only make me feel worse than I already did. It was best to leave it up to someone else to decide what happened to Ophelia. The whole thing was a mess. Her covering for her father, only for Mr. Graham to just *die*. I overheard an officer telling another that they found a small amount of fertilizer in his system, which probably caused him to be disoriented and lose his balance. He *fell*.

But when Rafe walked over to them and asked why a grown man would eat fertilizer, they were stunned.

The police had asked so many questions. I'd thought the end would never come. I should've said something about Ophelia then, but the timing had seemed way off. To be completely frank, I'd been too busy fighting the bloody imagine in my head to even think about her. I'd known Mr. Graham my whole life, and now he was gone. Ophelia's dad. Three days passed, yet somehow, I was still stuck in that moment of us seeing his body. Hearing my dad scream. The questions. Endless, endless questions. Three days, and I still hadn't fully realized I'd never see that man again. Just some hollow, soulless vessel rotting in the ground. Soon a bile of bones and nothing more. Morbid, but we all end that way, don't we? The police let us go but warned us to be careful. Three days, and they still hadn't released a statement.

Dad wasn't over his initial shock, so I tried to stay close by in case he needed me.

The eggs were already sizzling on the pan when I walked into the kitchen. I grabbed a slice of bread and a butter knife.

"Dad? You okay?"

"I'm fine, don't worry about me," he replied, placing strips of bacon on the hot pan. "We'll talk about something else."

He always gave me the same answer. He couldn't afford to fall apart, not even to mourn his closest friend. Warren Repairs was his entire world and it needed him. It always needed him, and he always gave it his everything. The problem was that he wanted me to do the same. If being away from home had helped me realize one thing, it was that I didn't want to stay stuck. I wasn't a tree with roots. I had college to go to.

I put the knife down and picked up slices of ham and cheese instead. "Dad, have you thought about what I said before? This might be the best opportunity I'm going to get. I'd be stupid not to take it, right?"

"Lucas, this isn't what I meant. We've discussed this topic, and I thought we agreed that you would stay close by. Now, more than ever, you must understand." His voice was strained, eyes downcast. His jaw and cheeks had become sharper. He'd lost some weight while I'd been gone, not to mention the gray creeping into his hair.

"I get it. I do." My voice softened. "I don't want to let you down." I sighed. "Dad, I'm happy to help here and there, but I cannot sacrifice myself for this. It's my choice. It's unfair of you to try and take it from me. The city can offer me so many experiences and the school looks great." It was as if he wasn't listening at all. We'd talked about this a million times.

I was happy to be home again but I never planned to stay there forever.

Dad placed his hands on the counter as if he'd collapse without the extra support. For a moment I worried he actually might. "You can have a degree whenever you want in the future, there will always be time. But what about all the work we've put into building this business up? My life's work. Now, as I said, we're done with this topic. This isn't the time, the town's mourning. The funeral's on Sunday, straighten out your suit."

I bit into my sandwich. I didn't want to fight with him. He was my dad, I loved him. For years we'd worked side by side, and for years we'd discussed the future. *My* future. Coward or not, for this I would fight, because I was done letting him plan my life for me. "I'm sorry, it's already decided. I'm going. You cannot make this decision for me. I'll be there for you, and I hope eventually you'll accept my choices too." With everything going on in Whitewood, who would want to stay anyway?

There was deep hurt in his eyes. I felt sorry for him, but I also had to think about the little boy who'd missed out on birthdays and playdates because he had to help his daddy with the work. And I had to think about the man who I wanted to become. Life could end at any moment. Better go after my dreams while I still had time. There were people who didn't.

The sea was a distant noise, familiar waves crashing against each other. The beach wasn't far. I could just make it out down the road. I kept walking the path towards it, imagining my toes in the cold water, the curling sea foam, and the sticky sand. I would stay there until day turned into night if I could. Until my muscles would hurt from swimming. Until I no longer feared going home to face my terribly disappointed father. Two seagulls soared past me. I listened to their shrieking mixed with the sound of my footsteps.

They weren't just my footsteps. They were someone else's too.

I stopped, bracing myself for the world to be aflame.

"What are you doing here? I thought you said nothing would ever make you come home."

Ophelia tilted her head. "*Someone* did." Her eyes were red, puffy. They became shiny as she spoke.

I groaned. "What do you want? I'm done fighting, just leave me alone. I don't want to see you, and this really isn't the time." But then I stopped and realized she might've meant her father not me. "Ophelia, why are you here?" I asked cautiously. I wasn't sure if she knew, since no one would've known to tell her. She might've read about it.

She took a shy step closer. "I'm sorry. I don't want to fight either. Is it true that my father's dead? I saw it on the news."

A stone dropped in my stomach. It wasn't fair. She'd come all this way because her dad was dead. I hadn't even thought to call her, she had to find out on her own. "I was there. I saw him. His head was all messed up." I coughed. "I'm so sorry. It was horrible."

Slow, fat tears streamed down her cheeks, but when she spoke, her voice was clear and crisp. "Who did it? Do they know?"

I wrapped her in a hug, mumbling into her hair. "The police are still searching, but don't worry, they'll find them." Although they hadn't told us a thing yet.

"This really does change everything."

But in my mind, I was thinking, *you lied to me.* What did this change?

Hey everyone! I have some interesting news to share. Meet at my place. It's kinda important.

ZACK: About what?

Uh hard to explain over text

KATIE: Right now? Is it an emergency?

ADAM: Or maybe you just miss us and it's not (please)

Okay no. It's about u know who, she's here

KATIE: Oh.

ADAM: Voldemort? Who?

ZACK: For fuck's sake

RAFAEL: Sorry, I didn't get the notifications. Are you talking about Ophelia? How much have you told her and why is she here? How is this happening?

You can ask her yourself. So, can everyone make it? **@LUCY @ARABELLA** ?

ARABELLA: Yes, I'm coming :)

LUCY: Me too. This is crazyy omg

27 / Rafael

When there's a storm, don't let go

My every nerve was rattling, like vines stretching away and pulling me in every direction possible. I knew my father finding out about the case was inevitable, but I had to at least try to prolong it. Luckily or not, his hands were full, allowing me to blend into the background. I'd planned to talk to him, but the moment I'd seen that butchered body I'd known I couldn't. In a way, Mr. Graham's death was my fault. If I'd told the police, they'd lock us in a room until we'd have no choice but to tell them everything, including how we'd acquired most of our information. My father was starting to suspect me, but he was far too busy to give it much thought. Still, I promised myself I would do whatever I had to in order to protect my friends. Even take all the blame if it came to it.

After today I might have to.

Taking a deep breath, I caught a whiff of coming rain in the wind that told me a storm was brewing. I was wearing jeans instead of shorts, a hoodie covering the top of my head. My eyes had looked dull in the mirror before. Void and tired, so much that I didn't even feel frightened anymore. I caught a glimpse of a ghost in them. He was convulsing with laughter, waving at me from beyond the grave. Who knows, maybe he was warming a spot for me in hell.

I knocked on Lucas' door, searching the sky for raindrops while I waited for him. There's something freeing about smelling rain and knowing the sky is about to weep. The door creaked open. Ophelia Graham was gawping back at me in flesh and blood. It was a jarring sight and I sucked in a breath.

"Hi, Rafael," said Ophelia.

I tried to say *hey*, but it came out more like *he-yehmm*. Heavy clouds vanished from my thoughts, and I focused on following her. Judging from her blotchy face, someone had told her about her dad.

She rushed ahead while I fell back, listening in on some secret conversation between Katie and Adam in the depths of the kitchen. They didn't see me, and I only lingered for a moment, too embarrassed to steal more of their privacy.

"Why do you hate me? You always have," asked Katie. The kitchen door was barely open but her voice carried without effort. It sounded like they were having another fight.

Adam produced a strangled laugh. "Hate you? *Hate you*? And what if I did?" He drew a sharp breath. "Katie, you could do so much better than this, and you know it. I mean, take a long, hard look at me. You know it's true. This is the rest of my life. You don't belong here, and I'm not going to trap you here with me. If me hating you is what it takes to make you realize that you deserve better, then so be it. I will continue to hate you because I can't have you." Adam paused. Whatever passed between them, I couldn't hear.

"Stop talking like you don't matter! What about what I want?"

I strode after Ophelia, not wanting to intrude anymore—for once not giving into the temptation of curiosity. Their words weren't meant for my ears.

We reached the living room.

"Rafe, isn't this exciting? We can finally question Ophelia," said Arabella, her voice filling the quiet.

"Uh … yeah." I sat down next to her; sure my legs would crumble beneath me otherwise. It wasn't the cold that had got under my skin, but a raging storm yanking at my seams. As if my body sensed something. I couldn't remember the last time I'd slept well, or been happy, or felt entirely safe. Every day I realized something about myself—some new part—that I hated. Was I a bad friend, or a bad person entirely? Mr. Graham's death (read: murder) was a tragedy, but the fact that I still had no idea who was stalking me was equally tragic. I'd hoped to solve the mystery quickly so my friends would never have to know about it. Now enough time had passed that I was just ashamed to tell them.

Ophelia sat on the couch between Lucas and Lucy. Zack was leaning against the wall. Everyone seemed unnerved, but while they could keep it hidden, my leg wouldn't stop bouncing, announcing my anxiety to the world. The room was dead quiet. I wrapped a hand around my wrist. A quick squeeze to ground me.

The kitchen door opened, and Adam and Katie walked out. Katie had her arms crossed as she went straight to the other side of the room. She took a cautious peek at Ophelia without the latter noticing. Adam stood next to Zack.

"So," I started, "you've been in New York this whole time, hm?" *Bounce, bounce.*

"Not the whole time," Ophelia replied. "For a while I moved around a lot, then decided to settle somewhere and got a job in New York. I made some friends who helped me. Good people who saw me struggling." She smiled weakly.

She didn't want to be there. She didn't want to tell us anything. Her eyes kept skipping back to Lucas or towards the door. What was she looking for? *Bounce, bounce.* Was she on our side or not? *Bounce.*

Arabella slid her hand towards me and rested it gently on my knee which relaxed instantly. She pulled her hand back, but my leg was like foam remembering her warmth and the feel of her hand. I held onto it until I calmed. Arabella and I were like two sides of the same coin. She was the light to my darkness. When I felt like a storm cloud, she was there to dance in the rain. And sometimes, she felt like a burning flame on cold skin. It was nothing I could make sense of, everything my head was telling me to stay away from. All I knew was that I was very lucky to have her by my side through everything.

"You had that phone with you, why did you take it? And Lucas told us a bit about these rich friends of yours, how much do they know?"

She glared at me. It was like throwing spikes at me or shooting lasers with her eyeballs. "Yes, we're close. They don't know about my past, if that's what you're asking. They don't need to, and I don't want them to."

Katie snorted. Ophelia turned briefly towards her old best friend. It was clear they were both hurting but curious about one another.

"And the first question?" I asked.

Silence and more glaring. How original.

Adam crumbled. "Don't you think you've been enough trouble already? Fess up." He pushed his hair back, arching against the wall. He had an easygoing smile on his face as if the conversation with Katie had never happened.

"I couldn't stay. It was all too much."

"Bullshit," muttered Katie.

"Excuse me?"

"You heard me," she spit back. "No one told you to go, did they? You made a choice, now own up to it and stop with the poor excuses." Katie's hand twitched, fury in her eyes.

"My father is dead."

"Yes, and we're really sorry we—" I started to apologize.

"My father is dead, and I'm afraid I've made a horrible mistake. I realize it was stupid of me. So stupid. But I was a kid, I didn't know any better." A pause while fat tears made their way down Ophelia's cheeks. "You want to know? Fine. I found that phone hidden in his clothes. I'd never seen it before. People had just died, and I thought—I thought he did it. That he killed them. When that man, Martinez whatever, died, he came home with his lip all beat up. He wouldn't tell me where he'd been. He stood outside for an hour, smoking. Wouldn't let me talk to him.

"He is—I mean was, my dad. What was I supposed to do? I couldn't turn him in. I tried; I swear I tried so hard! I couldn't do it. He was a great dad, and I thought that it was an accident, you know? Some misunderstanding."

"Both of them?" asked Zack.

Ophelia shrugged, wiping tears away. "I wanted to talk to him one last time. I wanted him to explain and tell me I've got it all wrong. We fought. I told him I'd turn him in, even though I knew I could never bring myself to do it. I was scared and confused. I just left. It was easier to leave, forget everything. So, when I had the opportunity, I did."

"And you took the evidence with you?" Adam asked, anger prickling his voice. His features were taking on a sharper shape, more angled. Icy eyes, square jaw, and wide shoulders. Even his platinum hair gave the impression of a stingray.

Ophelia sniffled. "He was my dad. But if someone really did kill him, then it means he was innocent all along, right? Which means I was wrong. He didn't do it." She turned to me, hopeful. Freckles stark against her light skin.

"I don't know," I admitted. "Did you look on the phone?"

Ophelia nodded. "Yeah. It had, like, a bunch of phone numbers. Nothing else. Just phone numbers. He was keeping secrets."

"Drugs," said Zack.

"What?" I asked.

"He was a dealer, obviously." He rolled his eyes.

"Come to think of it, remember when we saw him being all weird and suspicious that one night? And we saw Jeremiah right afterwards?" said Adam.

"He *did* tell us he sold pills to Sheldon. The man wasn't exactly hiding it," agreed Zack.

Jeremiah had been twitchy—I'd thought he was just drunk. And the random hidden stash of paper bags? It would all explain why he was reluctant to tell us certain things. The phone calls, the late nights away from home he refused to explain. Yeah, it added up.

One mystery solved, I supposed.

"And the call he got in the parking lot," said Adam. Not an accomplice, but a *client*.

Zack *tsk*'d. "Yeah, drug dealer."

"What? Is that why he was killed?" asked Ophelia, her voice thin and full of tremor. She pulled her legs up, wrapping her arms around the knees like a little girl.

"Possibly." *But not likely* I wanted to add. If I hadn't got so many threats recently, I might've believed it too.

"But why now? Who had reason to murder him?" asked Katie.

Silence, until Lucy spoke. "You were right, Rafe, we should give everything to the police. In fact, we should have done that a while ago. There's nothing left for us to do. Besides, it's too dangerous. None of us signed up for all this crap. The police have better equipment and skills. This is their job. They won't hurt us if we cooperate and we can all agree on a story so none of us would have to go in blind or say something they shouldn't." She wet her lips while speaking, eyebrows drawing closer and closer.

Zack kissed her cheek which meant he agreed.

Next to me, Arabella smiled, but there was nothing happy about it. I didn't need to hear her say it, I knew she didn't want this to be over. She wanted the truth as much as I did, if not more. I wanted to give it to her. I was letting her down. Quit the game, lose the prize. It wasn't only about the truth anymore, or Arabella. It was personal. My safety was gone, my peace was gone. I wasn't me anymore. I had to find the person behind it all. The question was, if I was willing to trust the police, or trust myself one last time?

The mood was sour as we walked towards the station. The clouds were still hanging above us, being all ominous, but my mind wasn't on them anymore. Ophelia was quiet. It was difficult for her, but I supposed there was some relief in knowing your father wasn't a murderer. Funky that in this case being a drug dealer was the better option. Either way, he was still dead, and Ophelia still had to tell the story exactly how she'd told it to us. It would change the whole narrative, forcing the police to admit that there was a killer out there who'd murdered more than once. It could tie well into our story. We'd leave out the illegal parts and be fine. It would be over and I might finally be able to sleep soundly.

Katie and Adam were pouting too. A common interest for secrets had united them, and I think they were infuriated to be giving up.

Giving up—the thing none of us were saying but all of us were thinking. Once the police knew, they wouldn't allow us to be involved anymore. Yes, we didn't want the mess and the danger and the problems, but we still liked to hang out together and solve old mysteries. After everything, maybe we could still be friends. Surprising how much I'd grown to like my new friends. I figured I'd miss even Lucy.

My stomach was in knots about what to say and what to keep to myself. I'd have to try and stay strong no matter how hard they'd interrogate me. I'd stick to my story, and the others would do the same. Some truths are better left as secrets.

A pine forest ran along the road, treetops rattling with wind. We walked in silence, and my fist held tight to the burner phone in my pocket. It would back up all our stories. Katie had Martinez's journal. The only thing we could not share were the pictures we'd taken in the archives.

Chills ran down my arms. It was knowing I'd be ending something I didn't want to end. Letting down people I didn't want to let down.

A car sped by, forcing us into a smaller bundle, stirring up dust from the road. Katie kept as far away from Ophelia as she could.

Suddenly, the car was turned around, picking up speed, and then charging at us again with such force that my foot twisted and I stumbled back.

"Hey!" yelled Zack, "watch where you're fucking going, asshole!" He waved his arms and yelled at the driver.

The car windows were tinted, making it difficult to see any faces. The vehicle was old, black paint coated with dust, and rusting along the bottom. It didn't have a license plate.

Adam opened his mouth, but we never got to hear a word from him. The car drove straight at us. Lucy screamed.

My legs gave in and my face hit dirt. I felt my knees bruise, but there wasn't any time to worry about that. We scrambled up the other side of the ditch we'd landed in, running into the dark, gloomy woods. I'd never ran that fast in my entire life. Because I knew they'd come for me.

They'd warned me.

The wind was blowing in my face, pine needles crunching under my feet. I couldn't hear anything besides my own heavy breathing, not even my sprinting heart. I had to keep swallowing to keep my ears from becoming blocked, but there was nothing to swallow. My throat was scratchy and dry, horror flowing through my veins. Pure fear not like anything I'd ever felt before. I wanted to tell everyone to stick together, to not be separated, yet I couldn't speak. I watched as my friends divided. Adam followed Zack to the right, into thicker woods, more shadows. Lucy and Arabella went straight ahead. Lucy peeped over her shoulder towards Zack, but it was already too late to go with him. Katie, Ophelia, and Lucas went left, disappearing behind trees, only flashes of red hair here and there. They changed their course so suddenly, I almost tripped over them. I couldn't follow them. Too many people would've been too big of a target, I realized. I went right instead, pushing a little harder to catch up with Adam and Zack.

I didn't look back to see if anyone was behind us.

I tasted iron, and suddenly there was a warm, rising sensation at the back of my throat. I swallowed it, a weak cry erupting from me. We tucked behind some trees, lying low. I couldn't see my surroundings without moving too much, so I stayed down. I forced myself not to make a sound, almost blacking out, only holding onto my conscience by closing my eyes and taking slow, deep breaths.

The forest was quiet.

They'd come for me. They were going to kill me. We were going to die. *I don't want to die.*

I don't know how long I stayed like that. It felt like hours. I was shivering, covered in cold sweat, afraid to even wave mosquitos away. How much longer? I thought of my father. What his face would be like when he got the call that eight kids had been murdered in the woods, one being his own.

Adam met my eyes, too scared himself to comfort me, but strong enough to still keep me going. If only I was more like him, we wouldn't even be in this situation.

A piercing blast went through the howling air. I pressed myself tightly against the spongy ground while Adam held back tears next to me. It was a gunshot. I wanted to cry and laugh at once. Of course they had a gun. A part of me hoped they were a good shooter—our deaths would be quick. When I was younger, I'd thought about how old I'd live to be. Like most kids, I'd wanted to live to be a hundred years old. I'd never imagined I'd die at eighteen.

If I could only get help. I had my phone with me. I fished it out of my pocket, dialing 911. It took all my courage—and I had little to begin with—to make the call. But there was no signal. Not in the middle of nowhere. I slapped my phone, and reached my hand as high as I dared. One bar. not great but it would have to do.

"911, what's your emergency? Hello? Is anyone there?"

I lowered the phone to my ear, but I couldn't get a single word out of my mouth. The dispatcher must've heard my breathing, but if I didn't say anything soon, she'd hang up.

"H—help." I didn't recognize my voice; it was barely a whisper.

"Sir? Can you please speak up? I can't hear you."

I took a look around, not seeing anyone. "Woods. Please."

There was a noise—a rustling of leaves. I tucked the phone, the dispatcher's questions drowned out by static before I ended the call.

Someone screamed. High. Shrieking. Sharp.

Lucy.

I gulped, a sinking feeling in my gut.

Zack was up and sprinting towards the voice in a second. Adam called his name, but Zack didn't stop. I pushed myself up, and Adam and I bolted after him.

Katie, Ophelia, and Lucas were already there, in a semicircle. The first thing I saw were the horrified expressions on their faces.

The second thing I saw was Lucy in the dirt, crying. She was soaked in blood. She couldn't breathe because of the swelling panic. She was shaking. I didn't think my blood could turn any more ice. I was wrong.

The third thing I saw was Arabella on the forest ground.

Crimson blood was seeping through her shirt, running down her fair skin. Her long sandy hair was pooled around her, the tips sticky with red. It was shiny, fresh, terrifying. Arabella was blinking furiously, fixating on her blood, and then at all our faces. When her eyes met mine, I felt a stab. I couldn't move, stoned in place.

No, I thought. *Not her. Take me. She can't die.* I took back all my wishing, this wasn't what I wanted!

Arabella was gagging, eyes wide. Her face streaked with sweat, a strand of hair glued to her forehead. Lucy pushed it aside with a trembling finger. Bells' nails were digging into the mossy ground, pulling at the dirt.

Zack tried to peel Lucy off Arabella, but she shoved him away.

"Someone ... someone call the ambulance," I mumbled with effort. "Someone call 911!" I then screamed, forgetting I already had and forgetting that the killer could still be around. I fell to the other side of Arabella. Her eyes flashed between me and Lucy. I took her hand. "Tell me something. Anything. A memory. Something you love. You have to—" My voice broke. "—keep talking. Stay awake. I'm here, you're not alone."

Her mouth hung open, but she didn't seem to get any sound out. A tear slid down her cheek and I wiped it away. It felt like fire burning through my skin. Not the usual kind that set me ablaze from the inside. This fire hurt me.

Lucy spoke through uncontrolled sobs, "you'll be okay. Don't close your eyes, look at me! Please, please..." She forced Arabella's eyes on her. There was so much blood. How much longer did she have? "Please don't go. Please don't leave me, you can't die. You can't leave me, Bells. You hear me? You can't leave me alone. You'll be okay, it's just a little blood."

Arabella was silent. The corners of her mouth turned up, and for a moment it looked like she was smiling.

Please, I prayed to the God I didn't believe in.

"*Shhh* ... you'll be okay," said Lucy. Who she was trying to convince, I didn't know.

I thought about kissing Arabella but how do you kiss a dying girl? Her eyes drifted to the stormy sky as the first drops of rain fell, landing on her colorless cheek. She closed her eyes. All I could do was watch her slip away from me, down a path I couldn't follow.

In the end, the rain did destroy the sunshine. The sky wept, and wept, and wept.

"No! No, no, no! Open your eyes, damn it! You have to stay awake; help is coming!" yelled Lucy, but when Zack pulled her away this time, she didn't resist.

Arabella's body was limp, the twitching was over. Blood was everywhere, moss and mud on Arabella's clothes, under her nails.

I couldn't feel anything. Weirdly, it was easy to understand that she was gone. Not accept, but understand. Because of course good people are taken from this world while people like me get to live. And I was so tired.

She was so pale. I'd never seen someone that pale.

"It's my fault. It's my fault," said Lucy between sobs.

Zack turned her around, holding her by forearms. "No, don't say that. Never say that. It was not your fault. Someone tried to kill us. None of this is your fault, you hear me?"

Water hit my face. I looked up, and it was pouring. I was soaked and I hadn't even realized. Thunder echoed in the distance. I stared at the sky. This was all wrong.

28 / Lucas

Do not run, do not flee

Everything the police told us since the moment they found us, drenched and scared, was a blur. I hadn't paid attention to a single word. Didn't care about the warm tea and blankets they tried to give me.

All I could smell was blood and rain. Hear nothing.

The police had about a thousand questions, and they all sounded the same to me. *Yes. No. I don't know. Maybe.* What was the question again?

I should've done *something*. Anything. I could've saved her if I'd been faster.

I remembered shots—two, maybe three. Holding Ophelia, telling her to be quiet. Pressing her so tightly against my body that her tears wet my shirt too.

I didn't remember when we'd regathered, or when the police and ambulance had arrived. My memory was in pieces. A flash here and there, a familiar voice or scent. I didn't remember when it had started to rain, only noticing that I was cold and wet when they'd sat me down in the station. It had been silent for a while. I'd watched the water drip from my hair onto the white tiles, muddy with footprints.

Another person gone. Who would be next?

I felt powerless and weak. And I couldn't even do anything about it, because the previous plan of talking to the cops was off the table. These days, the narrative was changing awfully a lot.

Of course, it was Ophelia who they were boiling in another room. I could imagine the questions they were asking her. *Good*, I thought. I wouldn't have to worry as much about her if they kept an eye on her. The fear I'd felt for her under those trees—I never wanted to feel that kind of fear again.

We waited in silence as our parents picked us up one by one. All except Ophelia. I was sure she'd stay there, at least for the night. She was safe there.

Unsurprisingly, dad had so many questions it was like being interrogated all over again. I didn't feel like answering any of them.

"What happened?" he asked. Eyes dancing between the road and me. "You'd tell me if you were mixed up in trouble, wouldn't you? If you were … if anything was wrong. I never want you in the middle of somethin' so horrible ever again. A person your age shouldn't have to see death and violence." He waited for a reply I wasn't going to give. "Well? Say something! I want to hear you say it. Promise me."

"Dad, I'm fine." A classic. Stolen right from his own vocabulary.

"Lucas, you could've been killed! You've been getting into all sorts of trouble. I can't even begin to understand where your mind's at." He shook his head. His forehead wrinkles grew inches.

"Can we not do this right now? I'm tired, and I don't feel like talking."

"Lucas, this is serious," he hissed. "Tell me what happened. I've been worried sick 'bout you. What do I have to do to get you to talk to me? I could've lost you today," he whispered the last part.

I didn't reply for a long time, but the silence was coaxing me, and eventually I concluded that if I didn't tell him something now, he wouldn't leave me alone at all.

"My friend died. Well, not exactly my friend, but I knew her. We went to school together. Someone was chasing us, and we hid, and somehow, she got shot. Now, will you leave it? I don't want to talk about it anymore, dad. I swear I have no idea who or why."

His grip on the wheel tightened. "I know, son. I understand, but I only ask because I want the best for you. I need to know that these friends aren't a bad influence on you. The boys I trust, but these other kids seem like newer crowd, and it looks to me that wherever they go, bad things follow. They've been up to something all summer." His voice was gentle, like talking to a wounded dog.

Fury was never tamed by a quiet voice.

I held my head. "Who am I kidding? You don't realize what boundaries are, dad! I'm sorry, okay? I'm sorry you worry about me, but don't you dare blame my friends! They are the only people who actually care. God, you're so selfish, don't you see? If mom was still alive, she would accept my choices, and not pressure me when I say I don't fucking want to talk about things!" My voice cracked, then dropped cold. I closed my eyes.

I wasn't certain how to let go without spilling over. I needed a moment, just one moment to think and relax. Was that too much to ask for?

Dad didn't say anything as he pulled into the driveway.

I ran to my room and closed the door a little rougher than I'd meant to. Then I spent a whole hour showering, rubbing off dried dirt. Soaking myself from cold sweat and pine needles. But no matter how much I scrubbed, I still felt filthy. If only there was a way to wash memories off skin.

I was drained, but I couldn't find it in myself to sleep. Every time I tried, everyone I'd ever cared about left me one by one.

Mom, Ophelia, Mr. Graham, Arabella.

Who else?

There was a knock on my window.

I took a cautious glimpse, then opened the window wide. "What are you doing here? Are you crazy? Why are you sneaking around alone in the dark? Do you realize how dangerous that is?" I bombed Ophelia with questions.

"Don't worry, I was careful. Can I come in?"

I stood aside, and let her climb in through the window.

"You should lock your windows and doors," she said.

"Ophelia, what are you doing here? I thought they'd make you stay at the station for the night or send you home at least. I assume you're now back on the list of living?"

"I can't go home. And I can't stay in Whitewood." Her lip trembled and she bit it.

"What? What are you saying? You can't leave again." I should've expected it. She always ran when things got difficult.

She shook her head. "I can't lose anyone else. My dad, and then Arabella, and Eloise is sick. I can't lose her. And I don't want to lose you. I can't go home. No one wants me there. My mom's not the kind to make apologizing easy." Ophelia choked on her tears, loud spasms as she tried her hardest not to fall apart. She gave up trying to form any words, letting the tears fog her vision.

It was a flood. A river that saw no end.

She must've known. There was no leaving now. Not anymore.

There was a murder on the loose.

29 / Rafael

Nightmares always bleed through pages

I stared at the pile of muddy clothes. They reeked, reminding me of every bit of the horrors they'd been through.

Every time pops asked me how I was feeling I gagged on words. There was a lump at the back of my throat that wouldn't go away. Bitter. My head thrummed, skull threatening to rip open and pour the contents all over the carpet. Trapped in a cage of nightmares that I couldn't escape. Couldn't crawl into Arabella's warm arms, hear her silky-smooth voice. A war was gathering forces inside of me, waves clashing. It was such an intense pressure of a feeling it made me squirm and wrap myself into a tiny ball. As if every pained breath I took sliced me. It alarmed me how empty I felt without her. The time before knowing Arabella was foggy—nonsense, really. I'd begun to rely on her.

Every time my phone made a sound I wanted to throw it against my bedroom wall. A few times I almost did.

I warned you. You did this.

That first night I'd sat, unblinking, for hours. I didn't speak, I didn't eat, I couldn't even bother to clean myself. I was a zombie. Eventually pops told me I stank, and made me get in the shower.

I'd choked on salty tears, snot on my chin. Rested my forehead against the shower wall, water running down my face.

Pops treated me like a ticking bomb.

Bombs are fragile.

Bombs are dangerous.

Time passed funnily. One day would fly by and another drag on. Throughout all of them I kept replaying my memories with Bells. The fact that her death was my fault was like a rope around my neck. She never got to find out the truth. I'd let her down in every way I possibly could've. I couldn't recall my last words to her, if I'd ever told her what she meant to me. Waking up that day, had she known it would be her last? Last time brushing her teeth, last time eating breakfast. Last time she'd see any of us. Did she hug her mom goodbye?

Showering helped me gain some clarity. The more I took them, the more I liked them. Each time it was like shedding my skin and being reborn, because cleanliness was oddly like control. I'd turn the water so hot it would feel like a million needles stabbing me, and when I was sure the sound of water would drown out my wails, I'd let my grief run down the drain. I figured if I felt like I was drowning, perhaps I could also drown some of my demons with me. Pretend the pain in my head and the sinking feeling in my chest was from the scalding pressure of water. No one would hear me cry, and I could pretend I never did.

But then pops started complaining about the bill and wastefulness, so I had to find other ways to keep my body and mind busy. I couldn't rid myself from my mistakes, but for a short while I could avoid them.

I'd heard cleaning was therapeutic, and I started doing just that. First, the cluttered desk and unmade bed, then vacuuming. I picked up the empty water bottles by my bedside, and took out the trash. I was surprised by how well it worked as a distraction. The only downside was that eventually I'd run out of things to clean. I tackled the clothes on my floor.

I'd completely forgot about Mr. Graham's burner. I pat the pockets, not feeling the phone. It wasn't there. I'd lost it—probably during the chase. The killer might've picked it up. I sank to the floor and stared at the pants. I had nothing. No one. No matter how badly I tried, or how good I wanted to be, I could never manage to be anything but a failure. I could see the person I was thriving to be, in the distance, teasing me, taunting me—wanting me to keep running after them just to watch me fall. All summer I'd kept going, thinking that, in time, I'd manage to do something right, but every time I'd just made things worse. There was nothing I was good at, nothing I could call mine. My passions weren't mine; my joy wasn't mine; my dreams weren't mine.

Before I could think about what I was doing, I reached for the cactus on the shelf next to me, and threw it against the wall with all my strength. The pot shattered, dry dirt all over the floor. The cactus was broken, lying on its side.

I exhaled.

I had forced everyone into taking on the investigation with me. *I* had ignored the threats, and Mr. Graham had died after *I* wrongly accused him of murder. Multiple times. *I* had lost the evidence. *I* was the reason we'd been attacked, and *I* hadn't been there when my friends had needed me the most. When Arabella needed someone to take a bullet for her, I should've been there.

All I wanted to do was go to sleep and wake up in the past, but I couldn't even do that.

I got up, picked up the clothes, and tossed them in the trash. There was no saving them, not that I'd ever want to wear them again. It hurt too much to look at them.

I swept away the dirt and the ceramic shards.

When I was done deep-cleaning my room, I sat on the edge of my bed. My room had never been this clean. It smelled like bleach and lemon.

I heard muffled laughter.

Pops was having a date over. Vivianne. I hadn't heard her come in. He was busy with work all the time. He deserved a moment of happiness. They saw each other a lot at the station, of course, had lunch together and everything. But these past few weeks, ever since Mr. Graham's murder, their relationship had taken a bit of a hit. They were both too overwhelmed to plan daily dates. I supposed this was one of their few free nights.

I got up from the bed, and walked over to my desk. I left a note to pops in case he'd come looking for me. For the first time in the eighteen years I'd been alive, I climbed out my window, and snuck away under dusk's cover.

It was five years ago that Zack stumbled upon the lake. We'd spent almost every single day of that summer swimming in the mirror water. It was the one place not tainted by bad memories, so that's where I wanted to be.

"Hey you," said Lucy. She sat quietly next to me. Her hair was in a single braid, hanging over her shoulder. She was wearing jeans and a long-sleeved gray top. If I squinted, she resembled Bells a bit.

I hadn't heard her coming.

"Hey," I replied with a clearing of my throat, "what are you doing here?"

"I couldn't stay cooped up inside any longer. The walls were suffocating me. I've been coming here. The quiet helps me think."

Lucy's skin was ghastly, her eyes red-rimmed, smile feeble at best. "You?"

I sighed. "Dad's having his girlfriend over."

"Ah."

"Lucy, I need you to know how sorry I am. If I could undo any of it, I would, I swear. In a heartbeat."

They'd been best friends their whole lives and I'd stolen her. Lucy had more memories to count. I was mourning the ones I never got to make. Back in the forest I'd had a moment when I'd suddenly wanted to kiss Arabella. But I wasn't a prince and my kiss would've only made her wither away faster.

"Please don't blame yourself." She frowned. "Because it wasn't your fault. If anything, it was mine. She died saving me."

"Lucy."

"No, it's fine." She took a deep breath. "She only agreed to play detectives because she wanted to know the truth. Never because you asked her to. Look where truth got her."

Silence dragged. The water was perfectly still, the sky a fading blue. It really was calming out there.

"She was amazing at everything she did, I envied her for it," Lucy continued. "There are times when I forget she's gone. Everything is blurring together, and I can't tell the difference between a dream and the reality anymore." She shook her head.

I'd always feel Arabella's ghost hovering around. I wanted her there, always tethered together. I needed the reminder. "Have you talked to the others?" I asked.

"A little."

The lump in my throat was beginning to shift, and now it needed a push. "Would you mind getting the group together? They'll come if you're the one asking." *But not for me.* They wouldn't come for a loser who almost got them killed.

"Um, sure. Why?"

"You'll see."

They had a right to know. The mistakes. The risks. The gamble. I'd thought I had nothing left to lose, but I did. I had my friends. And now I was going to lose them too. The difference was that this time I was choosing to lose them. They'd know the truth, and then they'd be safe. It was the only way to make things somewhat right.

They had to know they shouldn't feel guilty about any of it because I was the one who'd messed up.

An hour later we were all in Adam's room. I was the only one sitting, everyone else was either pacing restlessly or staring at me rather angrily.

"Why would you keep this from us?" asked Katie, her voice tinged with betrayal.

"I am sorry. You have no idea how guilty I feel."

"You fucking better feel guilty." Lucy was seething. I deserved that. I was a little afraid of her, since five minutes ago she'd tried to hit me with a lamp.

"I do," I said, not bothering to hide the rippling guilt and sadness in my voice. No more pretending. All cards were on the table.

"I can't believe you risked our lives without even telling us." Katie wasn't angry, not like Lucy was. If anything, she seemed disappointed in me, and that felt even worse.

"I know now that it was a mistake."

"Oh, so if Bells hadn't been murder, it would have been fine to toy with our lives? You fucking bastard, who do you think you are?" yelled Lucy.

I rubbed my short hair. "I'm sorry. I would have *never* intentionally put anyone in danger. I wanted to do the right thing."

"You're lying! Admit it! You would have never stopped! You're a sociopath. You played us." Her hands curled into two fists at her sides. She paced back and forth.

"Of course I would've! I would have never—" My voice broke, and I took a deep breath before continuing. "If I'd known she would die, I would have never even started this whole thing. Never. Believe me on this."

"What about when Mr. Graham died? Wasn't that clear enough for you? Because, Rafe, I'm having a hard time understanding who the fuck you are trying to fool this time. Just admit you couldn't let go, and you used us to get what you wanted. You didn't care who got hurt."

"What? No—"

"*Admit it*." Lucy's stormy eyes burned into me.

I jumped to my feet. "I never wanted anyone to get hurt! At first, I didn't want to worry you—"

"No. You didn't want us to leave you. You used us."

I squeezed my eyes shut. She was wrong. *I made a mistake.*

"No. Yes. I'm not lying. After Mr. Graham died, it's true, I was too scared to tell you. I was already blaming myself, and ... you're right, I didn't want to lose you. If you haven't noticed, Lucy, I'm nothing without you guys. A nobody. But don't say I didn't care about Arabella. I did. You know I did. I *still* do."

Lucy stared at me like I was revolting to her. She'd already made her mind up about me. She wasn't listening. "You've had us chasing a murderer all summer, but here you are, not far from being one yourself."

I blinked at her, letting the words sink in. It was terrifying to think they might be right, and maybe deep down I already believed they were. After all, Lucy hadn't been completely off about me. I'd expected them to be angry but I hadn't thought how difficult it would be to face their judgement.

I stuttered to get words out. "I—I'm sorry. Please, tell me what I can do? How can I make this right?" Tears prickled my eyes. I held them back.

"You've done enough. You've ruined us, and I never want to see you again. Ever." Lucy stormed out.

She probably did the right thing. At least she would be safe from me. They should've all ran. The moment they'd met me, they should've ran for their lives.

"For someone this smart, you sure can be such a damn idiot," said Zack. I was startled to hear him speak. He gave me one last apologetic look before disappearing after his girlfriend.

Katie and Adam remained. We sat in silence. I was ready for the next blow to hit, but it didn't seem to come.

"It's not that I don't agree with her, because I do," said Katie finally. "It's just that I *know* who you are, Rafe. I know you always want to be the hero. I believe what you said too. I think you got too caught up with being the hero, so you didn't notice the danger. I get it. Sometimes I get lost in puzzles too."

I searched her sweet face. "Do you think she'll forgive me? Will any of you forgive me?"

She waited before answering. "You can't win trust back with one night. Get some sleep. Calm down. These things tend to work out the way they are supposed to." She rose with a heavy limb, and hugged me goodbye. She felt warm against my shoulder, but not as warm as Arabella had. Not nearly as comforting.

"I'm sure Lucas would agree if he was here," added Adam. We didn't hug but I was relieved to know telling them had been the right thing to do, although hard.

Lucy wouldn't answer any of my calls or texts. Adam and I went to her house one day, but she pretended not to be home. I only knew because the curtains moved. The problem wasn't that she didn't want to be friends anymore. I understood that, I'd accepted it. It was that she was so full of fury. I didn't want her to hate me forever.

Zack promised to talk to her for me.

Mostly I hung out with Adam and Katie. We swam, we played volleyball. Video games Adam liked. It wasn't perfect. None of it was perfect. But it was all we had left. It helped to be around them and have some normality. Lucas was busy, as always. Zack pulled away whenever things got to be too much. The boys and I were used to him dodging us when he needed space, then reappearing again some time.

I liked to swim a lot. A new hobby of mine. I mean, showers were great, but being outside was way better. Morning swims, afternoon swims, night swims. All swims. No one else went to our meetup place anymore. I would swim until my lungs burned, and then I'd slip under the surface until they burned even more. I was never lonely, because underwater there were faces too. Sometimes I'd see Mr. Graham, often I'd see Arabella. I'd see her long blonde hair, how the strands moved with the water. I'd reach my hand out to touch her, but never manage to get close enough. She'd smile, and I'd smile. She'd blink, I'd blink. She'd be gone, I'd gasp for air. For a moment I could forget everything and focus on the fire in my lungs. It's funny how drowning feels like burning.

One day I let it slip about the swimming. Not about the faces. Just that swimming helped me grieve. It made me feel alive when I felt like I was dying most of the time. I still had a life to lose. Adam, the genius he was, thought scuba diving might be something fun to do with a small group. He thought it might take our minds off everything. It was hard not to show my excitement at the idea of seeing Arabella for a little longer than mere seconds.

He said he'd get some gear for us. It would be fun. We invited Zack and Katie.

Soon enough we were floating in the middle of the lake on a rented boat with rented scuba gear. Adam and Zack stayed on the boat to keep watch, Katie and I dove. They'd get their turn, but someone had to watch the boat (and rental isn't cheap).

The deeper I went, the colder it got. The water was soggy and dark, seeing anything was a struggle. I had trouble keeping up with Katie. She swam fast. My eyes narrowed to keep track of the tail of her short braid. Brown. Her hair was brown. I looked around, but there was no sign of Bells.

Suddenly I was alone. I moved around, panicky, waving my arms and legs. Hoping Katie would catch sight of me. When she didn't, I swam around looking for her. Maybe I'd gone too deep. Or I hadn't gone deep enough. I swam, trying to calm myself all the while. I didn't know what to do. Should I return to the surface and tell the guys? Maybe she was already waiting on the boat.

I started for the surface, but then, to my relief, Katie reemerged in the distance. She was slower than before. I picked up my pace, swimming towards her, worried something might've happened. A cramp. A hurt ankle. Maybe a fish bit her toes.

It wasn't Katie at all. I took me a moment to recognize the face.

It was Sheldon Rogers, chalk white skin deformed. His face was mutilated by time spent underwater, but I still recognized him from all the pictures I'd stared at.

Rigid, colorless, dead. And he wasn't a hallucination. He was *real.*

I scrambled to the surface, breaking the barrier with force. Adam and Zack heaved me aboard. The sun on my face stung compared to the cool of the water. The water that had a corpse in it. The water we'd been swimming in for years. He was right there under our noses. I was gasping for air. It didn't matter how much air I tried to suck in, it didn't help. My head was spinning. A sob trapped in my throat. It made me lightheaded.

"Rafe! Rafe! What happened? Tell me what happened." Adam was at my side, unzipping the slippery costume.

I gagged even more trying to speak. Zack patted my back. I heard splashes and talking, and then Katie was there too.

"He looks like he's seen a ghost. What happened?" she asked Adam.

He shrugged. "I think he's having a panic attack."

"Rafe, look at me. Breathe," she then said to me.

I was about to pass out. "I—"

It happened so fast. One moment I was on my knees, the next I was throwing up over the ledge.

Katie twisted water out of her hair as I told them about what I'd seen. There had already been so much death surrounding us lately that another body was anything but a surprise. After giving it some thought, at least. I'd hoped things would get better after everything we'd went through, but as it happened, the worst was yet to come.

We called the police. There was nothing to do but lie again. And we were getting good at that. Especially me.

We'd just gone scuba diving, we told them. To cheer up after everything, we told them.

It was our spot; we'd swam there before—which wasn't a lie at all. We said that we hadn't planned to find another body—which wasn't a lie at all.

That death followed us. Which wasn't a lie at all. Turned out, there were no more lies to tell.

30 / Lucas

If I were ever to fall into slumber deep

People like to stare when they see someone who is supposed to be dead. They stared at Ophelia wherever she went. Behind her back, they called her names and came up with stories as to why she wasn't six feet under. Stories spread like wildfire. I was just glad I'd convinced her to stay.

Most days I let her stay at my house. She spent her time alone, since I had to work, but she never complained. I encouraged her to talk to Katie or her mom, but nothing came of it. I think she was afraid of them, or rather what they would think of her.

Dad got used to her presence, mainly by ignoring her. He didn't really think she was dangerous or anything. He couldn't have. Initially, he'd been shocked like everyone else. Ophelia existed so quietly he probably didn't even notice her much.

However busy my days were, I liked to make time for Ophelia in the evenings. We watched a ton of movies and read books together. And we finally had time to talk a bit more.

I hadn't seen my friends in a while. My fault, for keeping myself so busy. A couple of days ago, there were news of another body found. Arabella's uncle. That's three bodies, now.

It was another day of hard work. It was already dark outside and crickets were chirping. I rushed home, hungry and tired, but excited to see Ophelia. Father was still back by the car, grabbing his things.

The house was silent.

No sign of Ophelia. What if something had happened while I was gone?

No, I was jumping into conclusions. The house was alright. The lights were on, nothing was broken, and there was faint music coming from outside.

Wait, what?

I listened hard, following the sound into the backyard.

"You're home," said Ophelia, holding a string of lights. Her hair was in a messy bun, a bit of sweat on her forehead.

"What are you doing?" My eyes locked on the lights, then the yellow tent in the middle of our backyard.

Ophelia cleared her voice. "I wanted to do something for you. You've been so kind and patient, so I thought we could spend the night out here. I got snacks and picked out a movie we can watch. It should be a clear night, no rain." She gestured at the sky flimsily.

"You did this for me?"

"Of course," she replied happily.

No one had ever done something like that for me.

She gasped softly, pointing at the sky again. "Look at the size of that star! It's gorgeous."

I smiled quietly. "That's not a star. It's Saturn. Did you know that Saturn is the least dense planet in our solar system, which means that it could potentially float on water?"

Her eyebrows shot up. "How do *you* know that? I remember you not even knowing the difference between Uranus and Neptune."

My smile drew wider. Yeah, I wouldn't make that mistake twice. "Is it still your favorite?" I asked instead.

She didn't answer but her face told me everything.

After a moment, Ophelia wiped her hands on her pants, grabbed my hand, and led me inside the tiny tent. It was quite tight, and I had to slouch so my head wouldn't hit the ceiling. The inside was also decorated with fairy lights. Bags of chips and marshmallows waiting to be eaten.

Ophelia threw a blanket at me. "Here."

I caught it clumsily.

"If you listen closely, you can hear the sea from here. During the day, there's too much noise, but at night..."

I sharpened my ear. She was right. The soft roll of waves. I smiled, meeting her eye. My hand wrapped around her waist. I kissed her gently. She smelled of lavender.

"Here, try this," she said, reaching towards the snacks. She took two chips and put one massive marshmallow between them, it looked like a monster smore.

"It looks disgusting," I commented. The nacho cheese went all over my fingers. The squished marshmallow was coated in it. It was a beastly thing barely holding its shape.

"Come on," she groaned. "On three. One, two, three—"

We took a bite at the same time. The chips crunched under my teeth, bits and pieces flying everywhere. Weirdly, the combination wasn't too horrid. The sweetness of the marshmallow and the saltiness of the chips canceled each other out, and the texture wasn't terrible either.

Ophelia giggled, stuffing another marshmallow in her mouth.

We ate another two or three of those monstrosities. Then we washed it down with soda. I felt like a kid, but not in a bad way. It was silly. I could put all the bad stuff behind me and enjoy myself for a night. Tomorrow I'd wake up, and it would be a memory I'd never forget. But for the time being, getting a little lost with Ophelia was the only thing I wanted to do.

Ophelia threw her arms around my neck, kissing me. Her back hit the tent's floor, arching. She pulled my shirt over my head, nails running across my hot skin. Her hand lingered at my waistband. I pulled my mouth away from hers, instead trailing down the low neckline of her top. Her breathing sharpened; I could feel her wiggle under me. I pushed her hair from her face, teeth grazing Ophelia's neck and shoulder.

Just us, in a tiny tent under the stars.

I could get used to that.

31 / Rafael

Her memory is my curse

Pops had never yelled at me before. He was a calm man with few words. All week he'd been patient with me, but now his generosity was running out. The corpse I found didn't help, and, worst of all, he'd finally had time to properly think.

"Why is it, that wherever you go, death follows?" pops' voice rung. "You are grounded. You are never to leave this house again!"

"You can't ground me, I'm eighteen," I counterattacked.

The look pops gave me convinced me otherwise. "You will not leave this house before you've told me something I believe. Tell me what's going on." He cracked open a beer. Pops' dark skin radiated heat, his cheeks taking on a reddish tint.

As much as I wanted to tell him everything, I couldn't. It would only create more trouble. "What truth? You already know everything. Besides, shouldn't you be happy that he was finally found?"

Pops slammed the beer can on the table, making me flinch. "Happy? Happy! You think I would be happy? This is the third dead body you and your friends have reported. What am I supposed to say to that?"

"Thank you?"

"This is not the time to be smart with me! What have you been doing all summer?"

I wanted to strangle something. "Dad, I don't know what you want me to say. I have told you everything and if you don't believe me, then fine. At this point, it doesn't even matter what I say. You've already decided." It wasn't the same as lying to my friends. I'd been a coward when I'd done that. I knew pops well enough to say for certain that nothing good would come of him knowing the actual story.

For a second, his mask slipped and he looked unsure. Then his face hardened again. "OK. If this is how you want things to be. You are grounded, end of story. Whatever it is, it ends here and now. If I find you in another mess, I swear I'm shipping you off to your grams in Argentina."

I went to sleep, but again sleep didn't come. In the dark, I sat on my bed cross-legged, letting shadows creep up on me and bear their bites. Ivy was with me, sleeping on the edge of the bed, purring softly. I was glad to have her around and not be completely alone.

Quiet, wet tapping echoed from my bathroom. It sounded like watery fingertips against the shower glass. I got up from the bed, and opened the bathroom door. Lucy's words were in my head, from when she'd told me about how her dreams and reality were becoming one. I hadn't slept well in so long.

Water was dripping from the sink. I released my breath, not bothering to stop the leaking. I just needed some rest. I had to get back to bed and close my eyes. Tomorrow would be a new day and a new chance to patch things up.

I looked into the mirror, and jumped back, holding back a strangled scream. My hands shook, covering my face and mouth.

Sheldon Rogers was in my shower, naked. His mouth opened, but instead of words, soggy water poured out. He gurgled; his chalky jaw wide. The dark water ran down his body like thick goo, catching on seaweed that was stuck to his chest and legs. When it reached the drain, the water turned into wiggling slugs, moving frantically. Some tried to crawl back up Sheldon's legs, some went down the drain willingly. Some tried to come towards me, gray and slithery.

I ran out the bathroom, and closed the door with a bang. I backed away, watching as the light inside turned off by itself. I was in complete darkness. I waited to see if Sheldon would come after me. He'd been like a puppet strung up on a wire, right from the waters I'd found him in. I waited, but nothing happened.

It's just a dream, it's not real. I'd fallen asleep.

"What? You've never seen a ghost before, you little shit?"

I swiveled, gasping.

Mr. Graham tilted his open skull, blush, slimy brain out to see. His dark gaze drifted over me.

"You're not real, this is a dream," I forced out.

He smirked. "How can you be sure?" His whisper echoed as the ground below me vanished and I fell into a damp, pitch-black hole. I reached around for something to grab onto, but there was nothing. I kept falling and falling and falling with no end in sight. Time and space transformed around me, everything spinning, until I couldn't see my room anymore.

I was at school, standing alone in a hallway. It was deadly quiet, except for the buzzing lights. I narrowed my eyes, the light hurting me after being in the dark. I walked up to one of the classrooms. There were people inside. Why weren't I in class? I was supposed to be in class.

Then I saw *her*. Arabella. Her nose was buried in a book. History. I opened the door, and walked in. No one looked up but her, like they were all frozen in time or something. Her eyes followed me slowly. She was glowing like the heavens had bathed her in sunlight. Just that little bit too translucent that I might've been able to reach my fingers through her, touch her heart, and see if it was still beating.

"Why weren't you underwater?" I asked because suddenly that was the only question on my mind. There was disappointment in my voice. Worry. She hadn't come to see me.

"I had school," she said as if that was obvious. As if all dead people went to school.

"I miss you, come back."

"No, I can't. This is the best part." She gestured to her book. "You'd like this one."

"*The bell jar*? I have read it. I'll tell you the ending. Please come back."

She closed the book and folded her hands in her lap. There wasn't a speck of blood on her. No sweat or dirt or fear. Arabella was an angel. How else could anyone explain her radiance? I'd never laid my eyes upon someone more mesmerizing.

My face dropped as I remembered her death. This was only a dream, and I couldn't bring her back. None of it was real.

"Arabella—"

"Wake up. You need to wake up."

"What?"

Her ears prickled. The rest of the people vanished, only she and I remained. The walls of the school shook, disappearing, then reappearing. Like a glitch. The dream was falling apart. "Someone's at the door."

Pain burst in my chest. Vines blossoming, twisting inside me.

I woke up in cold sweat.

Someone was knocking on the door downstairs. I took a deep breath, remembering Arabella's face in my dream, and then I pushed myself up from the bed.

I crept into the hallway, and sat on top of the stairs, hidden from the view. Pops opened the door, letting Vivianne and Maya inside.

"Hey, I'm sorry, I forgot my keys here. Do you mind if I..." Vivianne waved her hand.

"It's alright, do you remember where you put them?" asked pops.

They kissed each other briefly. Maya turned her head away. She appeared tired. Maybe she had nightmares too. Though now I wasn't quite sure if mine had even been that.

"Oh, they must be somewhere here. I'm sorry, I should've called. I just thought it best to come grab them right away or I'd have to borrow yours tomorrow. It's such a chaos at work."

"Mm-hm. Yes, I won't be free until eight tomorrow. You can let yourself in, I don't want you to have to wait around."

Vivianne smiled, and another kiss landed on pops' cheek, closer to the mouth. "Oh! Here they are." The keys jingled in her hand. "All right then, thank you. I'll see you tomorrow." Another kiss.

The door clicked shut behind them.

I went back to my room.

How long had Vivianne had a spare key to our home?

32 / Lucas

It's a lonely world without you

My eyes flew open, trying to make sense of where I was.

The tent. I must've fallen asleep. Ophelia was beside me, her arm resting on my chest. I set it aside carefully, pushing myself half-way up.

It was already light outside. The sunlight reached the tent's opening. It was starting to heat up in there, hardly any air to breathe.

Ophelia stirred, groggy with sleep. "Hey." She pulled me back down by the arm.

I gave her a peck on the cheek.

She held my chin. "I'm sorry." She noticed the question on my face. "For how I reacted and what I said when you confronted me back at the mansion. I'm sorry for not going with you when you asked me to. I'm sorry for being so stuck in my own head that I couldn't be there for you. And most of all, I'm sorry for ever leaving you. I shouldn't have. You were right. Oh, and, sorry for trying to run away from you in New York. That wasn't nice of me."

My face twitched as I opened my mouth to speak, but Ophelia wasn't finished yet.

"Lucas, I want to exist again. I want to be a person again, not just a shell of one. I want my life back. The police know I'm alive. The people know, although they can never find out the true reason. They'll always look at me differently, I've accepted that. It's all so messed up. I just want to go home and not be afraid anymore. And you've been there for me, even though I didn't deserve it. There are so many things I should've done differently."

"What do you want from me?" Her pulse was under my finger, a relentless drum. She just had to say it. Just once.

I just needed to hear it.

Ophelia clung to my shirt. "I want you. I want to fix what I broke. It is my fault people died. That my father died. Please, Lucas, how do I fix it?"

"You didn't kill them, Ophelia." Words were not enough, everything meaningful was in the things we did not say.

"No, there must be a way."

"We'll figure it out together. Who cares what people think? They don't know you like I do. I thought I didn't either, but all along it was you. You ran from everyone but me." I cupped her face, inches apart.

"I want you too, although you keep littering my bed with way too many plushies. We'll need some rules about that."

Ophelia smiled.

We'd figure something out. Take it one step at a time.

33 / Rafael

How come sadness reminds me I'm alive?

I couldn't dream of anything anymore. My body had reached its limit, and when I slept, I slept like a log. The first time it happened I startled myself awake out of surprise. It was blissful. Nothing could wake me. Not my alarm, not a blaring car on the street, not even pops.

I missed the lake, but I wasn't sick enough in the head to still go swimming there. I had to find other forms of exercise.

On a gloomy Tuesday evening, when the walls started to close in around me, I snuck out again and went to the beach. Sticky sand stuck to the bottoms of my trainers. I promised myself this would be the last time. I'd say goodbye, and let her go.

I was thankful there weren't any people at the beach.

I folded my clothes and took off my glasses, placing them neatly on a flat stone. I shivered, making my way into the biting water, pausing only to take a deep breath through my mouth and smooth out a wrinkle in my swimming shorts. My teeth clattered together. It wasn't night yet, but it was already so cold I feared my muscles might cramp. Deeper and deeper, until my toes couldn't touch the bottom anymore. I pushed myself off the ocean bed, and swam against the strong current, fighting against the waves and seafoam crashing in my face. My head fell back, and I watched the cloudy sky. Would it rain like the day she died?

It wasn't until my chest burned that I let go. I allowed all my strength to fall into my legs and pull me under.

I'd never been afraid when doing it, but in the arms of the stormy sea, I was somewhat petrified. I was completely crazy, I knew that. Again, I remembered how I'd missed my chance to kiss Bells. I hadn't even known I'd wanted to until she was dying in my arms.

I forced my eyes open. It was dark, the sandy bottom seemed almost black. It didn't feel right. My lungs were on fire, but it was nothing compared to the sting of the saltwater in my eyes. I couldn't hold my breath much longer, and still she was nowhere. What if it didn't work anymore? I'd never see her again. I breathed out bubbles, thinking of all the things to blame this on.

I'd have to resurface soon.

It was never about hurting myself, but always about Arabella. Swimming cleared my mind, letting go helped me remember the good.

Unusual, I knew, but it was the only kind of peace I had left. Pretending like I'd never lost her was the trick. A hoax. If I never lost her, there was no reason to be in pain. No reason at all to cry myself to sleep and wake up with fresh tears in my eyes. But the pretenses were gone now. Taken.

But then, maybe not.

Two slender hands reached for me, pulling me upwards. I let her tug me closer towards the light. Her skin was cold like mine. We were the same. Two sides of the same coin. Light and darkness.

I gasped for air. Everything hurt, burning as if I'd sunk deep enough to touch my toes to the ceiling of hell. Crawling towards the shore on my knees, I fell into the sand.

"What were you thinking?" yelled Lucy. Not Arabella. *Lucy.*

I couldn't answer. I was coughing up water. Tears gathered in my eyes against my will.

"You would be dead if I wasn't here!"

"I—" God, speaking hurt.

"Were you trying to get yourself killed?" She fell beside me, running a hand through her soaked hair. She was shaking all over, like a leaf in the wind.

My heart sank. "No." It was all I could get out. "Water." I waved at my throat.

"*Shit*. Hold on." Lucy jumped up, waddling through sand. She came back in a minute, and handed me a half-empty water bottle.

I chugged the entire thing, wheezing afterwards. It took me a good few minutes before I felt steady enough to speak. "It's not what you think. I wasn't trying to die." I started putting my clothes back on. They stuck to my skin, but at least it was a little warmer than being half-naked in the cold wind.

This wasn't something I'd ever imagined having to explain.

She folded her hands. "Then what were you doing? I saw you walk into those waves. You looked like you were in a trance. You had this empty stare, and then suddenly you were gone, and I couldn't see you anywhere."

I felt my cheeks heat. "I don't know how to explain this. You won't understand."

"Try me."

I bit my cheek. "After Bells died, I felt lonely and guilty, and I missed her. The only way to drown the pain out was to sort of … drown." I paused, and looked at her. When she didn't stop me, I went on. "The first time, I was swimming and I don't even remember how it happened, but suddenly I was underwater, and she was there. For a moment it was quiet as if the whole world was on pause. The next time I tried it on purpose, out of curiosity. I like to swim, it helps. But seeing her helps more. It's like bringing her back to life, if only just for a second." The words rushed out of me, as if they'd been waiting for a patient ear to listen. I shook my head, aware of how stupid it all must've sounded. It wasn't something I could easily put into words.

"What is she like? Down there?" asked Lucy, unexpectedly. It sounded almost like she believed me and didn't think I was a nutjob. I'd imagined I'd be on my way to the psych ward by now.

It took me a moment to reply. "Happy. Beautiful. As if she never died at all. It's easy to pretend she didn't."

Lucy slid closer to me. She grabbed my hand, making me face her. "Rafe, you can't keep doing this."

"I know." *Last time*, I'd told myself. I hadn't got to say goodbye. Secretly I damned the sea.

"It's dangerous. One day you might not make it back up."

"I know that too."

"Then why?" Her caramel eyes searched mine.

Wasn't it obvious? "It reminds me that I'm alive, and when I see her, I don't feel so terrible about it."

I should've died that day, not Arabella.

Lucy's face was a little blue. She'd saved me. She'd listened. I pulled her into a hug.

It felt good to talk to someone. Good to allow myself to feel.

Katie propped her phone up against a bag of flour, so I'd have a good view of her as she baked chocolate chip cookies. She'd already started before the video call by the appearance of the kitchen. All the ingredients were hauled together behind her on the counter.

"Can I have some?" I asked, stretched out on my bed like a cat.

"If my dad doesn't eat them all, then yes." She picked up a measuring cup, then stopped, staring at me. "Oh, wait." Nope, just ogling the flour.

Katie picked up the phone, and set me up against something else, giving me a wider view of her as she started filling the cup with flour.

"Have you talked to Lucas lately?" she asked.

"Barely." I shrugged, but she didn't catch that.

"Anything interesting going on?"

"You mean Ophelia?"

Katie looked at me, answer clear enough. She picked up sugar.

"Sorry. Maybe you should just call her. Have you?"

She mumbled to herself when fine sugar spilled all over the marble countertop. She left it there, and moved on. "No. I'm not calling her. She should be calling me."

"Maybe she's shy."

Katie snorted. "She has never been the shy type. She didn't even try to talk to me, why should I?"

That was right after Ophelia's dad had died. I doubted talking to Katie had been on her mind at all. And it wasn't like she'd been so forthcoming herself. Katie always kept a wall up.

"Okay, how about the fact that you miss her, and I'm sure she misses you too. Just talk to her, will you? Just once."

Katie rolled her eyes. She'd think about it.

"Hey, how's it going with Adam?" I asked.

Katie turned red. "Funny you should ask."

That was my que to grin and kick my feet in the air. "Tell me more. I thought you two didn't like each other. Don't tell me those cookies are for him, his favorite."

She cleared her throat, fumbling with the eggs. "There's nothing to say. And no, these aren't for him. He hasn't earned a cookie." Katie shook her head, blushing.

I laughed. It felt good to laugh. It made Katie spare me a glance, and when she saw my smile, she couldn't resist smiling too.

"How are you doing?" she asked. "Be honest."

I thought about it. "Not great. But I've been worse too, so right now this feels like a step towards something."

It felt like a forever had passed since Lucy and I had talked, but it had only been a day.

Katie gave a brisk nod. "Good," I heard her mumble. "That's good."

Pops called for me from downstairs. I told Katie I had to go and to leave me some cookies. I ran downstairs, steps creaking.

"House arrest is over." Pops was standing at the landing, holding car keys.

"What?" Shortest house arrest in the history of house arrests.

"But I need you to go pick up Maya from school. You can drive my car just this once."

I leaned against the staircase. "She's sixteen, can't she get home herself? It's not that far."

He raised an eyebrow. "I feel like you're asking for more house arrest." He jingled the keys in front of me.

I crossed my arms over my chest. "What's your game, old man?"

Instead of answering, pops started counting down from five. I raced down the last steps, and launched myself at the keys he was holding. "Fine. I'll go."

The drive to school was weird. There it was—the street I used to ride my bike down every day. And there's the neighbor's dog barking again. And that way is the shortcut I used to take when I was especially in a hurry, but not when it had recently rained. Never then, because the road would be muddy and splash all over me when I sped through it. Learned that one the hard way.

Making me pick up my future little sister was probably dad's way of trying to get under Maya's skin. Better yet, Vivianne's.

"My dad sent me to pick you up," I told Maya as she opened the passenger door, throwing her backpack between her legs and settling into the faux leather seat.

She barely looked at me. "Yeah, thanks. You really didn't have to; I usually walk or take my bike."

"How's, uh, school?" I asked.

"I suck at geography. Think I need a tutor."

"Hm."

She squinted. "What's that supposed to mean? *Hm*."

"Nothing. Tutoring is good. Sorry." I pushed up my glasses, focusing on the road.

We arrived at her house a minute later, but Maya didn't get out of the car.

"Do you think they'll get married?" she asked.

"Maybe." I hoped they wouldn't.

"I hope they won't. I mean, obviously nothing against you. It would just be weird. I've never had a father, or a brother, I wouldn't know how to act. I'm used to taking care of myself." She scrunched up her nose. She was cute liked that, big-eyed, pixie cut. Long, thin limbs.

"Yeah, me too."

Maya looked at me like she was trying to see *through* me. "Maybe if we got to know each other more, it wouldn't suck as much if they got married."

She had a point. I hated that she did. She'd asked me to hang out before. To be fair, it had slipped my mind.

"Sure. I'll see you around," I replied, making sure to smile.

Maya got out of the car; backpack slung over her shoulder. She turned at the door, and waved at me before heading inside. A few minutes later I got a text.

MAYA: Thanks for the ride. And thanks for being my friend. I feel like it's different for you and me. We're so similar. :)

We were, in some ways. Thinking back, I'd been trying too hard to push her away. To distance myself from her and Vivianne. Maybe Maya had been right. If we got to know one another we might not hate the idea of being a family so much.

Family is supposed to be there for each other.

34 / Lucas

Always better together

"I have missed reading," said Ophelia, huddled between my legs with her back against my chest.

I replied by gently stroking her hair with one hand, while the other entwined with her fingers. She moved, not closing the book. I turned her head and kissed her. We sank deeper into the soft couch. Ophelia smiled against my teeth.

A high-pitched creak of the door pulled us apart.

"It's my dad," I whispered.

We scrambled up, smoothing down our clothes. I kissed Ophelia's temple hastily before dad walked in.

"Hey, dad," I said.

His eyes shifted from me to Ophelia, eyebrows raised. "I think we need to talk."

I scratched the top of my head.

He lowered himself into a chair.

"I read about you in the paper, but I never expected—" Dad sighed. "—you to come here. I let you stay, but I didn't think this arrangement would go on for so long. Don't your mama worry 'bout you?"

"It's a long story," answered Ophelia. "I completely understand if you want me to go, I know I've overstayed my welcome."

Dad pressed his lips together into a tight, uneasy smile. He slapped both his hands against his thighs and stood. "A word, son?"

My throat went dry, but I still followed him into the dim kitchen dutifully. Only the last of the day's light was breaking through the blinds, casting an orange glow over the room.

I opened a cupboard, took out a glass, and filled it with cold water.

"Is she the reason you're in such a hurry to get away from home?"

My eyes widened. "What? What are you talking about? Of course not."

He didn't believe me.

"It's true dad! She has nothing to do with this." I pushed myself away from the counter, and sat at the table, across from dad.

"She's bad news, kid." Dad massaged his shoulder.

"She's not bad news! Just trust me, will you? I know what I'm doing. I can take care of myself."

He shook his head, tossing his arms in the air. "Fine. No need to shout. A few days. Tell your girlfriend to go home."

I ran a hand over my face. "Yeah, will do."

Dad reached for my arm. "I'm glad you're here, son."

"Missed you too, dad. I'm sorry about what I said before. You're just worried about me."

He pulled back. "Listen, about the getting away—it's not the worst idea. With everything that's happened, this place isn't exactly the safest. When things calm down, well, I was hoping we could talk more about it. As long as you're not doing it only for her sake. I love you, kid."

"Yeah ... love you, dad." My heart did a cartwheel.

Later that night, the group chat came alive for the first time in two weeks.

KATIE: Hey, how are you guys doing?

ADAM: Fine I guess

> I think everyone is pretty freaked out by everything that happened. Maybe it's best if we take a break for a while.

KATIE: Yeah, you're right. I just can't believe it.

It'll get easier

KATIE: I hope so

ADAM replied to KATIE: It will, Lucas never lies

RAFAEL: This sucks ... I feel so bad for how things turned out. What a mess.

> We should all try to move on. It was no one's fault

RAFAEL: **@LUCY** Are you OK? Sorry about the other day

KATIE: Wait what happened the other day?

LUCY replied to RAFAEL: Don't worry about it. Glad you're feeling better, tho. Oh, and **@ADAM** Zack sends you kisses and wants me to ask you if your parents realize that two wrongs don't make a right. I think he means you.

ADAM: What :(At least Jesus loves me

KATIE: Jesus might love you but everyone else thinks you're an idiot

ADAM: Be that as it may be, you know you love me star girl

35 / Rafael

The time I went to a family dinner

Pops had the flowers and I had the wine. He rang the doorbell, and shot me nervous look. I scooted back.

The door flew open and Vivianne all but strangled pops with a hug.

The whole house smelled like vanilla scented candles and chicken spice. Everything was neat, down to the freshly wiped windows and polished silverware.

I sat awkwardly at the table, swaying my legs, hoping for the smell of burnt chicken to disperse. Maya sat opposite of me and didn't look half as fiddly. She was quietly studying me. I smiled, and she smiled back. I was in a good enough mood. I'd slept for most of the morning until early lunch when Katie brough some cookies over. We'd chatted for an hour before she'd had to rush off.

Somehow my mind was clearer, as if the fog had lifted enough for me to see past my own two feet.   It was easier than ever to forget what had happened. I cast Bells from my head, evicted her from my mind. No more reminding myself of her death. I let the pain ease into a dull ache.

"I'm glad you came," said Vivi to me, "I was worried about you, is all. I know this might be a little difficult for you—both of you." She looked from me to Maya. "But I want you to know, that your father and I are taking things slow, so you'd have time to adapt. This will work out, you'll see."

If she and pops married, she'd become my step-mother. I knew she made pops happy, but if we were to be a family, shouldn't we all get a say? Frankly, it was a little too soon for me.

Tonight, Vivianne wore a plum dress, simple in cut and cheap in material, but pretty nevertheless. "Should we put some music on?" she asked.

"That would be wonderful, yes," agreed pops.

Vivianne stood from the table, moving over to the cabinet behind Maya, and tuned the radio on to some old song I didn't recognize. It filled the awkward silence and I was grateful for it.

"I'll go get the salad and some dressing." Vivianne vanished behind the corner. The candles on the cabinet flickered.

I ran my eyes over the photographs on the walls. There was something familiar about them. Most of them were of nature or travels. Some had Maya in them. Her posing in front of some church, at beach, or on a boat. There was one that I particularly liked. Maya was standing in a massive rain puddle with the biggest grin plastered across her face. She had this funky yellow hat on that covered most of her eyes, and she was in the moment of pushing it out of her face. Couldn't have been more than eight years old. Now she was almost seventeen.

Footsteps echoed from the kitchen, coming towards us. "Be nice," pops whispered in my ear.

I smiled. "Aren't I always?"

"Greek salad. If it's too bland, there's some salt and pepper on the table." Vivianne put the bowl between the chicken and the barbeque sauce, gesturing for us to dig in and eat.

I reached for the salt.

"I wanted to thank you, Rafe, for picking Maya up the other day. That was kind of you," said Vivi. I was out of her reach, so she fixed her hand on pops' arm instead, flashing me another sweet smile.

I ignored the obviousness of whose idea it had really been.

She turned to dad. "Darling, have you read the papers yet? Those wretched reporters…"

Pops scratched his temple. "Yes. There's nothing we can do. We can't give any statements yet, so they're allowed to spin any story they want." He quirked his head to the side. The long days were starting to wear on him, and he hated work talk. But he still answered Vivianne.

I bit down on a barbeque sauce coated potato. "How are things going? Have you found anything yet? About the poisoning, perhaps?" My curiosity was plain as day. I thought to try my luck too.

Pops shook his head. "Can't say, bud."

"But—"

"Times are heated right now. People are worried, rightfully so. We'll keep looking. Something will come up eventually. Sometimes it just takes a little longer. We found some prints on the stolen car near the woods, and they match the ones we found three years ago. Sadly, that does circulate some questions whether the fertilizer poisoning could've been an accident or not."

A lot of accidents in Whitewood. Drowning, burning, poisoning.

Vivianne dabbed her mouth with a napkin. "That girl—Graham. Has she been any help at all?"

Pops cleared his throat, eyes downcast. "She's a strange one, but I don't think she knows any more than what she's told us. Now, enough of work. It's best if this information doesn't spread yet."

I scoffed. And how many people had to die exactly until the police could piece the puzzle together?

Maya yawned, kicking me in the leg. "Do you want to go to my room?" she asked.

"Sure."

"Show him your shell collection, darling," said Vivianne, trying her hardest not to combust into fairy dust.

We got up, and Maya showed me down the hall. Her room was the second door from left. It opened with a slow creak.

I blinked, taken aback. It was all purple. The walls were purple, the rug on the floor was purple, even the notebooks on her desk were all purple. A unicorn must've vomited in her room.

Noticing my expression, she blushed. "It's a lot. Mom won't let me paint the walls. I've had this stupid lilac since I was a baby. Maybe you can get your dad to help me convince her. She thinks I'm a child."

Maya had a lot of paintings and photographs on her walls. Shelves, too. No books. What a bummer.

"Did you do these yourself?" I asked, gesturing to the paintings.

"Yeah." She turned an even darker shade of pink. I noticed the washed-out red paint on her sleeve—a fading pink, really. She had some on her collar too that she must've missed.

Artist, then.

"They're good. You've got skills." I winced at how badly the compliment tumbled out of me.

"Thanks." Maya sat on her bed, letting me have a quick look around.

She had a couple of awards. Art competitions, one for photography, and one for dancing from when she was seven. Her room smelled good. A strong scent of vanilla and coconut like in the dining room. I looked at the walls again, at the photographs. Vivianne had probably taken most of them. I flashed back to the photos we'd found in Sheldon's room. And yes—there was another. On Maya's shelf was a selfie of Vivianne and Sheldon.

She must've been the mystery person behind the camera on the road trips.

36 / Lucas

She returns

Ophelia hardly had many options left but to turn to her family, and she worried about that. She had nowhere else to go if dad decided to kick her out. It had been so long since she'd seen her mother. I would've done anything to see mine.

But she was scared, and I could understand that.

It couldn't have been Mr. Graham's face greeting us, but for a split second before the red door opened, I couldn't quite catch myself from imagining his stubbled face. Instead, it was Mary, Ophelia's grandma, at the door. It took her a stumbling moment to allow us inside, like she hadn't expected her granddaughter to show up at all.

"It'll be okay, you'll see," I reassured Ophelia. "They love you."

Mary sat us down in the living room. Ophelia held her breath in anticipation.

Mrs. Graham was small and thin in the swallowing chair by the window. Quiet, and disheveled.

On the other hand, there was Mary, who was strangely composed. She sighed occasionally in agitation, and it took me a moment to realize she must've been waiting, like me, for Ophelia and Esther to say something.

"Mother…"

Esther turned her head.

"Mom," Ophelia said, this time with less tremble in her voice. "Can we talk about this? I'm sorry about dad."

Mrs. Graham crossed her arms, angling herself away like a pouting child. She wouldn't say a word.

"Grandma?"

Mary grunted. "Esther, I think you should hear her out."

The woman shot a pained look at Mary.

"Oh, don't be difficult! After everything this family has been through, your child is home and she is well. This is a happy day. Now smile and hug each other."

No help. Esther only narrowed her eyes and continued her stare.

I gave Ophelia a nudge, coaxing her to continue.

"Mom, I'm so sorry about dad. You have no idea how much I missed everyone. I missed you. I thought about you all the time."

Esther jumped up from the chair, and walked over to the window. "It's too late now. Nothing you say changes anything. The daughter I had is gone. She died three years ago."

My chest tightened. I squeezed Ophelia's hand a little too hard, making her yank it away from me. How could she say that? To her own child?

The silence was deafening.

"Yeah, maybe she is," whispered Ophelia, her voice cracking.

"No, no. No one is leaving until you two figure it out," said Mary. "I am not letting either of you tear this family apart again."

"Grandma, there's nothing I can do."

She stood up.

Mary glared at Ophelia until she sat back down. "Figure it out. Both of you. I'm going to make tea."

I had to admire the old lady. She was unyielding. "Has it always been like this?" I whispered into Ophelia's ear, trying to sound calm.

"Kind of. We shouldn't have come."

"I heard that," said Mrs. Graham, side-eyeing.

"It's true, isn't it? You clearly don't care. Why bother?" She leaned back against the couch, hands and legs crossed. "I came here to talk to you and grandma, but obviously you didn't want me to. I wondered why you hadn't called. Now I know."

Mrs. Graham flinched.

Facing each other, they looked so much alike. Same hair, same lips, freckles. Both stubborn to the bone.

"I thought you'd be happy to see me."

"We had a funeral for you," said Esther, sounding bored and unattached from the conversation.

"Right."

I was unsure how I could help. Mary came back with a tray, balancing cups of tea and almond biscuits.

"Well? Have they made up yet?" she asked.

I shook my head, biting into a treat.

"Esther, apologize to my grandbaby."

Mrs. Graham's eyes shot to Mary like she'd said something outrageous. Something so scandalous she couldn't believe her eyes and ears.

"Oh, hush now, do it! Hug her. Both of you, actually. Come now, stand up, hug." She ushered both Ophelia and Esther together. It took a minute before they were close enough to reach their arms around each other. "Oh, how lovely! Doesn't that feel nice?"

It looked like they were a step away from a hysteric breakdown, tears in their eyes. But perhaps it was a necessary discomfort, and after a few times they would get used to it.

Either way, they did look a bit funny. So rigid and stoic.

Now we just had to do the same with Katie.

37 / Rafael

The twisted dangers of fantasyland

"Is that an actual smile on your face?" teased Katie, finger pointed at me. Her head was hanging off the armchair she was curled up in, brown hair everywhere.

"Oh, there's a lot you haven't seen," Zack said.

I frowned. I *was* smiling, wasn't I? Showing teeth and everything.

The two of them chuckled to themselves.

"Hey Rafe?" asked Katie.

"Hm?"

"What did the white whale say to the blue whale?" She snickered to herself.

I adjusted my glasses. "I don't know."

"Breathe, mate." She snorted, twisting a strand of hair around her finger. "I just thought of it, isn't it funny?"

"I don't get it." Adam was lying on the couch, a dark gray pillow under his messy platinum hair. "I thought it was going to be something with Smurfs, like *'How is Smurfland, papa Smurf?'* or Smurfette? Is the blue whale boy or a girl?" His words bled together. Buzzed.

"Why would it have anything to do with Smurfs?" Katie sat up straight. "How did you not get the joke? Now you've ruined it."

Adam groaned into the pillow.

I waved a finger between them. "By the way, are you two a thing now?"

Panic flooded Katie's doe brown eyes. Adam turned his back to us, acting like he hadn't heard me, or simply choosing to ignore me.

"Adam?" I poked carefully.

More people had walked away from Adam than he liked to admit. I wanted him to know that not everyone would do that. He deserved better. The time would come when it could be him. Why not him? Why *didn't* he deserve good? But I knew better than to say any of it out loud. Pity was the last thing he wanted. Once he decided he didn't deserve something, there was no arguing. Adam looked at Katie like she was the sun and somehow, he was scared to burn her. My chest ached. Adam was better than me, because he would never hurt the people he loved.

Gosh, I was getting mushy and emotional. This was the exact reason I never got drunk.

"You know," said Z, "I called it from the very beginning. No one fights like you two unless you secretly want each other. It was painfully obvious."

That got his attention, and Adam sprung up. "What? I called Rafe and Bells from the first moment they ever met. You know nothing."

I wheezed. "Please don't."

It was moments like these that hurt the most. That reminded me too much of the girl I couldn't save and the place I couldn't follow her to. Moments like this that told us all that life would never be the same. We'd seen too much death, and too much of it had been our faults.

"For the record," said Ophelia from where she and Lucas were sitting, "the whale joke made me smile."

"Good. It was a brilliant joke," agreed Katie, lifting her chin.

Adam shook his head, laughing.

She narrowed her eyes. "Shut up, silly goose."

"I didn't say anything, star girl." His voice was raw, low like a whisper.

There was a high-pitched *ding* of the doorbell, and all our faces snapped alert. Who would be at the door so late at night?

"Hang on, I'll get it." Zack arose, stretching his long legs, and brushing strands of black hair from his face, He dragged his feet towards the door.

To my right, Lucas snuggled closer to Ophelia, like he might doze off at any moment. The girl kissed him softly.

"Oh, gross!" Katie winced. "Get a room, you two!"

"I don't mind." Zack said, reemerging, hands in pockets.

Katie beat him with a pillow. "Gross! Gross! Gross!" She stopped when her eyes landed on Lucy, silently standing at the doorway.

I could barely breathe. It took me a whole second to pick my jaw off the floor and refocus. I still saw Arabella everywhere, in everything and everyone. Lucy sat next to me, and I craned my neck away from her, tensing when I felt the couch shift with her weight.

"Rafe, are you okay?" she asked.

I shook my head, forcing my eyes on her. "I'm fine, thanks."

I laced my trembling fingers, feeling the warm blood pool in my fingertips. My heart wasn't racing *yet*. It was more like a steady drum, and I felt every beat. Everything was quiet except for that. How could a feeling be so loud?

I took a deep breath, exhaled slowly.

I had to distract my mind.

I grabbed a beer, sniffling as I cracked it open under Lucy's watchful gaze.

Zack grabbed the pillow Katie was still holding and whacked her over the head with it. Adam fixed him with a scornful look. His eyes were glazed.

"She started it!" exclaimed Z.

"I know."

Katie used the moment to get one last whip at Zack.

Zack ignored her, puzzled. "Man, what the fuck are you doing?"

I glanced up from my phone, shielding it from Lucy. "Er, I have an idea?"

Bells deserved justice, and the police were getting nowhere. Dad had said it himself; they had no leads. At the very least, I knew how to be smart about my plan this time. Well, the drunk Einstein on my shoulder did.

"Why'd you say it like a question? What's the idea?"

I fidgeted uncomfortably. "The cops are getting nowhere because everything takes forever to do. And pops is going to kill me anyway when he finds out I got drunk. I might as well make the most of the situation."

Zack whistled, pulling out his cigarettes. "Where is this going?"

"I'm, uh, texting him."

He arched an eyebrow. "Who?" Lighter out, cigarette to his mouth.

I hesitated. "My stalker."

Zack's response was a stoic puff of smoke. Not everyone was like him. Unconcerned.

"You can't do that!" yelled Katie.

"It's dangerous, I don't think It's a great idea," said Lucas, ever the calmest.

"Yes!" yelled Lucy. "Are you crazy? Give me that!" She lurched for my phone, but I managed to jump away from the sofa, clutching it tighter and typing my message as quickly as possible. At least this I could do. It was something. It was more than the police were doing.

"Rafe, no!" she kept yelling. I held my phone away from her.

"Why don't you just call? Honestly, I hate texting! It's so annoying," said Adam.

"I can't—" Again, I had to escape feisty Lucy.

"You have his number? Why didn't you do this earlier?" asked Zack, then held up his hands. "Don't get me wrong, totally not a good idea or anything."

"I can't call him. It's an unknown number."

"Give me the phone, *genius*," hissed Lucy. She was getting tired of jumping around me by the sounds of her tortured breathing.

Zack pulled her into his lap, holding Lucy by her waist, a burning cigarette in his other hand. She scowled, eyes still trailing me.

I tried my best to keep my mind straight when typing out my message, but the buzzing in my veins made it impossible. I kept missing letters and having to go back.

I pressed send, waiting until a gray speech bubble appeared. I didn't wait long.

I couldn't look. Katie stood next to me, and together we managed to read through the response.

It's over. I know who you are, maybe I always knew. The police have your fingerprints!! Tomorrow 10 PM at the warehouse, the door will be unlocked.

I'm not scared of yuo

You*

Agreed?

Fine. Have it your way. See you there, Rafael.

38 / Lucas

Big bang

I was worried I'd fractured my skull and had a supermassive black hole in my memories. I forced my eyes open, watching as the world started to spin into place. For a moment I stayed there, under the covers, piecing together everything I could remember from the night before, and praying that in the meantime the nausea would wear off and that the early morning light would stop making me want to gauge my eyes out.

I was in my room, Ophelia asleep beside me, about a dozen pug-eyed plushies under her arm.

Zack's parents had gone out, and he'd invited everyone over. A small gathering to forgive and forget.

The memories were barely starting to flood back in when I stood.

I looked in the mirror. My face was puffy and shadowed, my lips red. I was itching for a cold shower.

The chilly water got my blood pumping, but it couldn't set my head quite straight. I closed my eyes, and let the water push against my eyelids, tickling my nose on its way down my bare body.

The headache remained as I wandered through the halls towards the kitchen. I held my hand to my forehead as if that would fix anything. But then I realized it wasn't only my head that was thrumming, but also the door. I dragged myself towards it, and it practically flew open at the slightest touch of my hand.

My friends—close and less—stood outside, as ragged as me. Adam was still wearing what he'd worn the night before. The bunch of them looked like the definition of a hangover. But something else glinted in their eyes. Panic.

"What is going on?" I asked, my voice dry and scratchy, and still coated in sleep.

"We fucked up. I really, really, really fucked up," said Rafe, rushing to get the words out. "Again."

"What are you talking about?" I asked drowsily, hand traveling up my neck. "Can you slow down?"

"Focus!" yelled Zack, making me jerk back.

"Guys, I just woke up. Please stop yelling."

"Lucas, I am literally going to die tonight, you better fucking listen!"

I had never heard Rafe shout like that. He sounded like a trapped animal, afraid. Wait—did he say *die*? "You're what? What time is it?" I searched my pockets for my phone, groaning when I remembered I'd left it on my bed.

Zack pointed at the sum of them. "Can we come in?"

I nodded, and stepped aside. They walked in like geese, dragging me alongside into the kitchen. Zack sat me down, and handed me a glass of water.

"Last night, I messaged my stalker/probably killer," explained Rafe. "I'm supposed to be meeting him tonight. I need a plan or else I might end up as Whitewood's next big accident."

I choked on water.

"I have twelve hours to come up with one. The meeting's at Warren Repairs warehouse, and I was hoping you would make sure that no one else is there. Please," he added.

"Well, can't you just not go?" That earned me a smack on the head.

"If I do not go, he *will* come after me, because, by the way, I told him I know his identity. Before you start yelling, I understand that it was stupid."

Rafe *did* look like he'd been lectured already. "Call the police?" I offered next.

"And explain the texts? The murders? Explain *everything*? Do you want to be the one to go to the cops, say we stole information from them, and hope they won't press charges? I sure as hell don't. My pops is already watching me like a hawk."

I sighed. "How'd this even happen? Why do they think we know who they are?"

"I was drunk," explained Rafael. "I could hardly make decent decisions."

Zack waved his hand. "So what? I remember Lucy trying to stop you and you didn't let her!" Zack didn't lose his cool very often. It was serious, then.

"That's true, I did try. Once an idiot, always an idiot." Lucy tucked her hand under her chin.

"I wasn't exactly thinking clearly! Why didn't *you* stop me?" He stared at Z.

"Why didn't *I* stop you? Fuck this, man."

"Okay," I said, standing. "Okay, we'll figure something out. You said we have all day, right? But first, I need a coffee."

"Double that," murmured Adam.

I smiled softly. "How about I make a cup for everyone?" It would be a long day, better get my thoughts straight fast. Can't show up to a fight jet-lagged.

39 / Rafael

Water has no mercy on blood

My steps against the solid concrete sent shivers down my spine. My eyes were trained on my shadow, which always stayed a step ahead, mocking me. *Catch me if you can.* My shadow was joined by another flickering outline. I waved my hand, ushering Lucy back into hiding.

It was almost ten o'clock. I was hot and cold all at once. Terrified but ignited with a sense of righteousness. All this pain and fear would be gone soon. It would be alright. I remembered something Arabella once said to me. She said, "If you're afraid and you don't let it show, no one would be any wiser. Bravery is what they see." I took a deep breath, rolling back my shoulders.

Sweat prickled my forehead and neck as I continued pacing in the dim lights.

What I hadn't told anyone was that I was secretly glad for my ferocious, drunk self, and what he had done. It sent a pulsing thrill all over me to know that I'd finally meet the one person I hated more than anyone. All along it should've been me to die in those woods. Death had been tempting me since then with the prospect of seeing Bells again, and I knew—*I knew*—this was my one chance to either avenge her or die trying.

Fuck it.

No more holding back.

I checked the time again. My nemesis was running late.

As I thought that, I caught sight of blonde in my peripheral view. The lights above me flickered furiously. I was being watched. I drew a sharp breath, searching the dark. A slender silhouette stepped into the light. I hadn't even heard footsteps.

"Rafael," she said. The whites of her eyes were red. She was out of breath, like she'd been running.

"Vivianne. You." There had once been a moment I'd considered it, but defused it from my mind as quickly as it had come. Vivi wasn't a bad person.

She had a wild look on her face, as if all the heavens would come crashing down any second. "Listen to me. You must listen." She searched around, breathing hard. "Tell me what is going on. I saw her take the gun, and when I hear about that poor—" Vivianne choked, nostrils flaring.

All along, she had been right there. I was just too blind to put the pieces together.

"I should've known it was you." I took a threatening step forward. The clues had always been there. I'd been stupid. So, so, so incredibly stupid. My blood turned to ice.

"W-what? No, I—"

"Just tell me this, was my dad part of your plan too? I can't imagine you ever truly cared about either of us." I grit my teeth; jaw so tense it hurt. "If you've hurt him, I'll destroy you."

"Please, listen. I would never do anything like that. I followed her, but she got away. I thought you might know what is going on. Will you let me speak?"

"Oh, drop the act. You can't possibly think I'd believe a word you say. Not after what you've done," I sneered.

"And what has she done?" asked a third voice.

My eyes skipped to Maya's curious face, widening. I didn't need another person to worry about, she would only get hurt in this mess. The poor girl probably had no idea what kind of danger she had walked into. Besides, there was no good in her hearing about all the horrible things her mother had done.

"Maya you shouldn't be here." One of the girls could take her outside and keep an eye on her while I kept Vivianne talking. Before I could say more, my gaze locked on Maya's hands emerging from behind her. On the object she was holding.

"I think I'm exactly where I'm supposed to be." The barrel of the gun was pointing straight at my head.

I gulped, dizzy. *No way.*

Vivianne gasped. She took a tentative step towards her daughter, but the latter made her come to an abrupt stop.

"I really wish you hadn't followed me, mom. I didn't want you to see this." Maya motioned Vivi's hands forward to duct tape the wrists. "This is the only way to keep you safe." Her voice was sharp, a steel look of superiority in her eyes. Vivianne was too shocked to stop her from also taping her legs and mouth. Her silent tears made the tape curl at the edges.

"I don't understand," I said. But no, that wasn't entirely true, was it? Because the one thing Vivianne didn't have was a motive. "Sheldon was your dad, wasn't he? Why kill him? How could you kill him at, what, thirteen? That's impossible."

I wanted to scream. Outside, the wind was picking up.

Maya resembled her mother a lot, but besides that, she resembled someone else too. Big round eyes and light hair, although Maya's was a shade or two darker. She was another version of her cousin.

Vivi's body shook, her makeup smeared with tears and bullets of sweat. Her eyes darted like arrows between me and Maya.

"He was my father, yes. Not that anyone ever bothered to tell me that." Maya stepped away from Vivianne, focusing solely on me. "I'd always been curious. Always felt like there was something missing, some part of me. I went to talk to him, and guess what I found out? Mom never told him either. He wanted to spend time with me. I thought he wanted to get to know me."

I took a step, and Maya lifted the gun again, finger digging into the trigger. I froze, but it didn't stop me from speaking. "So that day, you two..."

"He wanted to go somewhere alone. He said it like he was embarrassed of me or something. We drove up the canal to a lake. He kept talking about how he had no idea. He asked me if it was money that I wanted. *Money.* It wasn't like he had any. I couldn't believe I'd felt sorry for him. I was so angry. We talked, but it didn't help because all I could think about was how everyone had been lying to me all my life, and the more he said the angrier I got. It was this freeing, euphoric type of anger. It felt so amazing to finally exist loudly."

"You decided to kill him?" I yelled. "What were you thinking, Maya? You were a child!" My vision swam. We weren't siblings, but she'd been the closest thing to one I'd ever had. There was no undoing what she'd done. No reset button to take us back in time.

"I never meant to kill him! He didn't understand what it was like for me! I had no one. No friends, no father. Mom was always working. I was tired of being invisible, and having people look straight through me like a ghost. No one ever chose me. I was alone in a war, battling demons no one else cared about. People never asked me why I was hurting, they just told me to keep smiling. Always getting pushed around like a plan B when the only thing I ever wanted was to be a first choice for at least *someone*." With her free hand, she stroked her short hair. "I pushed him. I didn't think I'd be strong enough, but he was weak. I didn't mean to kill him; I was just angry. He fell. His leg—he couldn't swim. I tried to save him, but he was too heavy for me to lift. I watched my father die, and I knew what it would look like, so all I could do was hope no one would ever find him. Now you have. Congratulations."

I scowled. My almost little sister. She disgusted me.

"Don't look at me like that, Rafe," she said like she was in pain. Maya licked her lips. It was agony watching her, knowing everything. "I know you don't believe me when I say this, but you and I really are the same. We feel so much it destroys us sometimes. We can't control the hurricane. Cut from the same cloth, always expected to live in everyone else's shadows, cold and uncared for. People don't think twice about us."

"We are nothing alike," I replied coldly.

Maya took a deep breath. There was a pause while she accepted my unwillingness to side with her. She should've known no brotherly love would save her. But Maya collected herself quickly, and was searching for her next words when a sneeze stopped her. She narrowed her eyes at me, then at the containers behind me where my friends were hiding.

My mouth went dry. There were six of us, and one of her. She had a gun. I was good at math, but I wasn't sure what the odds in a situation like that were.

Maya *tsked*. "I'm not an idiot, Rafe, but maybe I was naive thinking we had an honest deal. Your friends can come out."

We surrounded Maya in a semi-circle. Fear was creeping back up on me now that we were all sitting targets. Still, rage was a steady flame in my chest. Maya was the killer. Maya, who cried when she nicked her knee. Maya, who got lunch for her mom, and who needed tutoring in geography. *This* Maya did all this damage?

"I still don't understand," said Adam. "What about Martinez and Ophelia? How is any of this making sense?"

"He saw you," I whispered more to myself than anyone else.

Maya caught my mumblings. "Yes. He thought I was drowning him instead of trying to save him. I was scared." She sighed. "I'm not scared anymore."

Martinez tried to keep it from Esther. It must've been hard for him. In the end, none of it mattered.

"He went up in flames." Maya's face was blank. No remorse or guilt. I didn't recognize her at all.

"You didn't have to kill him!" exclaimed Lucy. She was crying, furious. "You could've talked to him, told him about what happened." Lucy's hands curled into two tiny fists at her sides.

"Maybe. I panicked. Either way, it wasn't a risk I was willing to take. What's done is done. After all, I am what the world made me."

The barrel of the gun wasn't quivering anymore.

Maya wasn't blinking anymore.

"And before you ask, I hoped you would listen with Joseph Graham, but you never do. I told you to stay away, but you don't have it in you to listen to anyone but yourself. His death is on you, and your friend's death is on you too, Rafe. If you'd just left me alone, none of this would have happened. We could've been each other's family one day. I wasn't always too happy about the idea but then I thought, why not? You are the only one who could understand me."

"I would rather die than be your family," I growled.

Maya's face twitched.

"Who do you think you are to play God?" asked Katie. "That's four people's blood on your hands. And for what? You can't make people love you by killing them!"

Maya huffed angrily. "I never played God. I have been a victim all my life, and I'm sick of it. Some things are just meant to be. Your friend is better off dead. Accept that. Would you really want her to live in this filthy world? She's in a better place."

Lucy yelled, storming ahead. Katie tried to catch her by the arm but failed. The click of the safety trigger, however, stopped Lucy.

"That's enough."

Lucy bit her lip, breathing heavily. "I thought you were going to shoot us. Go on then. Prove it. Prove what a monster you are. Who knows? Maybe mommy will finally give you a hug."

"You asked for it," chirped Maya with ease. She arched her hand and fired.

Adam jumped to the side. The bullet missed him by an inch. A jitter went through me at the bang, and I could swear I was back in that mossy forest for half a second. I could smell copper, rain, and feel the last of Arabella's warmth on my skin.

Maya smiled, but her eyes were searching for an exit. Her feet moved slowly. "There's no signal so don't bother. In this storm, no one is coming for you."

Another shot fired. My heart skipped another beat. A fowl cry surfaced from the back of my throat.

Everyone was screaming, Adam the most. He was the closest, saw it the best. He knelt, holding Katie, blood gushing everywhere.

40 / Lucas

In the end, the hero stands alone

I leaped from the bushes, and ran as fast as my legs would take me. My foot caught on an uneven part of concrete, and I fought to regain my balance. I wasn't stopping. It was a blur of events. One moment I'd been rubbing my hurting head, the next I was half-way across the lot. I put as much force into my legs as I could muster. I had the keys in my hand, knuckles turning white. Only another second before I'd reach the door.

I jumped through the threshold, locked the door behind me without a thought, panting as the rustling trees were replaced by the sound of distress. I still had the keys in case we needed to make a swift escape. We just had to stall until the police got there. I knew that warehouse inside and out; every possible hiding spot.

I turned around, trying to make sense of what was happening, but halted immediately. While I'd been MIA, things had certainly escalated.

My attention focused first on Adam, who was helping Katie sit up. He held her face in his palms, observing her bleeding shoulder. Katie whimpered under his touch. I searched around the warehouse for the rest of my friends. Thankfully no one else seemed hurt, though Lucy did look a little green in the face.

A girl I didn't recognize was standing in the middle of the room. Her head was turning in every direction, as if she was contemplating something, gun in hand. I exhaled audibly, surprised to find myself up against some schoolgirl. But that wasn't all; The police department's receptionist was tied up on the floor in a puddle of her own tears. Vivianne Reyes, if I remembered right. How hard had I been hit? Where had all these people come from?

I ran towards her, kneeling. Vivianne's sobs stopped as she gazed up at me. My hand rested on the corner of her mouth, pulling the duct tape away in one brisk motion.

"What happened?" I asked her, ripping at the tape shackles around her hands.

The woman didn't answer. The moment her mouth was free, the wailing only intensified. Her skin was cold, and it struck me that she hadn't understood a word I'd said.

"Great," I said to myself. I got up, leaving Vivianne to unwrap the rest of herself.

A loud bang splintered the room, echoing off the walls. The little girl was trying to break open the back door, which I'd locked. She'd picked up a hammer from the tool bar by a nearby wall, and was now slamming the door handle and lock, hoping it would buckle. She wasn't having much success, but managed to partially break the handle off the door, leaving it hanging. Despite it, the door remained shut.

My pace was frisk, hands ready to wrap around her and pin her down. While I was sneaking up behind her, she picked up speed and slammed her shoulder into the door. Her tiny body convulsed, cramping with the backlash of the hit. To her dismay, the body slam had done nothing to crack the lock.

In the time it had taken her to do that, I managed to get close enough to her to get a swing in. The girl turned, stumbling back, eyes wide. She was backing away, adjusting her grip on the gun, so she could point it at me.

"Get out of my way," she snarled, burning with hatred.

How someone that young could be so evil I didn't know. Maybe evil doesn't ask for age. Maybe that is the most sinister thing about it.

I waved at Adam to tell him to go, and without hesitation he picked Katie up. She squealed in his arms, staining Adam's white T-shirt dark red. Zack ran to meet them, dragging Lucy along too. Having broken the door, the little girl clearly had no other option but make her escape through the only exit left—which happened to be on the other side of the warehouse.

"Hey, what's your name?"

She stared at me. My question had surprised the sneer off her face.

"Sorry, it's just that you look familiar and I can't seem to figure it out," I explained. My head still hurt; she'd hit me hard. I pushed the pain aside, focusing on keeping her busy and buying time.

"It's Maya."

Amazing. Yes, I'd definitely seen her around.

Maya continued, "And I did not come this far for you all to ruin everything for me. Now, step aside." She took a confident stance, letting me know she wasn't afraid to shoot me if I wouldn't listen.

"Please put the gun down," I pleaded, holding out my hands.

Clearly Maya didn't care much, because she pulled the trigger and ran. I jumped, my whole body and ears ringing. Apparently, angry, weaponized teenage girls were hardly the sort to be reasoned with. I had to subdue her, make it easier for us to not die. Most of the doors in the building (not counting the entrances) were unlocked, which was a great problem since Maya had probably bet on it and was now on the run while the chaos she'd created was raging on.

I was right behind her. A little more and I'd catch up. To my left, Rafe seemed to snap into action. He pushed up his glasses, and charged after Maya. We were side by side, so that when Maya suddenly stopped running, we both almost slammed into her.

"Mom? What are you doing?"

Vivianne had freed herself. Her skin was blotchy and bone white, her body had stopped shaking.

The three of us stared at her, waiting. Rafael whispered something to me, but my ears didn't pick up what. Another second passed when nothing happened. Maya was torn, her shoulders slumping forward.

Rafael let out a war cry, sprinting to push Maya down. The gun skittered across concrete. His fist connected with her cheek, and although it was a weak punch, tears sprung in the girl's eyes. She grabbed hold of Rafe's hand, biting it. He yelped.

"Rafe!" I rammed at Maya, and before neither of us could properly catch our breaths, I hit her in the kneecaps. That sent her sprawling on the ground. I felt a little sorry for her. Her body would be utterly bruised. I was even a bit impressed with how much she could take. Maya's nails dug into me, scratching, and drawing blood. I winced, trying to pin her hands down while she struggled to break free. At last, Maya shoved her knee into my stomach, rolling away from under me.

"Get away from him!" Lucy yelled. She was holding that damn gun.

Slowly but steadily, Maya pushed herself onto her feet. She had a slight wobble to her, still regaining her balance. Lucy and Vivianne were both still in shock and not making the situation any better. Rafael and I had taken a couple of punches, but we could count on each other to push through.

Although, for me, the world was starting to spin more and more. And with that, intensified my headache.

"Lucy, give me the gun. Get out of here," I said.

She looked between me and Maya. "Arabella was my best friend." Her hands shook with the weight of the weapon.

I slipped the keys out of my pocket. "Take these. Go through the storage room and out the front. Walk until you get a signal. Call the cops. Then wait. Take Vivianne with you, and make sure Adam and Katie are okay." Adam was only steps away, clutching Katie like they were glued together. Katie looked like she might lose consciousness any second now.

"She's not going to shoot me," stated Maya. Her hands were in the air, slowly, as she backed away.

She was going to run for it.

I reached my hand out, but, suddenly, there was Zack, grabbing Maya from behind and lifting her off the floor like she weighed nothing. The girl kicked and screamed in his arms, trashing like a wildling.

Lucy met my eyes. I gave her a reassuring smile, and held out my palm for her to grab the keys. She yielded. I grabbed the gun from her, and didn't move until the lights in the next room flashed on.

Zack settled on the ground, holding Maya tight to his chest. "You guys should go too."

"I think I'll stick it out," I replied, emptying the gun of its remaining ammo.

"Me too," agreed Rafe. He grabbed the roll of duct tape Maya had used on Vivianne to tie Maya up.

Her mouth fell open, releasing a disbelieving gasp. It was over and she had lost.

"Where did you get the car? You can't drive," Rafe asked Maya. I was confused for a second, then I remembered the woods. He sat down, taking off his glasses to examine them. They were cracked, but had somehow retained their shape.

"Wasn't exactly hard. Everyone in this town drives some beat up heap of rust on wheels. I watched a video on how to wire a car. Dumped it later. I guess I wasn't careful enough."

"Yeah," agreed Rafe, "you sure put in a lot of effort, didn't you?"

Maya smiled.

I took a deep breath, centering myself. Then another, but the there was nothing that would stop the spinning and blurring of my sight. My muscles burned, and so did my head. Everything turned foggy. I moaned, touching the back of my head where it seized with pain.

Rafe was watching me.

"I'm okay," I uttered.

A concussion, probably.

I relaxed my body, closing my eyes and focusing on my breathing. I opened them to a loud shrieking of metal.

The warehouse door had finally collapsed in on itself, and through it rain poured in. Outside, it was pitch-black. The storm was bad. I was hit in the face by the freezing wind, like ice spikes scraping at my chin. I held a hand in front of me, squinting.

Z's black hair, already damp with sweat, caught a hit of cold rain. Streams of water sprayed the floor.

I exhaled through my mouth.

"I will enjoy seeing you rot in jail," said Rafe to Maya, calmly.

"Hope you'll visit me, big brother." Her eyes sparked. There was so much fight in her. "I haven't felt fear since my father drowned." Her voice cracked.

Zack couched, resting his back against the wall.

If I didn't move, the world would stand still.

Somewhere in the distance, there was a siren.

"Let me go. Please let me go. I don't want to go to jail." Maya swayed on her spot a little, but the guys held her unyieldingly. "Rafe, please. I'm sorry. I'll disappear. You won't ever have to see me again."

I thought he would never answer, but then he said, "I'm sorry, I cannot."

Maya stared at him in disappointment. Then, she leaned her head back, shutting her eyes as tears streamed down her face. "I hope they won't make me look at my mom," she murmured to herself.

I felt numb. All I knew was that I was still standing, and the only thing left to do was wait. I was just glad it was over. A moment to breathe.

A blink, and the officers were there. They took Maya away. She was quiet the entire time, even as her mother screamed her name. They had to restrain Vivianne until she calmed down. The medics spent some time patching us up. They took Katie to the hospital. She'd be okay, they promised. They wanted to take me too, but I said I wouldn't go before my dad got there. They left me to wait while they checked up on everyone else.

Lucy ran into Zack's arms. He kissed her forehead, reassuring her. Reporters were surrounding the area, begging for an interview from one of us.

My phone buzzed in my pocket as I got all the notifications I had missed during the fight. I'd missed a call from Jeanie. I forced myself to set it aside for the time being. I was too injured and too tired for it. I'd give her a call back later.

I needed my dad.

I shivered in the cold night. The storm was passing, turned into a light drizzle of fine rain. My ribs and head hurt. My knuckles were turning an ugly shade of purple, but the pressure had lifted from my shoulders, and I'd never felt more at peace.

"Lucas!"

Ophelia fell into my arms, burying her head in my neck. I'd snuck out without a word. How insane that that had happened less than two hours ago, when it felt like a lifetime had passed.

"Thank God you're okay."

I couldn't summon any words, but having her so close to me eased my pain more than any medicine. She helped me breathe.

Dad stood right next to her. A wave of sorrow hit me. Softly, I pulled away from Ophelia, so I could hug my dad, and finally feel like I was home.

THE MORNING DAILY

Whitewood's double homicide: cold case solved

Gale Kennedy
August 16, 2018

Yesterday evening, a missing person's case dating back three years was solved by a group of local Whitewood teenagers.

Three years ago, three citizens named Sheldon Rogers, Link Martinez, and 15-year-old Ophelia Graham disappeared shortly after one another. The police conducted intensive searches and investigated possible leads, but without success, the case was ultimately closed. Both men were announced dead after a period of time. Rogers was assumed to have drowned, and Martinez deceased due to the fire to his home. Ophelia Graham, however, was recently discovered alive and well after years of being missing. She has since been questioned by the authorities, and reunited with her family. The specifics regarding her disappearance have not been made public as of yet.

The friend group used their connections and wits, which lead them to be able to uncover the person behind the vanishings. One of the members of the group was the local police department chief's son, who has refused to comment on the events.

On the photo: police on the crime scene on August 15th

However, it is important to note that although after years, the justice is finally being served, it was not without consequence. Since the resurfacing of this case, two more Whitewood citizens have passed under unusual circumstances. Maya Reyes, a 16-year-old girl, has confessed to killing Rogers and Martinez when just thirteen. She has also admitted to her involvement in the deaths of Arabella Rogers, and Joseph Graham, who is Ophelia Graham's father. In addition, Maya Reyes has been connected to various other infractions of the law, such as breaking and entering. We have yet to learn more about her arrest. As of currently, the investigation is very much ongoing.

Epilogue / Rafael

I am what you made me

The sun was shining that day, but the leaves were already a jarring shade of red. A breeze ruffled my fresh buzz, tinging my ears with cold.

I knelt, wiping moss from Arabella's gravestone. She would've liked moss, but she wasn't there to stop me. I hadn't seen her in a long time. It was a relief, feeling stable and steady again, but it didn't free me from the aching in my chest. A couple of months had passed, but the missing didn't go away so easily.

Gently, I set the flowers down, and let my thoughts drift. I could still hear the reporters screaming my name. All our names. A story was all they'd cared about. When I'd just walked out of the darkness, and they'd been already waiting there with flashing cameras. It'd been a long night, and an even longer day. Probably the longest of my life. I hadn't let myself think about it in the past months. Only now, when back at home, did I remember.

My friends were waiting for me. Everyone was so busy that it'd been a while since we'd last seen each other. At least for Thanksgiving we'd made time.

Lucas, Ophelia, Katie, and I were studying in the city. Zack and Lucy, however, were taking a gap year to travel together. Lucas and Ophelia spent plenty of their weekends in Whitewood with their families and I'd made him promise to keep one wary eye on pops too. Adam kept his distance from Katie. He'd come around, I knew. Once enough time had passed and he'd get his act together.

Today we'd all meet again. One more chance to be kids. To reunite, and never let go. Eagerness prickled my cheeks; hands numb from the November air.

I'd missed my friends.

I let my fingers trail the soft grass, moist with last night's rain.

Then, I stood, and faced the misty morning sun.

Author's note

All my life I've been haunted by stories. I've always loved to read, and always felt the need to write. I often think back to the first wobbly lines I wrote, and how they've morphed me into the person I am today. How without them, I wouldn't have written this book. My best decisions have always been the ones I never imagined myself making.

For the longest time, I've feared not being good enough. But all a writer can do is smear their soul across the pages, and hope people love it. I knew the pressure of people expecting a great story from me would crush me, and the book would never see daylight at all, so I didn't tell many people about this story. But to the few people who did know, I want to say thank you. This next part is yours.

This book would not exist without your undying support. All those times you helped me work through a problem, small or big. When I doubted myself, but you never did. You believed in my story when you hadn't even read a single line of it.

Thank you, Elisabeth, for being the first to listen. For knowing I could do it way before I did.

Thank you, Clara, for bearing my ramblings. I always felt seen by you.

Thank you, Marit, for being the first to read my story, and for accepting the task with such grace and joy. Your part in this has been exceptionally important to me.

Thank you, everyone else, who helped me by simply existing.

And I thank you, dear reader. It excites me to know you've met these characters and followed their story for a while. You matter.

Milton Keynes UK
Ingram Content Group UK Ltd.
UKHW020033271124
451585UK00014B/1608